Drop Dead Dallas

KIM BLACK

Published by Kim Black Ink, Steepledog Productions
PO Box 50814
Amarillo, TX 79159

www.kimblackink.com

Printed in the United States of America

Cover design by Sean Black.

ISBN 978-1-946846-21-1 Paperback
ISBN 978-1-946846-22-8 E-book
ISBN 978-1-946846-23-5 Hardback

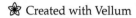 Created with Vellum

For Riley, with all my love.
And to the memory of my mother, Bobbie, and my mother-in-law,
Wildeana. I miss you both.

Acknowledgments

Special thanks to Tammie, Becca, James, Kim, Donna, Kristine, Brandi, Kay, and Val. Your input, encouragement, and feedback have been priceless to me.

To the classic noir storytellers and players, Raymond Chandler, Dashiell Hammett, Humphrey Bogart, Joseph Cotten, William Powell, Veronica Lake, Myrna Loy, Peter Lorre, and so many others. Your work inspires me.

To Dad, Sam, Whitney, and Sean. Thank you for all you do every single day.

To my readers, I couldn't continue without your support.

CHAPTER 1

The Lie

I LEANED against the front of my apartment building, a late Gothic Revival called the Kirby, on Main in historic downtown Dallas and waited for the afternoon drizzle to let up before my one-block walk to the Kirby's sister building, the Adolphus. I wore my favorite red patent stilettos and had no intention of letting the rain or my terrible judgment ruin them.

Today's adventure was courtesy of my twenty-ninth birthday, which I spent alone in my loft with a six-dollar bottle of Prosecco and a handful of other bad ideas. The next morning, still holding a little buzz on my lips, I made the call and hired Dallas's most eligible bachelor, Cotten Hammond, Private Investigator. I didn't have a case. I had a crush.

When Dad passed away last year, I took over the reins of the family business—Petra Energy Resources—as well as the Diane Pawley-Peters Memorial Women's Foundation, named after the mother I never knew. Hammond was one of our donors, and I had the privilege of honoring him at the foundation's banquet last month. He stood taller than I expected, with dark brown eyes and a jaw that could part a crowd. He balanced the obligatory black tux and white tie with a well-groomed five-o'clock shadow that emphasized his cleft chin. On top of that, his handshake was firm, warm, and respectful. I was in lust.

On that night of bad ideas, I devised my scheme. When I called the following day, he assured me he knew who I was and that he'd help in any way possible. I explained that I believed I was being followed, maybe stalked. It wasn't true, but I figured he couldn't prove how I felt, so I went with it. According to my scheme, he would follow me for a couple weeks, take a few pictures, and then give me his guarantee that I was perfectly safe.

In my rich imagination, he'd see my exquisite taste in food, friends, and fashion, and fall head over heels. I realized —about two hours and three aspirin after the call—that I had ruined any chance I had with the man by creating this ridiculous charade. That's what I do, though. Meet a man, become infatuated, sabotage the relationship, and end up alone with a bottle of bubbly. Rinse and repeat.

I glanced at my watch—ten minutes to four. My neighbor's gray kitty, Marlowe, loped up beside me and purred a damp figure-eight around my ankles. "What are you doing out here? Spencer will be so worried." Marlowe was well-known for escaping his apartment and had become somewhat of a mascot for the Kirby. "Now get back inside before you catch a kitty cold." I held the door open as he slunk into the lobby. Marlowe was the only soul with whom I'd shared my scheme.

My absurd scheme. Now or never.

I stepped back into the drizzle. I couldn't be late for my follow-up appointment. The whole thing was a mistake, but I'd look good making it.

Walking into the back lobby of the freshly restored Adolphus Tower office suite, I did a little shimmy to lose the clinging raindrops and let my trench coat drop from my shoulders. A digital office directory on a loop with announcements and five-second ads hung between the modern staircase and the glowing brass elevator. I checked my lipstick in the monitor's reflection and noted that Hammond's office was Suite 202. To the stairs.

I froze in front of the stained curly-pine door and studied the hand-painted lettering on the translucent glass panel. *C. Hammond, P. I. By Appointment.* Do I knock or just walk in?

I reached for the brass handle, but it turned when I touched it, and my hand instinctively drew back. I stifled a gasp, which spoiled any sultry entrance I might have otherwise made.

"Ms. Peters, it's a pleasure to see you again." His baritone was as deep as his eyes and as warm as his handshake. "Please, come in and have a seat."

"Call me Ronni." I tilted my chin, and he directed me to a Bordeaux leather wingback on the client side of his mahogany desk. Behind me was a wall lined with old leather books. I hesitated at the chair and drew a full breath, inhaling the sweet scent of Eastern spices and first editions. He took my coat and placed it on the hook by the door before he rounded the end of the desk and, with his eyes, asked me again to sit down.

I took a quick appraisal of the office. His desk, two wingchairs, and a credenza behind the desk. On the wall opposite the books was another door with frosted glass—this one marked PRIVATE. I lowered myself into the chair and sighed. I let my lashes rise and fall a few times. I was all in. No confessions.

Drawing another deep breath, I simpered, "I appreciate your time, Mr. Hammond."

"Please, you should call me Cotten. Can I offer you some water or a Coke or something?" He smiled, gesturing vaguely to the door beside him, but the crease in his forehead grew more pronounced. Something was off.

"No, thank you." I crossed my legs and shifted forward in my seat—the most effective pose when wearing a faux-wrap dress. "I hope I haven't wasted your time."

He shook his head and opened the drawer at his knee. He maintained eye contact, but it was all business. My seduction foundered.

He centered a black file folder on his blotter, and his gaze finally broke. He seemed to look me over for the first time. He released an almost imperceptible chuff and then sat back in his chair.

"Do you know the name *Steven Wexler*?"

I took a moment to mentally flip through my contacts. "I don't think so." Before I could guess where his questions led, he slid a photo of a man from the file and positioned it in front of me.

"Maybe you recognize his face?"

The photo might have been a mugshot or an employee ID

tag. A middle-aged man stared dead ahead with artificially orange hair, a black mustache, and bags under his eyes. A chill, maybe from the persisting rain, ran down my spine. I shook my head and pushed the picture back, touching only the corner of the photo with my fingertips. "No. I don't know him."

"You don't know any reason he would be following you?" He stared as if he thought I might slip up and he'd catch my lie. My therapist would suggest that was my guilty imagination.

"What?" I tried to do my part in the conversation, but my brain sputtered.

"This man, Steven Wexler, has been following you for the last two weeks. At least, but who knows how long before that. You've never met him before?" As he spoke, Cotten opened the file and spread out at least a dozen photographs of me, with Wexler somewhere in the background.

My mouth went dry, and every other part of my body broke into a cold sweat. I don't know whether Cotten said anything else because, for the next several minutes, all I could hear was the pounding of my heart. My vision blurred. I blinked several times, trying to clear it enough to study the snapshots.

At the grocery store. At the park. On my walk to work. In the lobby of my apartment. In each picture, Wexler was staring at me. No mistake. He knows where I live. Where I work. Where I do everything. I had no idea I was actually being followed. I'd never even caught a glimpse of Cotten in the last two weeks.

I leaned closer to the photos, hoping to see a mistake.

Were they photoshopped? Maybe it wasn't me in the pictures, or it wasn't Wexler. But it was.

I looked up at Cotten, who flipped sharply on his side. His arms reached out to me across the desk, and I heard him calling my name from far away. "Veronica. Ms. Peters!" All at once, someone turned out the lights.

CHAPTER 2
The Damsel

I OPENED my eyes and found myself horizontal on a tobacco leather couch under the window in Cotten's private office. The blinds were drawn, but the sound of the rain on the glass assured me the storm had picked up again. Lightning flashed, and I could feel the rumble of thunder as the window frames rattled. The room matched the dark tone this day had taken.

My scheme had been ridiculous, and now everything had gone sideways, quite literally. I should have known better.

I started to sit up, but as soon as I moved, a two-ton rhinoceros plowed into the side of my head. I had no idea that those little stars you see circling cartoon characters' heads were real until this moment.

"You hit pretty hard." A voice soothed from somewhere nearby.

I turned to find the owner of the voice, but the rhino hit again. I squeezed my eyes shut and clutched at the sides of my head. My ice-cold fingers soothed my temples, and then just above my left ear, I felt it. A goose egg. Maybe from a small goose. Okay, maybe a duck.

"Let me help you." This time I was sure it was Cotten.

I inhaled and exhaled slowly, allowed my eyes to open a slit, and then a little more. Cotten knelt in front of me. He slid his arms around my shoulders, and in one strong lift, I sat upright. My shoeless feet dropped to the floor, and my toes flexed on his fluffy white rug.

Without a word, he held out a glass of water in one hand and two white pills in the palm of the other. "I think you'll be all right." He waited for me to take the chalky tablets.

Proving my judgment as faulty as ever, I allowed my fingertips to linger a second too long on his skin as I gathered the pills. My breath sputtered. I laced my fingers between his as I took the cool glass from him. Electricity. I parted my lips as seductively as possible and slipped the pills between them.

Aspirin. Plain aspirin. Bitter on my tongue.

I gulped down the water quickly and handed the glass back to him, all my sexy gone.

"What happened?" My voice sounded scratchy and raw.

Cotten furrowed his brow. "You fainted. I showed you the pictures, and you went down like a house of cards in a March breeze. If I'd known you'd take it so hard, I'd have been by your side. You collapsed before I could get around my desk." He narrowed his eyes. "And your head made a quick stop on the arm of the chair on your way down." He sounded embarrassed.

But I was the one who fainted. I tried to remember that moment. We were talking. Cotten said something about a man. A man following me. He had pictures. It couldn't be. I didn't really have a stalker—I made that up. But the photos were real. And that's when everything got a little fuzzy.

"I have a stalker?"

Cotten moved to sit in the chair beside the couch. "Yes, but don't worry. I have his name and ID. All we have to do is file a complaint with the police. I have a buddy who's a detective."

"But *you're* a detective." Things were still a little fuzzy.

Cotten squared his shoulders. "I'm a private investigator. My friend is a police detective. I can gather evidence for the complaint, but you have to file to get the law after the guy in an official capacity. It's not like on TV." He leaned forward with an intense stare.

Oh, those eyes. I longed to dive in and take a full-body bath in those eyes.

"But it's not a problem," he continued, snapping me back to attention. "I've got you covered."

How I wished.

Something clicked over Cotten's shoulder. I turned my head to see what it was; this time, the rhino was only about four hundred pounds. Progress.

"You want a cup of coffee?" He sauntered to the coffee maker and poured out a cup. "It might help with the headache. At least warm you up a bit."

"It'll hold me over 'til I can get something stronger into me." I took the mug from him and wrapped my still-chilled fingers around it. A quick glance let me know he disapproved of day drinking. Well, I disapproved of his judgey look, so I guessed we were even.

Cotten sat down and watched me sip my coffee for a moment. This would have been the perfect time for me to be charming and seductive, but the bump on my head still throbbed, my ego lagged, and some freak stranger was following me around downtown Dallas. Seduction would have to wait.

"If you know who the guy is, can't you just call the police and have them throw him in jail?" I really had no desire to spend the evening at the police station.

"That's not quite how it works. We'll go in and talk to my friend. He'll take your statement. You'll tell him how you first suspected you were being stalked. He'll want specifics. Did you see Wexler wherever you went? Did he make threatening remarks? Was he intimidating you? Have you met him before? Did he have a grudge against you or someone in your family?"

I flinched a little more with each question. No matter how hard I tried to keep a poker face, my expression and resolve crumbled.

He leaned forward in his chair. "What's wrong?"

"I can't. I don't know. This is all too much." My cool shattered, and something else broke through. My damsel-in-distress—or   I'm-caught-in-a-lie-but-now-the-truth-is-so-much-worse panic breakdown—seemed to work wonders with Cotten. He shifted from his chair to sit beside me on the couch.

He shushed me as he took the coffee mug from my trembling fingers. "Don't worry. I'll be right by your side. The photos I have are all time-stamped and geo-tagged. It won't be a big deal. It's not the Spanish Inquisition."

I held my breath for a minute, releasing it only when the throbbing in my head melted into the sound of my heart beating in my ears. "I'm not sure what to say."

"Just tell the truth."

The truth? That wasn't going to work for me. I pasted on my best helpless expression.

He shook his head and almost reached for my hand. When he didn't take it, I nearly lunged to grab his. But I didn't. I was just a client to him, and I did this to myself.

"I'll help you." His tone was calm. "First things first. Do you know, or have you ever met, Steven Wexler?"

"No." Maybe the first honest word I'd spoken all day. Then my mind started second-guessing. "I mean, I can't say that I've never seen him before in my whole life. This is Dallas. I might have passed him in the street or something."

"But not to speak to?" Cotten glanced at my hands again. "You didn't know his name or have a relationship with him?"

"No. For sure, no."

"Good. Easy enough." Cotten clapped his hands together and laced his fingers into a church-and-steeple configuration. "And how many times had you seen him before you suspected he might be following you?"

Now we arrived at the problem. I'd never seen him. Ever. Wexler had been following me for at least two weeks—apparently quite closely—and I hadn't even noticed him. At all. But I couldn't say that. I couldn't tell Cotten Hammond that I had only made up this crazy story to spend an afternoon gazing into his beautiful, brooding eyes.

But I also couldn't tell him I had seen the man before. I knew that if I lied and said I'd seen him on this date at that place, well, somewhere, someone would prove that it couldn't have been. And then Wexler gets away with it, and I'm the crazy one.

Ridiculous.

CHAPTER 3

The Statement

I WAITED in the lobby as Cotten pulled his black sedan to the canopy at the front of his building. I shivered, not from the chill of the rain or the gloom that melted down from the clouds but from the cold terror that clutched at my lungs.

In just a few minutes, I'd be at the police station, doing my best not to lie to a detective about why I hired Hammond. Explaining that—despite making the whole stalker story up—I was indeed being followed by a man I did not know. The entire situation was implausible.

The car stopped, and Cotten hopped out. As I stepped out of the building, he rounded the front and pulled open the passenger door. He took my hand, steadying my shift from standing on the curb to sitting in the car, causing a ripple of heat to wash through me. But when he closed the car door on my side, another chill rushed down my spine. Beside me on the seat sat the black file folder filled with evidence. My evidence.

Cotten watched the road as he navigated the short drive to the precinct. Once we were parked, he tucked the folder under his arm and came around to escort me inside. He barely glanced at the officer at the door. A nod as we stepped through the security arch and up a few flights to his friend's office.

Detective Damon DuBois, as the door and the desk plaque indicated, hunched over his desk, studying a photograph with a magnifying glass. When Cotten tapped on the open glass door, DuBois pushed the photo into a file and swept it all into his upper desk drawer. The man was nearly as wide at the shoulders as his desk, which gave the strange impression of an adult sitting at a child's table.

I expected DuBois to greet Cotten with a smile. Instead, he released a disappointed sigh and maybe even rolled his eyes. He shifted his gaze to me and adjusted his expression to a pleasant serve-and-protect smile.

"Can I help you?" DuBois inquired as though he'd never met Cotten.

"Ms. Peters," Cotten said as he directed me into the small glass room. "I'd like to introduce you to my friend, Detective DuBois." He pulled out a chair for me, and I sat. "Detective, this is my client. Ms. Veronica Peters."

DuBois focused in my direction, but it was clear that my presence—at least Cotten's—irritated him. I offered my hand across the desk, and he shook it. Sitting there, I could see the desk was normal-sized for a typical office. The man really was just that big. His palm was so broad that my fingers only half-folded around his grip. I also noted his hand was a good twenty degrees warmer than mine.

"And what can I do for you, Ms. Peters?" DuBois' eyes cut to Cotten with a flash of what I guessed was contempt.

"Well," I cleared my throat more for effect than necessity. "I have a man. I mean, I don't want him. To be after me." My face flushed hot, and my voice vaporized. "There's a man following me."

A smile cracked DuBois' stoic expression. "You have someone following you?"

I shot a glance at Cotten, and he took up my cause. "Ms. Peters hired me about two weeks ago. She thought she might have a stalker. I followed her movements, took a few pictures, and learned that she did, indeed, have a man following her."

Cotten plopped the folder onto the desk. "The man's name is Steven Wexler. He's a small-time crook who usually gets off with nothing more than a slap on the wrist. And no, Ms. Peters has never seen him before."

DuBois flipped the folder open and glanced down at my stalker. His face didn't change as he looked back at me and flipped the folder closed again. "I'm sorry to hear about that, Ms. Peters. But your friend here," he waved his hand dismissively toward Cotten, "has misdirected you. I'm a homicide detective. You'll need to file your complaint with Officer Green out there." He slid the file in front of me and pointed to the woman officer at one of the desks in the larger common room.

I turned and smiled at the woman, who looked up when she heard her name.

"She can take your statement." With that, DuBois was finished with me. With us. He folded his arms over his desk and returned to his hunched position, waiting for us to leave.

A swift wave of relief swept over me for a second. I was

done. I could go home. No. Not yet. Green gestured to the chair at the end of her desk as I stepped out of the glass cubicle.

Cotten waited for me to sit and explained my situation to Officer Green. She nodded automatically with each sentence. I think I did, too. Everything sounded better when Cotten said it. His voice was deep and graveled in all the right places. But it was more than that. He was confident. He didn't stammer or trip over his tongue; he knew what he was talking about.

He gave Green more details. Who Wexler was. Where he had followed me. The more I heard, the more frightened I became. Why would anyone want to follow me anywhere? I still didn't quite believe it. Why would a known crook be stalking me? I mean, I had money in the bank, but I didn't live like it. Daddy taught me early on not to flaunt my blessings. Don't flash cash. Don't dress like a celebrity—except for the shoes.

Green tugged open a file drawer and shuffled a page or two under the clamp of a clipboard with a broken corner.

"I understand." Her voice sounded low and consoling but insincere. She heard all kinds of things every day. My case wouldn't raise an eyebrow. "Please fill out this page with as much detail as you can provide, and I'll review it when you're finished."

I drew a deep breath. "Thanks." Just what I wanted, a high school essay.

She slid the clipboard to me and took a few seconds to hunt for a working pen. Once found, she handed it to me and turned her attention to Cotten. "You can have a seat over there." Green gestured to a row of connected plastic chairs against the wall by DuBois' door. "She needs to give her statement without your help."

I watched Cotten amble back to his *friend's* glass office. I'd have preferred to keep him close, but I could fill out a form myself. And I was pretty sure I could remember all the details he'd just given to DuBois and Green.

Name. Address. Phone. Employer. Every number I'd ever memorized. Who to notify in case of emergency. That one stopped me. This was the first time I'd had to answer that question since Dad had passed away. My heart lurched. Who was my emergency call now?

Leave it blank. No. There must be someone. But there wasn't. Just leave it blank. Yes, I'll come back to it.

A few checkboxes. No drugs. No felonies. No misdemeanors.

I stared down at the white expanse of space allotted for my statement. My brain flashed back to junior English. Explain the symbolism of at least three colors from *The Great Gatsby*, 500 words minimum. My heart pounded in my ears. I touched the pen to the first line. I started with the most obtuse statement I could think of.

On the evening of June twenty-first, I had the idea that I might have someone following me. This was not untrue. That was the night of my idea. I continued my essay in the same manner until a loud scream stopped me cold.

A person rushed into the common room, wearing blue and white striped overalls and not much else. He, or she—I couldn't tell—yelled so loudly the sound bounced and rattled all the glass doors facing the center.

"Johnny Depp stole my identity, and I want justice!" There were a lot of swears and curses and other crazy accusations, but at the end of each breath came, "Johnny Depp stole my identity!"

Green hopped up from her chair and shot me a stay-where-you-are look as she hurried toward the person. Two more officers joined the effort, and within a few minutes, the person was down another hall, and the yelling had stopped.

By then, I noticed Cotten had returned to DuBois' office, and they were talking. In the exaggerated quiet of the common room, I could hear their conversation easily.

"Because I'm homicide, and this isn't a homicide." DuBois sounded tired more than angry. "Maybe you hired someone to tail her for a while so you could get a little extra now that the old man is gone."

"I didn't lose my job. I still work for the company. I'm not charging her extra for this. And you know I would never try to scare someone into hiring me."

"She's just your type. Maybe she's worth the risk."

Cotten's voice strained. "You're still angry about your CI?"

"You know as well as anyone how long it takes to get a good informant. He's dead, Cot. He had something big. Now he's dead." DuBois lowered his voice to just above a whisper, and I had to concentrate. "He said he was offered a murder for hire that could set him up for life."

"That was nearly a year ago." Cotten's gravel became raspier, and I wondered if he was getting emotional. "I didn't chase him. I didn't want him to run. I still don't know why he did."

"He was a criminal. That's what they do. You approach. They run. And my guy just happened to run in front of a bus."

I cringed at the idea of anyone getting hit by a bus. I realized that if anyone watched me, they'd know I was eavesdropping. I checked my expression. *Finish the statement, girl.*

As I filled the white space with all the little details I could think of, I heard Cotten apologizing. Green returned, and I handed her my paperwork. She looked it over and frowned.

"I can start a file for you." She tapped the end of a pencil on her desktop. "But I'm not sure I can do much more right now."

Cotten joined us. "Why not?"

Green shuffled through the photos and then paperclipped them to her file. "Is the street door of your apartment always locked?"

I answered with a shrug. "It's supposed to be. But the lock's been broken for months. We had a doorman when I moved in, but they replaced him with a camera, and I doubt that works either."

Green pressed her lips into a thin line. "That's my problem. See, you're in public places in all these pictures. If we try to pick this guy up, his attorney will argue that he just happened to be in the same public places as you. Even the lobby of your building could be explained away."

I pounded my finger into Wexler's face in the top picture. "But he's staring at me. In all these photos, he's staring right at me." I couldn't believe I'd gone through all of this to be dismissed so easily. Twice.

She pulled the pictures from under my hand. "I get that, but his lawyer will say, 'Of course, he's looking at you. You're pretty.'"

This was going nowhere. It had all been a silly made-up story just a few days ago, and now I was struggling to stay calm. My thoughts scrambled. "How does everyone know what his lawyer will say?"

"Because Wexler has one of the best lawyers in Dallas." Green and Cotten said the words in unison.

My stomach churned, and I fought the urge to vomit. My vision blurred again, but I was determined not to faint. Everything was wrong. Everything.

I glanced from Green to Cotten and then to DuBois, who was now standing beside me at the desk. What wasn't true before suddenly was, but now that I had proof, everyone told me they couldn't do anything about it.

A thought popped into my mind. A voice. A scream. *Johnny Depp stole my identity, and I want justice*!

CHAPTER 4

The Promise

"IT'S HOPELESS." I took Cotten's hand as he helped me out of his car in front of my building, but I was so frustrated I hardly noticed his firm but oh-so-gentle grip. "There's nothing they can do to help."

"Not yet," he added. "We know who this guy is. We have the advantage. You started the file, and that's the biggest hurdle. We gather more. We add to the file. It's a process."

"And you'll keep me safe until it's over?"

Cotten opened the door without bothering to enter the key code. "I will."

I started toward the stairwell.

"Don't you live on the third floor?" Cotten kept hold of my hand.

"Yes, but I usually take the stairs up." I looked up to make eye contact for the first time since we left the station. "I always thought the stairs were safer for single women."

He cocked his head toward me. "You're right—when you're alone. But you're not alone now."

"You're coming up with me?" My thoughts raced with my pulse. I wanted to bring him up. I did. But was my place clean? How had I left it this afternoon? I hadn't expected company. What had I been thinking? I figured I was in for a hard crash and burn and a bottle of bubbly. Maybe a Hall-mark movie. I'd never expected my dream man to accompany me home, let alone become my personal bodyguard. Well, he hadn't actually used that word, so maybe I shouldn't jump to conclusions.

"I'll come up for a little while. I'll check out your place—make sure it's secure. Then we can work out short-term and long-term plans of action." Cotten led me into the elevator after making sure the car was empty. He punched 3, and we made the slow and creaky ascent.

We passed Marlowe, in the middle of a bath, in the hallway to my place. I smiled in his direction as I unlocked my door with my phone app.

Cotten proceeded inside with a quick sweep. "It's clear." He motioned me in and closed and bolted the door behind us. "How often do you change the code on your door lock? I assume you can change the password, right?"

"Yeah." I glanced at my phone and twisted my lips from side to side. "I can't remember the last time I changed the code."

"Then that's the next thing we'll do." Cotten peered into the short hallway to my bedroom. "May I use your bathroom first?"

A flash of panic swept over me. The bathroom was a

wreck, even if the rest looked decent. The fear must have shown on my face.

Cotten took a quick breath. "Unless you'd like to go first?"

I smiled. "Thanks."

"Just let me know if anything is out of place."

Out of place? My bathroom was always in shambles. I entered and closed the door, grateful I hadn't let him see it first. Towels heaped on the floor. Lipstick-smudged Kleenex spilling out of the wastebasket. Brushes filled with tangled blonde hair. Toothpaste bits in the sink. Makeup everywhere.

I scraped all the countertop contents into the top drawer. I cleaned my hairbrushes and then squished the trash down to a sensible level. Picking up a still-damp towel, I wiped down the counter and the sink, then tossed that towel and the others into the hamper by the tub. I picked up a perfume bottle and spritzed the air a few times. Good enough. I flushed the toilet before I realized that I still had to pee. Well, now that would have to wait.

"Your turn." I gestured to the bathroom with a casual breeziness.

As soon as Cotten closed the door, I raced into the bedroom and blitzed it, too, throwing blankets over the bed and shoes into the closet. A quick spray from another bottle of perfume, and the place was presentable. I hurried back to the main room and popped a few wine glasses into the dishwasher. By the time I made it back to the sofa, Cotten was out of the bathroom.

"You have a nice apartment. Different than what I expected, but still really nice." Cotten took a seat at the opposite end of the couch.

"Can I get you something to drink? I have bottled water,

orange juice, and wine." Maybe if I played the proper hostess, it would give both of us something else to think about.

"Water would be great." Cotten pulled out his phone and held it up. "Do you mind if I check my messages?"

"Not at all." I got each of us a bottle of water and pulled out a small block of cheese from the fridge. In another minute, I assembled some raw broccoli and celery sticks and found an apple rolling around. I grabbed a knife and some napkins and threw everything onto a tray. It wasn't much of a dinner, but it was better than nothing. "What *did* you expect from my apartment?" I set the tray on the coffee table.

"Considering who your father is, I thought it might be a little bigger." Cotten opened his bottle and took a long draw.

"I like the charm of the historic building. And I grew up in a big house. I don't need that much." I didn't want to clean that much and didn't care for housekeepers going through my stuff.

"I don't suppose anyone really needs that much."

"So, how do you know my father? I mean, I heard you talking to DuBois about him. Like you knew him." I didn't want to sound rude. I had been eavesdropping, but with everything else going on, I figured it was a risk I could take.

Cotten furrowed his brow and set his bottle of water on a coaster. "You don't know?"

"Know what?"

"Your father was my boss. And he was one of my closest friends." Cotten tilted his head at a slight angle. "You *do know* that I work for you, don't you?"

"I hired you," I started. My brain worked to process what he was saying. What I'd heard him tell DuBois—that he still worked for the company. "You work for Daddy's company?"

"I thought that's why you asked me to help you. I've worked for your dad for a decade. I run the background checks and oversee the security for Petra. I set up the security system in his home. I can't believe you didn't know." He shook his head and grabbed a stalk of celery. "Why did you hire me, then? Did you just find my name online?"

Swallowing hard and scanning the tray, I scrambled for something to say. I couldn't backtrack now. He wouldn't believe me. "No, I knew you from your gifts to our foundation. I didn't realize you knew my dad personally."

"Oh." He munched on the celery like a cigar. "I assumed you knew me. That your father might have mentioned me to you. He talked about you with me quite often."

Really? I wondered if I had said that out loud, but Cotten didn't respond. I guess this time, I had kept my mouth under control. "No. He never talked about you—with me." The gears in my mind cranked slowly. "I wish he had."

Cotten relaxed into the sofa. "Me, too."

I picked up a small piece of broccoli. "He was one of your best friends?"

"He was."

"You probably miss him almost as much as I do." I wondered if that was possible.

"Every single day." Cotten chewed another big bite of celery. "So, how much did you hear between DuBois and me?"

I swallowed hard—he wasn't letting me off the hook. "Something about a guy getting hit by a bus. That's gruesome."

"It was the worst thing I've ever witnessed." Cotten's

expression became solemn. "I don't know why he ran from me."

"What exactly happened? Can you talk about it?" I took a sip of my water and leaned back into the couch cushions.

Cotten picked up the knife and began slicing into the apple. He'd turned it into eight wedges on the tray in less than a minute. "A group of moms hired me. They all took their kids to the same park to play every few days, and they'd noticed a guy with a camera coming around and taking pictures. At first, they thought he was shooting the gardens, but they noticed he included their kids in the photos. They said they had called the police, but nothing was being done. So they hired me."

"That's creepy. Like predator-creepy."

"Yeah." Cotten nodded. "Human-trafficking creepy. I watched him, and it was obvious that he was up to something. I approached him, and he ran. I still can't figure it out. He just took off like a bat out of hell. Before I knew it—before anyone knew it—he was bouncing off the front of a bus and lying in a heap in the road."

The image he described burned into my mind. "Awful."

"The moms were crying. The kids were crying. Everyone saw it happen."

I stared at the apple slices in front of me. I suddenly wasn't hungry. "And DuBois was angry? He thought you chased him or something?"

Cotten rolled his shoulders and rocked his head back to stare at the ceiling for a second. "DuBois is upset because the dead guy was his confidential informant. His CI. He was a criminal, but he was also a snitch to the police about a lot of the dirty deeds around town."

"I see." I wasn't sure I did, but it seemed the thing to say. "But he was involved in human trafficking? Seems like getting him out of the picture is a big deal."

"That's what I believe, too." He took another sip of his water. "DuBois says the guy was about to dish dirt on a big-time hit about to happen. I told him that if it were so big-time, he'd be able to figure it out without a snitch."

I raised my brows. "Wow. You're pretty brave to say something like that to DuBois. He seems like he could steam-roll anyone that crossed him."

"Damon's tough now, but I used to beat him up in grade school."

"You beat *him* up?" I tried to picture it. Cotten was tall and muscular but nowhere near the size of DuBois.

"Let's just say that we were more evenly matched back then. As we got older, the difference became more defined. He was the star graduate of the police academy. I struggled. I had the brains but not the brawn. Not like him. I went the private route. He went into public service." Cotten picked up an apple wedge. Watching his teeth sink into the flesh made me hungry again. "We help each other out from time to time."

I grabbed an apple wedge, too. "Thank you for helping me with my problem. This whole thing is such a nightmare." I was careful with my next few words. "I truly believed it was all in my imagination. But those pictures of yours. They have me rattled."

"I won't let anything happen to you." He shook his head. "Whatever it takes. I promised your dad years ago to keep an eye on you. Of course, I didn't expect it to be like this, but I won't let you down."

We sat for a few minutes without talking. We finished the few bites of cheese and munched on the rest of the uncomfortably loud food.

Once the tray was empty, I pushed it a few inches away. "You mentioned a short-term and long-term plan of action. What do you have in mind? Do I need to pull out my couch for you?" I wished.

Cotten's left eyebrow shot high. "No, I don't think that's necessary. I think you're safe for tonight. But I do want to run through some situational awareness techniques with you. Then I've got to get home and check on my family. Don't worry, though. I'll come by in the morning to escort you to your office."

All I heard was *family*. My heart stopped beating for what seemed like forever. He had a family. Of course, he did. Why wouldn't he? He was smart. He was gorgeous. He saved children from predators. He was practically perfect in every way. And he belonged to someone else.

We spent the next half-hour going through self-defense tips and what to do in an emergency. Cotten was very hands-on, which I would have enjoyed under different circumstances.

He demonstrated where to pinch, pull, and kick an attacker to do the most damage. We practiced a few moves; he slid up behind me, put one arm around my shoulders, and clapped a hand over my mouth. His arms cinched around me perfectly, and all I could think about was his patchouli cologne and how close his lips were to my ear.

Reveling in his embrace, I hesitated for a second before I fake-bit his hand and fake-stomped his instep.

"You can't wait to react. You have to take charge of the

situation right away." He rested his wrist on my shoulder and stared deep. "If you don't, you're giving the attacker time to incapacitate you."

"But what can I do if they're even close to your size? I'm too small to fend off an attack."

His forehead tilted toward mine. "Have you ever held a bowling ball?"

What did that have to do with anything? "Of course."

"About ten pounds or so?"

"About."

"Would it hurt me if you threw a bowling ball at me?" Now he gestured to his torso.

I resisted the urge to touch his chest. "Yes, if you didn't dodge it."

Cotten concurred. "And you weigh more than ten pounds, right?"

"Yes, of course."

He patted his hand over his heart. "So imagine what would happen if you threw yourself at me."

That scenario was exactly what I had imagined for the last month or so. *Steady, girl. He has a family.* What was the question? I stared back into his eyes and focused. "Maybe I could knock you down?"

His lips stretched into a wide smile. "Yes! Now I'm not suggesting that as a first reaction. You have to try to escape first. It should be a last resort. But it can be effective." He hunched down to demonstrate. "Lead with your shoulder and aim for center mass. When the guy is bent over, bring your knee up. Head, throat, privates. Then you run like hell." He straightened. "Understand?"

"Yes, I think so." I wanted to be back in his arms. I wanted *him*. But he was taken.

"Now for the little stuff." He showed me how to use reflections in glass and mirrors to see who might be behind me. It was all useful information. I tried to listen. I tried to learn. But it was difficult to think of anything beyond his family.

A wife. A kid or two. A tidy house in the suburbs. If he worked for my dad, he would have everything he needed for a stable, secure little American dream. My dad was big on keeping employees happy and well cared for. I was a job to him. A good job, maybe, but a job nonetheless.

DuBois had said that I was just his type. Who cared? Just a job.

"I'll be here to pick you up around eight." Cotten carried the snack tray back into my kitchen and set it beside the sink. "How do you like your coffee?"

My therapist would have a heyday with this. I could hear him now. *The Good Lord will send the right man at the right time, but it will never be someone else's husband.* I would probably laugh about it later. Not today. Not tomorrow. Maybe in a few years, though.

"What?" I realized he'd asked me a question.

"Is eight o'clock too early? Too late?"

"No. Eight is fine." I followed Cotten to the door. "You'll take me to work in the morning?"

He opened the door. "Yes. And I'll bring you back home tomorrow evening, too." He scanned my hallway in both directions. "Keep your door locked and bolted. I checked your windows, too. So you're secure for now."

"Thank you, Cotten. I do appreciate your time." I held out

my hand to shake his. This was not how I envisioned spending the day with him, but it was what I'd been given.

"You can call me if anything happens between now and morning. If you get scared—whatever. I mean, call 9-1-1 if it's an emergency, but short of that, call me."

It was almost too much of a temptation, and I wasn't sure I was that strong. "Thanks again. I'll see you in the morning." I started to close the door, but he stopped it at the last minute.

"I forgot," he said in a hushed tone. "How did you say you liked your coffee?"

I grinned as politely as I could manage. "Black."

He gave a slight bow, and I closed the door between us, turning the lock and throwing the deadbolt.

Black, like my heart.

CHAPTER 5

The Office

THE EIGHT O'CLOCK-IN-THE-MORNING sun glared extra bright off the streets, buildings, and cars that made up downtown Dallas. I hadn't slept well. Visions of Cotten playing catch with little kids in his yard kept running like a loop in my brain. Under normal circumstances, I'd have drowned the images in wine, but I'd only had one glassful left in the bottle, and I didn't dare run to the corner shop for more.

Cotten was professional and friendly. He asked how I slept.

"Not too well." I picked up the paper coffee cup and sniffed at the cover. The dark aroma sent a strong shot of comfort into my lungs. "I'll be all right."

"You will." He pulled into the parking garage and parked in my reserved parking space. "I'll walk you up to your office. What time will you be ready to go home this afternoon?"

a deep breath. "I may have an appointment at four.
to check with Karen. If so, it will run for about an
n I message you when I'm ready to go?"

"Of course." He scanned the garage in every direction as
we made our way to the elevator. "Do you need me to bring
you lunch?"

No more temptations. "No. I can have something sent up.
I won't go out alone."

He gave my office a quick sweep—checking all around
the main room, the small closet, and the private bath. "Everything looks good. But don't hesitate to call me if something
comes up. I can be here in five minutes."

Cotten left me alone to work. As cluttered and cozy as my
apartment was, my office was the opposite—spacious, organized, and flooded with natural light. My desk was wide and
clean. Even my computer desktop was neatly arranged.

I opened my email program, as I did every morning, and
deleted the spam before starting through the business corre-
spondence. First I read the internal messages, then the rest.
Sitting at the bottom of my inbox was the final email I
received from my dad from July last year.

"Let's have lunch this afternoon if you're free."

I hadn't been free. He'd eaten alone in his office at the
other end of the hall. Baked salmon, tossed green salad with
raspberry vinaigrette, and Perrier. When he had finished, he
collapsed from a sudden and massive heart attack. The doctor
explained that sometimes things like that happen. Nobody's
fault. It was just Daddy's time.

I couldn't bring myself to delete the email. Probably never
would.

Tap, tap, tap.

The sound jerked me into high alert. Bev Muncy, one of the other vice presidents of Petra Resources, poked her head into my office. "You busy?" Before I could answer, she frowned. "Girl, you look terrible. Are you sick?"

I shook my head and tried to fix a smile on my lips. "Not sick. Just didn't sleep well last night."

Bev stepped into my office and closed the door. "I saw a man walking you in. Did he have anything to do with your lack of sleep?" Bev positioned a narrow hip on the corner of my desk and swished her long, auburn hair over her shoulder.

I swatted the idea away with a flick of my wrist. "Not in the way you're thinking. Do you know Cotten Hammond?"

"Petra's chief of security? We've met, but only through work. He's been voted the sexiest man in the building for ten years running." Bev raised her brows and licked her coral lips.

"He has?"

"By me, at least. He's yummy." Bev waved her hand as though she was fanning heat from her face. "Ooh, was he your escort this morning? Lucky you."

I laughed. "Besides the sexy thing, what do you know about him?"

Bev plopped down in the client chair on the opposite side of my desk. "Only what you tell me, honey."

"I only really met him ten days ago. He's doing a job for me."

Bev leaned back in the chair and grinned. Her voice was full of salacious implications. "I can tell." Her phone started to jingle. "Hey, listen, I'll come by about noon. We'll grab lunch at that new place on the corner, and you can tell me all about it." She waved to me over her shoulder as she hurried out, answering her call on the go.

I watched her leave, sighed, then took a long sip from my still-too-hot coffee. My desk clock said 8:20. Time to do a little investigating of my own.

I googled Cotten Hammond, thinking there couldn't be more than one in the Metroplex. Wrong. At first glance, there were six. After a few minutes of deduction, I had a Cotten Hammond Junior, a retired English professor, approximately 70 years old, with a Garland address, and Cotten Hammond III, Private Investigator, 34 years old, on Main Street.

I found three newspaper articles, dozens of social media tags, and a full-color magazine spread about Cotten. They all mentioned his philanthropy, quick wit, and high-powered connections—meaning my dad—while suggesting he might be the most available and sought-after man in North Texas. Nothing about a wife. No mention of a family.

The most recent post was from merely a month ago, a short piece about Dallas's ten most eligible bachelors. He was third on the list. So why would he tell me he had a family if he didn't?

Of course, there's only one reason to do that. It's an easy way to preempt unwanted advances. Story of my life.

What did I expect? If it hadn't been for the actual stalker, Cotten would probably have already forgotten me. He certainly wouldn't be coming to pick me up after work.

I spent the next hour working on my pet project, *The History of Petra*, a book about how my father built the third-largest energy empire in America from the ground up in a mere fifteen years. I'd intended to present it to him on his last birthday, but then everything else happened. After his death, the whole manuscript went on a shelf for a month. I'd finished it only a few weeks ago. I was determined to have it ready for publication by the end of the year.

Ten o'clock chimed on my phone, and it was time for my therapy session. I saved my computer work and took a quick bathroom break. I settled into my leather and wood Eames chair and ottoman and turned on the television just as Steve Harvey began his opening monologue. Okay, so I don't go to an actual therapist, but the man gives sound advice. And he's funny. The world needs more of that.

By the end of the show, I blotted tears of laughter from my eyes and cheered for the 63-year-old woman who went back to school with her granddaughter. Any hour I'm not having a pity party for myself is a good hour.

I checked with my assistant, Karen, whom I inherited from Dad. My four o'clock had canceled. I returned to work and finished editing the chapter about Petra going public. According to my outline, I had just five chapters left to proof-read. And maybe add an afterword; I hadn't decided about that yet.

Another tap at the door. Bev again. "Are you ready for a bite?" Another frown. "Honey, go fix your makeup. I thought you looked bad this morning. Have you been crying?"

"Therapy session," I explained as I hurried into the bathroom.

Bev laughed. "I had to give up my therapist when his wife caught us on his desk."

"Bev!" I never understood her need to overshare. "Did he lose his license?" I finished fixing my face and rejoined her.

"Who's ever going to know?" She looped her handbag over her arm.

"Umm, his wife, me, and anyone else you've told." I pulled my purse from my desk drawer and slipped the strap to my elbow.

"Oh, you worry too much." Bev waited for me in the hall while I locked my office door. "You're the oldest thirty-year-old I know."

"Twenty-nine," I whispered under my breath. Maybe she was right. I looked Bev up and down. She was a decade older than me. A little thicker at the ankles, but her curves were well-balanced, and she knew how to handle any man. Just ask her.

We headed down in the polished chrome elevator, picking up a few more passengers on our way to the lobby. I smiled politely. I knew faces, but I wasn't good at remembering names. Bev was a pro, at least with the men.

"George! I haven't seen you in ages." Another floor. "Bradley! How are you? Do you remember the last time we were in this elevator together? I'm sure you do."

All I could do was stand in the corner and blush. We finally made it to street level, and I was prepared. I was going to keep a constant watch on my surroundings. Nobody would follow me. I wouldn't let myself get isolated. I was ready for anything.

But as we walked to the main glass doors, I saw him. His bright orange hair caught the sunlight like a flame. He'd shaved his mustache, but it was Wexler. He stood at the sidewalk, watching people enter and exit. He was waiting for me.

I froze in my tracks. Bev walked another seven or eight steps before realizing I'd stopped.

"What's up?" she asked, spinning on her heel.

My brain didn't work. I couldn't take my eyes away from

Wexler. He was right there. I struggled to swallow and realized I was breathing through my gaping mouth.

"Hon, what's wrong?" Bev asked again. "You look like you've seen a ghost."

I took a step backward and pulled my thoughts together. "I forgot about a phone call I need to make before lunch." Another two steps back. "Listen, I'm not sure how long this will take. Why don't you go on without me? I'll take a rain check." And without waiting for her to answer, I turned and ran back to the elevators.

Getting into a car with four others, I started texting Cotten. *Wexler is here, at the front door of my building. Please come ASAP.*

"What floor?" a gentleman in a gray suit asked.

Before I could answer, another young man pushed *12*. "Come on, Jeffries. It's Ms. Peters. Her office is on the top."

Jeffries bowed slightly. "I'm sorry I didn't recognize you, Ms. Peters. I hope you're having a good day." The car made a soft ding, the doors slid open, and he got out.

The younger man and two other women shared the ride to the twelfth floor with me. We all exited at the double ding, and I headed back to my office, praying for a reply on my phone. It came just as I got my door unlocked.

"Two minutes."

True to his word, he was at my office door in ninety seconds. "I called the police as soon as you messaged me. I got to the front door just in time to see the patrol car pull up and Wexler walk away."

"Did they pick him up?" I didn't think I could handle the idea of Wexler waiting for me around every corner. Nope. Based on the last five minutes, I knew I couldn't.

"They can't pick him up. He's still on public property."

"But he was waiting for me!"

"I'm certain the patrol officer will ask him what he's doing here and probably a dozen more questions." Cotten gestured to my Eames chair, and I took a seat. "Look, we called it in. It will go into your file. This is how we make the case."

"Ugh. Why is he following me?"

Cotten strode to my mini-fridge, pulled a bottle of Perrier out, and handed it to me. "You should drink something. Take a moment and breathe."

I stared at the green bottle. The corners of the yellow label peeled at the neck. I handed it back to Cotten. "I just want plain water, please."

He took the water from me and opened the refrigerator door. He looked inside and then exchanged the green bottle for a blue one. "You have a dozen Perrier bottles and only two plains. If you don't like carbonated, why do you keep it?"

"Dad loved it." That was the simple answer. Explaining why I couldn't move those horrid green bottles out of my office was more difficult. I didn't know why, so how could I tell him?

Cotten didn't seem to need more than that. He cracked the seal on the silver cap. "Would you like me to ask your assistant to replenish your plain water?"

I gulped the cold water as fast as possible, feeling the icy fingers track down my throat and into my stomach. "Yes, please."

"Can you work remotely for the rest of the day?" Cotten scanned the room. "I thought this place would be safe for you, but I was wrong. I want to take you somewhere out of his reach."

Yes. I had to get somewhere safe. I needed this to end. But then I realized it would never end. Not as long as he could get away with it. I looked at Cotten, who stood at the window overlooking the traffic below.

I walked to his side and squeezed his forearm. "We need to catch him actually trespassing, don't we? If we could catch him on private property and call the cops, that would get him locked up, right?"

Cotten furrowed his brow. Through his sleeve, I could feel his biceps tense and flex. "But I don't want you in danger."

"I won't be in danger. You'll be watching. You'll be ready to pounce as soon as he makes his move. Please. I can't do this much longer."

"If he knows I'm there, he might do something stupid. He might get desperate. He could hurt you before I could stop him."

"You taught me some self-defense. Teach me more if you need to." I raised my gaze to meet his, and we stood toe to toe. I don't know what I expected, but what I saw sent a hot flutter to my stomach. His eyes shifted to my lips and back up.

"I promised your father." His voice was no more than a distant whisper of thunder.

I tightened my grip on his arms and felt his hands at my elbows. I leaned forward until our lips were only inches apart. "Now make your promises to me."

CHAPTER 6
The Plan

I WAS up to my neck in a manic-depressive state. Afraid for my life one minute and needing a cuddle the next. I wanted to be brave. But it was as though my whole body was one of those gelatin salads that languish at the end of the early-bird buffet.

We needed a plan. No, I'd had a plan. That's what started this whole fiasco. We needed a better plan.

"What if I went home for a little while?" I shut down my computer and grabbed my purse. "You can follow me while I walk home. If the police didn't pick him up, he might follow me, and you could follow him. If they did pick him up, I'd be safe anyway. We need to get him on private property, right? Can you set up cameras in my building?"

Cotten crossed his arms over his chest. "Do you own your apartment building?"

"No."

"Then, no." He scoffed. "We'd only be allowed to put up

cameras in your specific apartment, and if he's there, he can be arrested for breaking and entering. We need to get him on your turf. In this office, or...."

"Or what? Where do you have in mind?" I thought I saw a spark in his eyes.

"Do you have a go-bag?" He took a step toward me. His gaze floated up from the floor to my eyes. He looked as though he was devising a fool-proof scheme.

I took a step closer to match his. "I have no idea what that means." I thought I'd take a stab at the low, breathy voice Bev used to seduce every man she met. Instead, my voice sounded in need of a lozenge.

Cotten shifted his weight to his heels and leaned back on the corner of my desk. He painted an amused smile on his lips. "It's simply an overnight bag that stays packed all the time, just in case you have to be away from home unexpectedly. For a trip to a hotel room or safe house."

I swallowed hard and shook my head a fraction of an inch. If I didn't know better, I would say he was flirting. Most likely, it was my imagination, but a part of me wished. No, all of me wished. I could hear Steve Harvey's voice—*if wishes were horses*. Shut up, Steve.

"What do I pack in a go-bag? What will I be doing? What will the weather be like?"

His lip curled on one side. "The point is to be prepared for anything. For you, I'd pack a pair of jeans and a shirt. A dress. Some slacks, a blouse, a jacket or a sweater. Any accessories and underwear you need for those. Basic toiletries. Something to sleep in. You'll need an extra phone charger, copies of your ID, travel papers, credit cards, and as much cash as you feel comfortable carrying."

"I'll need more than that. Three outfits aren't enough for anything over 36 hours."

He laughed again. "When I take you on a week's vacation to Turks, you can pack everything you want. A go-bag is for basics. Bare essentials. The cash gets you whatever you didn't pack."

I was sure he spoke normally, but everything after 'when I take you' came out in slow motion. I had no idea how my face reacted. Thankfully, he wasn't looking at my face because when I heard Turks, my arm twitched, my purse strap dropped from my shoulder, and the bag fell open on the floor.

We scrambled for a minute, both suddenly on our knees, reaching for rolling lipstick tubes and an open tin of peppermints.

"Are you two playing Twister?" a voice called from the door.

Greg Oberman stepped into my office and cocked his head sideways for a better angle of the situation. Dad always had called Oberman his navigator because he always seemed to know what was coming next on the energy horizon.

I popped my head up and smiled. "I dropped my purse."

Oberman bent toward Cotten. "And you had to call security?"

"Ha. That's funny." I set my bag on the corner of the desk as Cotten helped me back to my feet. "No, umm, Mr. Hammond and I were about to grab lunch." I smoothed my skirt with my hands and stepped between Oberman and Cotten. "Is there something I can do for you, Greg?"

Oberman grimaced and raised his graying eyebrows high. "Karen wanted me to remind you of next Monday's quarterly board meeting. So send your report to her by four this afternoon."

"Do I need to send a report if I'm going to be at the meeting?" I hadn't made the last three meetings, but I felt strong enough to attend this one. I was finally ready to fill Daddy's chair at the head of the table.

"You're going to be there?" Oberman's face looked as though I'd slapped him with a fish.

"I think I'm up to the challenge now." I settled my hands on my hips, Wonder Woman-style, which had been one of Cotten's recent tips for making myself appear more of a physical threat. I could almost feel him beaming with pride behind me.

"Are you sure it's not too soon, Veronica? We all miss your father, but none of us can pretend to fathom the depths of *your* grief, child."

There it was. *Child.* Despite Petra Resources having a workforce planted primarily in their thirties and forties, I was the board's youngest member. By a decade. I took a step forward. Another tip. "Thank you for your sympathy, Mr. Oberman, but I know my father would want me to pick up his mantle and lead as he did. I'm anxious to make him proud."

Oberman must have realized his faux pas. "I didn't mean to imply anything unflattering. I know how proud your father was of you. Some of us watched you grow up here, and we share that pride."

"I understand." Sure I did. "If you could let Karen know I'll be there Monday, I'd appreciate it." I pasted on an intentionally patronizing grin and watched Greg shove his hands into his trouser pockets. "And if anyone asks, I have an out-of-office meeting after lunch. So I won't be back in today."

"Uh, yeah. Okay." Greg shuffled back into the hall, looking mildly miffed that I didn't crumble and send regrets for Monday's meeting.

I glanced at the wall clock. I'd probably crumble in another hour or so. By myself. With a bottle.

"And here I thought you weren't like your father at all." Cotten sauntered to the door and held out his elbow for me to take. "You're a lot tougher than... I don't know what I'm trying to say. You're tough."

"I think the words you're searching for are *tougher than you thought I was*, right?"

"Just so." Cotten walked me down the hall to the elevator. "And my underestimation speaks more to my character than yours, I confess."

"Well, aren't you the flatterer?" We got into the empty elevator. "I suppose everybody but me knows you're Petra's security man."

Cotten nodded. "So you made a smart call making this a social relationship. There's no need to worry the others that you might have threats against you."

I stepped closer and squeezed his arm as the elevator slowed halfway down to the lobby. Maybe it was for show. Maybe not, but I wasn't going to let the opportunity pass.

The door opened on six, and a young man clutching a too-big stack of files started to join us. "Going up?" he asked.

We both shook our heads. "Down," Cotten and I answered together.

"Sorry." And the man stepped back as the door slid closed again.

The elevator stopped, and we stepped out into the lobby. The space was filled with worker bees hurrying in every direction.

Cotten got a strange look in his eye. "I have an idea." He turned us toward the parking garage elevator instead of the street doors. A minute later, we were back at his car. "I'm going to drop you at your place. You put a go-bag together and meet me afterward for a late lunch. How about that bistro a few blocks down from your apartment?" He opened the car door for me.

"Don't you want to come in and wait with me while I pack? We can talk through some plans. Then you can put my bag into your trunk." I hated to waste a semi-clean apartment.

He shook his head. "I need to check on the situation status with DuBois. And I have to get a safe place lined up for you. Leave your bag just inside your door, and we'll come back for it after." Cotten steadied me as I lowered myself into his car.

We were back at my apartment a few minutes later, and Cotten cleared the place room by room. No obvious threats.

He seemed satisfied that I was safe for the moment. "I'm going to disappear for a little bit. At least *you* won't see me. I want you to meet me at the bistro in one hour unless I text otherwise. I'll be waiting for you in the back. That will give me enough time to get things straight. And don't worry, I'll be watching you from the moment you step out onto the street."

"How can you follow me *and* beat me to the restaurant?"

"Tailing from in front of a target is more of a challenge, but it's quite effective if you're watching someone being followed by a third party." Cotten pulled the drapes back from the window and glanced in both directions down the street.

"You're just making that up. Nobody can follow from ahead."

"I can."

"I'll see you." I was sure I'd be able to spot him if he was in front of me with all the awareness tips he'd given me. After all, I went for at least two weeks never noticing a man with traffic cone orange hair following me, and then today, I saw him right off.

"You won't see me. I'll bet dinner you don't." He crossed his arms over his chest, glancing down at the watch on his wrist. "I need to go. If you spot me before you arrive, I'll pay for dinner personally. It comes off my expense tab."

"And in the highly unlikely event that I don't see you? I'm already paying for your services." I walked him to my door.

"When this is all over, and Wexler is no longer a problem, you can buy me another dinner. Off the clock." His tone was playful. I felt sure this time he was flirting.

I tilted my head coyly. "Hmm. Then maybe I'll miss you on purpose." I had a terrible urge to throw myself at him, but resisted. "I'll see you in an hour if I don't see you on the way." I waited for him to walk away, but he just stood and waited.

"I'll go when I hear the dead-bolt lock." He tilted his head forward and gave me a stern look from beneath his brows.

I closed the door slowly and threw the bolt. Through the peephole, I watched him walk away. Nice.

Now to the go-bag. I took the overnighter from the top of my closet and found the clothes he suggested, putting together three ensembles. I debated with myself about which tops were the best for the bag. Most flexible, most comfortable, cutest—and then settled on the tee and the blouse compatible with the same pair of comfy shoes. Packing more than two pairs seemed unnecessary, considering bag space dictated how much hair and makeup stuff I could take.

I packed the clothes, underwear, shoes, ID, and paperwork, then moved the bag to the top of my hamper, where I could top it off with my toiletries. I filled my little zippered case with all the makeup basics that were almost used up and then with samples I'd collected over the last few months.

Next, hair products and tools. I was just about done when I thought about my hair accessories. I'd need a dozen bobby pins—at least. And several hair ties and bands. Combs, brushes, and a quick-dry hair turban. I shuffled through my things and saw a cute hair clip I had misplaced a few weeks ago. It was right there, on top of all the others. *Hmmph.* I had scoured the bathroom for it on my birthday—it was set with emerald green Swarovski crystals—but I gave up after looking for nearly an hour. Knowing me, I'd probably picked it up a dozen times to look beneath it.

Well now I had the clip, and I knew just the dress to match it this afternoon. I snapped it loosely on the side of my hair, just behind my ear.

I appraised my newly assembled go-bag proudly, zipped it up, and set it at the side of the door. Time to get ready for my date.

I took five minutes to dress, another five for makeup, and ten more to sit and review all the tips Cotten had taught me. I *was* going to see him, but I might *not* admit it.

And if that slimy Wexler was following me, I would spot him, too. That bright orange hair. He stood out like a sore thumb. Honestly, how had I not seen him before? A shiver ran down my back. *How had I not seen him before?*

I thought about what DuBois asked Cotten. Did he pay someone to scare me into hiring him? Hah! If only he'd known I had made the whole scenario up in my imagination. The idea was laughable. But why had that been DuBois' first thought? Cotten Hammond was a good man. He donated to a women's foundation. He saved kids from human traffickers. He probably had a dog.

DuBois was wrong.

Thinking about this got me nowhere. And I had somewhere to be.

CHAPTER 7
The Date

OVERTHINKING BECAME my new favorite pastime. Maybe Officer Green was right. Maybe it was just a case of me being in the same public places as this Wexler guy, and I was just some spoiled little rich girl. Maybe I didn't have a stalker at all. Only a wild imagination.

But I'm not a little girl anymore. I had no delusions about men wanting to be with me. Well, I did have the one delusion about Cotten, but that was beside the point. After all, even Cotten believed I had a stalker, and he was no spoiled little girl.

I walked to my dinner meeting with Cotten and recounted the last few weeks. I'd been all over downtown—the market, the salon, the department store, the office, the cleaners—and not once had I caught a glimpse of my creep. Until today. Was he getting sloppy, or had I gotten better at being aware, as Cotten said?

He *had* taught me a lot. I imagined his arms around me as

he pretended to attack. His strength, his smell, his family. But he didn't have a family, did he? *Girl, it doesn't matter whether he does or not—he used that excuse not to stay the night. He doesn't want you.* I forced myself to think of something else.

My reflection in a shop window reminded me to practice one of Cotten's awareness techniques. I stopped, stepping out of the way of other pedestrians, and scanned both directions in front and behind. Nobody stopped or appeared to duck into a doorway or around a corner. I used the window reflection for a long perusal of the others on the street.

No Cotten. No Wexler.

At any given moment, a dozen or more people used the public scooters to zip through the crowded downtown streets. The scooter program made sidewalks more passable and freed up parking spaces considerably. Scooter passes helped would-be pedestrians take ten or even twenty blocks with ease. It also seemed to help with pollution control. The one downside was discreetly identifying the people darting by.

I scanned the faces of the scooter operators as best I could. Most were in their early twenties, with earbuds in and bags slung over their shoulders. No one made eye contact. Good.

I pretended to check my lipstick in the reflection, but a dress inside the shop caught my eye. Red with creamy magnolia blossoms scattered over it. It screamed summer carefree. That's what I needed. The dress looked lovely, but I craved the carefree part.

As my eyes shifted focus, I noticed two young women in the store pointing at the dress and then at me. They made disparaging faces at the dress and then laughed.

At first I felt offended, but then I remembered I wasn't

shopping anyway. I was surveilling, and I had just surveilled them. But how long had they stood mocking me before *I* noticed?

I should practice more. I walked down the block before stepping into a doorway to "check my watch."

Nobody ducked or made quick, unexpected moves around me. No one watching from cars, scooters, or windows. Even from across the street.

Still no Wexler. And to my dismay, no Cotten.

I checked the time and realized I was almost ten minutes late for my date with Cotten. Dinner meeting. Appointment. Whatever.

My hair and nails looked fantastic, and I wore a cute sundress and heels. I could call it a date if I wanted.

But ten minutes—of course, Cotten would arrive at the restaurant first.

I entered the bistro and checked my surroundings again. No stalker in sight. I stepped through the door, and the smell of sunbaked asphalt faded into the lush aromas of smoked and grilled meats, buttered pastries, and cream-laden sauces.

The host shifted from behind his stand and tilted forward in a half-bow. "Good afternoon."

"I'm meeting...."

"Yes, Ms. Peters. Follow me."

He knew my name. Recognized me on sight. I'd never experienced this. I hadn't been to this bistro since I came with my dad. Everyone knew Daddy. It never occurred to me that anyone had bothered to see me.

"Thank you." I wished I knew his name.

Even with the dim lighting, I saw Cotten wave from the other side of the room. I followed close behind the host, both of us stopping short and side-stepping to maneuver between the tables and chairs of other diners and drinkers.

Cotten stood as I approached, his arms reaching out for me. His smile broadened as his gaze perused me from head to toe and back. My skin flushed when I detected a gleam in his eyes. He looked at me in exactly the way I wanted him to look at me.

Every move I made needed to be smooth and sultry. I made sure to shift my hips just enough. No jiggle. Keep it classy.

Almost there. I looked good. Cotten looked great. I was Grace Kelly to his Cary Grant. We were perfect together. Everyone in the bistro could see it. The host stepped aside for my final approach. Only a step away from him. Our hands inches apart.

And then the heel of my left shoe caught and held fast to the rug. My left foot lurched and broke free of the shoe a split second after my right foot came off the floor.

Cotten's hands caught me and pulled. I had my lips pursed, ready to kiss Cotten's cheek, when my whole body launched forward more quickly than either of us expected. My face crashed into the side of his head, leaving a stripe of Crimson Caress from his lips to his ear.

My right shoulder hit squarely in the center of his chest. Our bodies became horizontal, pushing over our table and at least one of our chairs. Water glasses flew, and flatware catapulted to other tables. The whole fall transpired in slow motion but ended in mere seconds. As the din quieted and the linen napkins settled, there were at least eight legs in the air, counting our table, and the chilly breeze on my backside made me acutely aware that the whole bistro now knew Victoria's secret.

Our host flailed his arms to assemble his waitstaff army as Cotten helped me to my feet. A server handed me my shoe and gestured to the short hall over her shoulder.

"The restrooms are right back here." She shot a glance at both of us. "We'll have your table ready by the time you get back."

Back? Oh, uh-uh. I had no intention of staying after that fiasco. I wanted to crawl under a table and hide, but with my luck, I'd probably just knock that over, too.

Cotten seemed to read my mind. "Don't worry about any of that."

"I'm not worried; I'm mortified. I can't stay here."

He drew a deep breath. "Hardly anyone noticed."

Note to self: Cotten was a terrible liar. "My underwear!" I whisper-screamed. "And I smeared lipstick all over your face."

He let his lip curl as if he enjoyed it. "You have a smidge on your own face, too." He allowed the smile to spread, and his expression resembled the Joker's.

I couldn't stop shaking my head. "I'm going to die of embarrassment."

"Let's go clean up our faces. Then we'll see, okay?" He offered his elbow toward me.

I agreed reluctantly and slipped my hand through the crook of his elbow. I took one limp-step and dropped the other shoe to the floor. I held a grudge as I shoved my bare foot into it.

We entered the hall, and Cotten went left. I went right. The ladies' room resembled a French boutique. White porcelain vessel sinks sat on a black marble countertop. The water closets were assembled from vintage doors painted eggplant. Each stall had crystal doorknobs, inside and out. An antique chandelier hung overhead, and the bazillion facets of the crystal droplets sent rainbows of light through their prisms, reflecting in the gilded mirrors on either side of the room.

The restroom was empty, so I entered the middle stall to relieve myself. I stared down at my stupid shoes. They weren't even that cute. Off to Goodwill as soon as possible.

I pulled a handful of translucent one-ply from the roll and began dabbing the lipstick stain on my face. This resulted in tiny bits of toilet paper embedding themselves in the smear on my chin. When I finally inspected my face in the washroom mirror, I was more than mortified. I looked like a drunk clown. Not only had my lipstick slurred down my chin, but with the stress, my mascara had blossomed around my eyes.

Running the water until it turned lukewarm, I grabbed a tissue from the counter and wetted it. Five long minutes later, I managed to get my face somewhat presentable. At least enough to hike back through the dining room and then home. How could this get any worse?

No, don't ask. Don't even think about it.

My adorable little handbag sat on the counter while I pulled everything out in search of my lipstick. I'd peeled my face off, and I needed to replace it with something. I dabbed my lips with the dark red crayon. They'd swollen from the thorough scrubbing, but I could make it work.

I had just finished up when the bathroom door opened again. A petite woman with green-black hair entered and stood beside me at the lavatory. When I glanced up with a forced smile, I noticed two things. The upper left side of her face was tattooed to look like a sugar skull, and she stared directly at me.

Wasn't that a gross breach of etiquette? I flashed her another smile, hoping she'd avert her eyes, but there they were. Golden cat-eye contacts looking straight at me. I prayed they were contacts. The woman didn't look away.

Nope. I wasn't going back out there if everyone was going to stare. This was my home now. It was a nice restroom, anyway.

"Are you Ronni?"

She said *Ronni,* not *Ms. Peters.* My heart lurched the same way my foot had only ten minutes ago. Who was this woman? Surely not a member of the waitstaff. Could she be an accomplice to my stalker? Do stalkers have partners? My mind raced through a dozen scenarios, all of which ended with me in the trunk of a car. I said nothing, but my expression betrayed me.

"There's a man in the hall. He's waiting for you to come out."

My heart thudded loudly in my ears. Wexler was right outside the door. I searched for another way out. None. Not even one of those tiny slider windows.

The woman held out her hands to stop me as I tried to side-step her. "Wait!"

"I gotta get outta here." I didn't know if I said it out loud or only thought it.

"Ronni, stop!"

I did. Okay, if my stalker were going to take me, I'd be ready. Aware of my surroundings, I'd remember everything. Every sound, every smell, every bump in the road. I'd be the best possible witness. I'd find a way to relay all the details to Cotten.

Cotten! If my stalker was outside, what had happened to Cotten?

Taking half a step backward, I inhaled a deep, calming breath. Sort of. "What do you want?"

"I'm just here to help." She raised her hands as if she was approaching a rabid raccoon. "Cotten is your boyfriend, right?"

Gulp. I couldn't think. I couldn't move. Not even a blink. "What have you done with him?"

"No. Nothing. What?" She gawked at me as though I had antennae. "Cotten is the guy in the hall. He asked me to come in and check on you. He's your date, right?"

"My date." My blood pressure started to pulse down, one heavy heartbeat at a time. "Yes, he's my date." My thoughts settled slightly. I took another step toward the door.

"But wait a second. I'm really trying to help."

"How can you help me?" I still wasn't convinced she was there to help.

"I didn't see what happened out there. I've been at the dishwasher for the last hour, but I heard it was bad." She raised her brows and crossed her skinny arms as she bumped her hip against the counter.

Exhaling, I shook my head. "Bad isn't the word. I'm not sure I can show my face out there. It was the worst possible thing you can think of."

"Oh girl, you have no idea what I've seen. What I've done. I once dropped a tray of sixteen cocktails on a former First Lady and got tackled by a Secret Service bodyguard. That night after my shift, I got hammered and did this." She gestured to her face tattoo. "And that was the week before my sister's wedding."

"Ooh." I sucked the word through my teeth. Yeah, that was worse.

"And I had just gotten my accountant certification. But looking like this," she gestured to her face again, "Nobody's gonna hire me. I'm stuck washing dishes to save up to have it removed. Until you experience this level of embarrassment, I think you'll be fine."

I grimaced. "I suppose it's not so bad."

She laughed. "You've been in here for nearly ten minutes. Most of the witnesses have already left the restaurant. If you stay here much longer, the ones still left will be talking about you for other reasons."

"Okay. I think I'm ready now." I tucked my handbag under my arm and squared my shoulders.

She furrowed her brow, putting a crease into the skull tattoo. "You're not going out there like that." She pointed to my left foot.

Shifting my weight to my right side, I looked down. To my horror, I saw a banner of onion-skin toilet paper secured to the offending heel. Stupid shoe.

Using a paper towel, I plucked the flag loose and deposited it into the trash bin by the door. "Thank you," I said as I washed my hands one last time.

Offering my freshly cleaned hand, I said, "I'm Ronni Peters."

The young woman shook my hand. "I'm Inez Delgado."

"Thank you, Inez."

"No problem at all. I figured you'd like to avoid any more attention." She tilted her head and grinned.

"I'm still not sure I'm brave enough to stay for dinner."

She shook her head and pointed again at her face tattoo. "Girl, you have to. Gavin ordered you a special spread—on the house—and your boyfriend is seriously good-looking. You get back out there and enjoy your date."

Inez opened the bathroom door for me. Cotten stood in the hall, waiting for me. As I walked past her I whispered, "Thank you."

"You got this," she whispered back.

Cotten and I returned to the dining room as Inez disappeared into the kitchen.

"Everything all right?" Cotten gestured to our table, which had been reset and now included a yellow pottery bowl of Caesar salad, a loaf of artisan bread, and two glasses of dark red wine.

Cotten put a hand to his heart. "Yes, thank you, Gavin."

Noticing that nobody in the room was staring, I nodded. "It's perfect."

The host floated back to our table as Cotten pulled out a chair. I sat down. "Please forgive us, Ms. Peters. Our rug is getting worn. I should have replaced it months ago, but I don't think of it. And now this has happened. There will be a dagger in my heart until I can make it up to you."

"Gavin, there is nothing to forgive." I took his hand, feeling terrible about making a scene. "You spoil me."

Gavin offered a quick bow. "I am so happy you have come back to my bistro. I've been afraid you wouldn't return after your father—God rest his soul—passed. I am pleased to have you again. If you wish for anything, you need only speak it, and it is yours." He bowed again before leaving us to our dinner.

"Well, you certainly know how to put a man in his place." Cotten tilted his head as he slid his napkin across his lap. "I was feeling a bit cocky about you not seeing me on the street. I had some witty thing I was going to say, but for the life of me, I can't remember what it was."

Picking up my knife and fork, I grinned at him. "I knocked it right out of you, literally."

"Mmm-hm, you did that. But not when you plummeted into me. No, my mind went blank in the five seconds you finally came to a full stop on top of me."

A wave of heat flashed through me. That was definitely flirting. But was he pretending we were on a date, or was this indeed a date? I knew which I voted for but felt a consensus was needed.

"What is the plan going forward?" I hoped we could get business out of the way quickly. "Did you figure out whatever you were checking on?"

Cotten swallowed a bite of salad. "Yes. I had DuBois look up something for me."

"But Green is the officer with my case." I chased a grape tomato around my plate.

"Yes, but I was asking about Wexler. DuBois knows everything to know about him." He put another bite into his mouth.

"If DuBois is homicide, does that mean Wexler is a killer?" My heart immediately pounded hard. I was getting in a week's worth of cardio.

"So far as anyone knows, no. Wexler is strictly misdemeanors. But he pays the bills as a leg man for some of the top offenders in Texas. The guys who snap their fingers and have enemies erased. While nobody has ever accused Wexler of pulling a trigger, there's a pretty good chance that he knows where a few bodies are buried." Cotten picked up his glass and started to take a sip. "Oh, excuse me." He held up his glass toward mine. "Cheers."

I quickly picked up my glass and clinked it gently against his. "Cheers," I echoed and then took a much longer drink than he did. When I finally set my half-empty glass back on the table, I motioned to him. "Please, continue."

Cotten looked a little judgey again. "Yes, well. What I wanted to be sure about was his lawyer. Wexler, as I noted before, always gets away with whatever crimes he's accused of because he has an excellent lawyer."

"You and Green both said so."

"So I called DuBois to make sure I had it right. I did. His lawyer is Marcus Humphrey. Humphrey has also done work for your company." Cotten poked his fork at me for punctuation.

I leaned toward him. "Are you sure? I thought my father's lawyer was April Todd. I'm positive."

"Your father's personal lawyer is Ms. Todd. But Petra Resources has used Humphrey half a dozen times in various small cases."

"Is that a big deal? I thought it was common practice for big companies to hire as many lawyers in town as possible for as many different jobs as possible. Daddy said it was to keep lawsuits to a minimum. If a lawyer has worked for you and someone tries to sue you, they can't hire your lawyer because it would be a conflict of interest, right?"

"Right, more or less." Cotten buttered a slice of bread and handed it to me.

"Thank you." I took a quick nibble. A thought popped

into my head. "I suppose I don't see a connection. Wexler uses a lawyer my family's company has used in the past."

"It may be nothing at all. But I think, and DuBois also suspects it, that Wexler gets his job leads from Humphrey. Let's say client Smith needs someone rubbed out. Humphrey happens to know a small-time crook who owes him for representation—someone who might be able to do the job without actual ties to Smith. He does the job and confirms it with Humphrey, who then hires another crook to hide a body, launder some cash, or dispose of a weapon. They all scratch each other's backs without ever meeting those whose backs are getting scratched." Cotten's brow crept low as he spoke in a hushed tone. "Understand?"

"Yeah, I understand what you're saying. When it goes to court, everyone has an alibi. Nobody can connect any dots because there's no evidence of personal meetings and no paper trail to connect the suspects." I found myself leaning lower and whispering, too. "But why is it important that Humphrey represented Petra? Do you think he's working with someone who wants to rub me out now?"

"No." That's what his voice said, but his expression hinted otherwise. "But I want to be sure. Because if Humphrey has had past access to Petra's financial statements, then someone could use that information to get to you."

"But why me?" My whisper came out more like a whine this time.

"You're the heir to your father's company. You're heir to his fortune. You're the controlling shareholder of the whole shebang." He inched his hand over mine. "One could ransom you for millions."

I swallowed hard. "You think Humphrey...."

"Look, it could be Humphrey or Wexler himself if he got access to some of Humphrey's files. Or it could be someone else working through Humphrey."

My whole body trembled. Cotten held my hand more tightly. I had never intended for anything like this to happen. How had this silly idea gotten so far out of hand? How did it become real? "Someone wants me dead?"

Cotten shushed me gently. "I don't think so. I think someone wants money from you. The most common motives for all crimes are love, money, or revenge. I can't imagine anyone wanting revenge against you. So it must be money." He kept his tone soft and controlled. "Even if you take a step further and include your father, money is still more likely than revenge."

"Of course. My dad was a saint."

Cotten chuffed a quiet laugh before he stifled it.

"You didn't think so? You said he was a good friend." I pulled my hand from Cotten's loosened grip.

"Your father was a great man. He was my best friend and, more, he was a second father to me. But he was no saint, Veronica." Cotten's casual smile turned into a knowing smirk.

"Name one bad thing he ever did."

"I can name a dozen without straining. And you could, too, if you took your idol down from the pedestal to dust it once in a while."

My face flushed hot, and this time not from embarrassment or lust. How dare Cotten accuse my dad of any impropriety? He wasn't perfect, but everyone loved and admired my dad. I reached for my glass and didn't wait for a clink. I downed the remaining wine in one huge gulp. Not very ladylike, but I was mad. "You need to take that back."

"Okay, okay." He held his hands up in surrender. "Look, I loved your father. I truly did. I just knew him differently than you did. I'm sure he told you things he would never tell me, just like he told me things he would never tell you."

"Like what?"

"I don't know." He shrugged a little too casually. "If I think of something, I'll tell you. I promise." Cotten flipped his hand palm up on the table between us as if he was inviting me to take it. "My point is that if this is about your money, which I believe it is, someone will soon be making a move toward acquisition."

Drawing a deep breath, I placed my hand in his. "You think they'll try to grab me soon?"

"I don't know whether it will be kidnapping, extortion, or something we haven't thought of yet, but chances are they won't wait much longer. If this person thinks you've hired me, or if they know you can ID Wexler, they'll act soon or not at all."

"Great." Sarcasm dripped from my lips. "On a related subject, did you find me a safe place to stay tonight?"

With his other hand, Cotten picked up his wineglass and took a baby sip. He laughed and then handed it to me. "I think you're gonna need this more than I do."

CHAPTER 8
The Ravishing

WE SPENT another hour and a half enjoying dinner and talking about my book on Petra. Cotten asked about how the company was doing. I explained that earnings had been down since Dad's passing—and morale, too. He suggested that we take the scenic route back to my apartment. It would give us more public visibility and a better chance to catch Wexler in stalking mode.

We finished our dinner without further incident, thanked Gavin, and left.

The streetlights flickered on around us as the summer sun finally surrendered to the stars peeking through the violet canopy. Everyone left on the sidewalk seemed to be between the ages of twenty and fifty. The older and younger sets had already retired for the night.

We walked back toward my home for my go-bag. I'd wanted this evening to be a date. It had such promise. But once the restaurant calamity was over, the real problems began. It wasn't just that we were wrapped up in the business of stalkers, kidnappers, and murderers. That was heavy enough. What really tangled my thoughts was the talk of Dad.

My memories of my dad didn't include anything short of sainthood. So what did Cotten know about Dad that I didn't? Did I want to know?

I had no reason to think anyone might be after me because of my father. I had no idea why anyone would be after me at all. Cotten was probably right. It had to be about money. He was probably right about everything.

We held hands as any couple on a date would. His fingers closed around mine. Our steps fell into sync. We exchanged mooning glances. And so we were officially on a date. A fake date, but I was still going to count it.

Cotten and I ambled more slowly than the other pedestrians on Commerce. "Anyone following us will stick out in the crowd," he explained.

A foursome of younger revelers hurried past us, muttering something about slugs getting squashed if they didn't get out of the way. I assumed they were griping about us. Cotten only laughed.

And then, from nowhere, he grabbed both of my hands and pulled me into a shadowed alcove in the front entrance to the law offices of Kirshner and Clements, yet another one of Daddy's legal teams. Cotten draped my arms around his neck and held me loosely pinned against the granite historical marker by the door.

He began by holding my face in his hands. His fingertips crept into my hair, pressed lightly behind my ears, and followed the curve of my jaw. My skin melted into his.

His thumbs brushed over my lips, and I puckered in response. Cotten barely seemed to notice.

My whole body heated as his hands slid down my neck and traced my collarbones. My heart pounded so loudly that I was sure he could hear it. He moved to my shoulders, around my shoulder blades, and then to my sides, slipping his fingertips under my arms.

I was glad I had shaved earlier, and now I just prayed my deodorant kept its promise.

As he inched down my sides with his hands, I became acutely aware of how thin my dress fabric was. I felt his fingers and thumbs trace the lower edges of my bra, pushing slightly at the underwires. I'd had several dreams similar to this, and I struggled to breathe normally as my diaphragm tightened. I wanted to say something, but my senses were overloaded.

His hands moved stealthily over my ribcage to my waist and then to my hips. My fingers clutched at the back of his neck as my stomach fluttered and my skin flushed. I had never experienced this kind of intimacy in public. Part of me wanted to tell him to stop, but the rest of me—the rest of me couldn't imagine interrupting the moment.

His grip tightened on my thighs, and before I knew what I was doing, I raised my right knee and wrapped my calf around his leg. His heated hand slipped to the bend in my knee.

My breath rasped, and I almost didn't hear when he whispered, "Now the other leg."

While I struggled to understand the statement, Cotten released my right leg and worked his fingers over my left, ending again at my knee. As he let go, I wondered if he could read my mind.

"Not here." His voice graveled low.

"My apartment is on the next block," I suggested. The sky above the city lights grew darker, but this part of downtown stayed busy well past midnight. I didn't want to be the star of anyone's viral video.

Cotten took a half-step back from me. My arms were still around his neck, and his hands rested on my hips. He smiled as if struck by a brilliant idea.

Before I could decipher his idea, his fingers began combing deep through my hair, ravishing every root and follicle. I could hear someone moaning in waves of passion. It was me. This was better than any of my dreams because it was actually happening. He continued for several seconds until he finally pulled my green crystal barrette free.

And as quickly as it began, the ravishing stopped. Cotten stepped out of the alcove and into the blue glow of the street-light on the curb.

He held up my clip and turned it over. My overheated skin cooled as I watched him peel a wire attached to a little magnet thingy from the back of my barrette. Before I could ask what it was, he held it out as if he was going to drop it on the sidewalk. But then he held his index finger to his lips in a shushing gesture. "I've got a better idea." His voice was still low.

He took a dozen steps to the corner and looked both ways down the street. He bent down like he was tying his shoe, and then he stuck the little wire doohickey under the fender of the nearest rent-a-scooter. He walked back to my side, and a group of pedestrians swarmed the bank of scooters, riding away on all of them.

He smiled as we watched them turn the corner, out of sight.

My brain was only just beginning to understand what had happened.

"What was that?" I asked when he handed me back my clip.

"Some kind of high-tech tracker." His eyes gave me an approving blink. "I don't know if it had a mic on it, but you did a great job anyway."

"You were patting me down? Searching for a tracker?" I was explaining it to myself, not asking questions.

Cotten moved closer again. "I knew it had to be on your person. They probably planted it while you were waiting for coffee or bumped into you in a crowd. It's easier to do than you think. The mark rarely notices."

I was the mark. And no, I hadn't noticed. Thinking back over the last several weeks, I could imagine half a dozen times someone could have stuck that thing in my hair. A shiver danced down my spine. The air was warm and humid, but my blood ran ice-cold.

"You did great, though." His soft voice was hardly reassuring. "Anyone walking by would have thought, well, that we were just...."

"Having a moment of passion?"

"Right. And the moaning. It was the perfect touch. You're a natural."

Great. I'm a natural. I fingered through my hair, grappling with my dreams and reality. I wanted to feel safe. I wanted to be back in his hands. I wanted to put that better-than-TSA body scan on replay. I wanted more of that.

But it hit me. Someone had been tracking me. Tracking every move I'd made. How long had I been wearing that clip? A week? A month? But it had been missing... until today. My mind raced. Someone had been in my apartment. No, Cotten had checked. And double-checked. Had I simply misplaced it? Did it make a difference? My hair clip had a tracker stuck to it.

As he had suggested, this was bigger than a single stalker. This was organized. Professional.

I trembled, and not from the cooling air. I was losing it. I grabbed Cotten's arm to keep from collapsing.

"Are you okay?"

"No. I'm not okay. I'm scared."

He wrapped his free arm around my shoulder. "Listen, Veronica. I'm not going to let anyone hurt you." He was on the job, not on a date. "I give you my money-back guarantee." He tagged his promise with a laugh.

I didn't laugh. I barely heard what he said. All I could hear was a scratchy little voice in my mind cackling, *Someone wants to hurt you, and he knows where you live.*

CHAPTER 9
The Castle

WE HAD RUN by my apartment long enough to pick up my bag and scratch Marlowe's ears. The stress of the whole day had morphed into exhaustion, and I was on the verge of a full-scale collapse.

"Where are you taking me?" I attempted to relax into the leather seats of Cotten's black sedan. I'd hoped he would usher me to his home, but he turned north when he should have continued west.

"To a more secure location."

I soon realized we were headed directly into the ultra-elite Turtle Creek neighborhood. Daddy's house. "You're locking me up in Dad's castle?" I drew a deep breath. "You know people will be coming and going from that house nearly 24/7, right?"

Cotten grimaced and cocked his head a quarter turn. "That's how it used to be. Not so much these days. But I designed and installed that security system. It can be zoned.

I'll control every camera in the building. Nobody can get to you—not even close—without an okay from me."

His expression revealed undeniable tension. His beautifully sculpted jawline tightened, making the short stubble stand straight out.

We drove through the wooded parkway, and the streetlights cast a shadowed, leafy pattern on everything.

I liked Daddy's house well enough. He designed it to be his castle, literally. The cut-stone façade created an impressive fortress with turrets on both front corners. The massive pecan double doors appeared impassable, with black hammered clavo nails and iron strapping at the hinges. Daddy never did anything halfway.

Just inside the security gate was a low bridge over his landscaped moat stream. Really.

I once considered suggesting that Daddy stock the moat with real alligators, but I didn't want to give him any ideas.

Cotten pulled the car around the curved drive and eased up to the front. I watched him as he studied every low shrub and shadow, searching for anything out of place.

"So, you're gonna lock me up in the tall tower, and I'll have to let my hair grow long enough for my beau to climb up?"

A smile formed at the corners of his eyes, and I believe he might have laughed. But then, a sudden change came over his expression.

"I'm sorry, Veronica." His tone dropped to a whiskey gravel.

"It's Ronni. Please." At least he'd progressed from calling me *Ms. Peters.*

He shook his head and stared at his hands. "I didn't even think to ask. I just assumed you didn't, but of course you do."

"I do what?" I tried to interrupt, but he continued as though he hadn't heard me.

He raised his eyes to mine. "I mean, you're smart, charming, and incredibly attractive."

"I'm what now?"

He finally took a breath. "What?"

"You said you assumed I didn't, but I do. Then you said I was attractive." I raised my perfectly-plucked brows high. "What exactly do I do?"

Cotten shifted his gaze to the steering wheel. He put the car in park, and I thought I detected a flush traveling up his neck.

"If you'll give me your boyfriend's name, I'll make sure he's cleared to come into the house—at the gate—to see you."

"My boyfriend?" The idea shocked me more than it had him, I think.

He shrugged. "Well, okay. *Boyfriend* might not be right. Too high school. But your significant other. Just because I didn't come across him while surveilling... it was rude of me to assume. But if you give me his name, I'll take care of it."

Cotten looked flustered. Calm, cool, and collected, Cotten. He seemed to be channeling, well, me.

"Oh!" I tried to be the calm one now. "I don't think you're rude at all. You're careful. You're taking care of me, and I'm grateful." I hoped I didn't come across as overanxious. After all, he'd just called me attractive. "Why do you think I have a boyfriend?"

He stammered slightly. "W-well, you said you'd grow your hair for your beau to climb up."

I laughed. "That's Rapunzel. It was a joke." I gestured to the stone wall in front of us. "A castle joke."

I saw the muscles in his jaw relax slightly. "But you do have one, correct?" He reverted to his professional tone.

"A boyfriend?" I paused only for a second. "No, not currently. I'm available—free—single right now." So much for keeping things breezy. I had to fight my impulse to ask him, *How about you?*

I watched his reaction. More relaxed. Almost a smile. But maybe it was just my imagination. I gestured toward the front doors. "I guess we should go inside."

Leaving his sedan in the circle drive, we climbed the stone steps to the entry arch. The porch was covered with a high-pitched, blue slate roof, making it seem a little too much like a Disney backdrop.

Above the latch on the door handle glowed a small glass square with a red line across the center. I placed my thumb over the stripe, and a bright white light flashed beneath, scanning my print. Two clicks and the door opened.

"You did this?" I asked. "I had no idea you worked so closely with my dad."

Cotten pushed the door open for me. "Everything as per your father's specifications."

That was an understatement. "Everything my whole life has been to Daddy's specifications. That sounds like I resent him. I don't. Didn't. He just really liked to be in charge. In control." I hoped I didn't sound too whiney.

"So, maybe not entirely a saint?" Cotten followed me inside and closed the door behind us. "I'm not trying to push the issue. Really, I loved your dad. My father passed away when I was installing this system, actually. He had pancreatic cancer. Your dad understood the situation and gave me more support than most employers would."

I took a minute to acclimate to being back in the big house. I didn't believe in ghosts, but if I did—they lived here. I drew a deep breath, hoping to catch a whiff of Daddy's cologne, but nothing. Everything smelled like lemon oil, the housekeeper's go-to for everything.

"I wish I'd known you before I hired you. Of course." I backtracked. "I knew who you were, but I had no idea you and Daddy were friends."

Cotten laughed as we walked through the entry and into the gourmet kitchen.

I made a quick, sweeping gesture as if I was suddenly the hostess of a grand party. "Can I get you a bottle of water? Or something else?"

"I'm all right for now," he replied.

I searched the white Carrera countertops for the snack basket. Empty.

"I haven't lived here since Dad passed. Celia stocks the kitchen before board meetings or events, so I'm not sure what we have on hand."

Cotten shook his head. "We can go out for supplies tomorrow if we need to. I'm still full from dinner. I mainly want to check that the security system is set on high for you."

"What do you need to change?"

"Right now, everyone with access to the house can go practically anywhere. Board members, house and groundskeepers, and everyone whose print is in the system. I'll adjust it so that only you can get into the bedrooms and wherever else you'd like to keep private. And I'll let the staff know about the changes. Probably should zone the garage for only you as well." He started down the back hall.

I followed him to the control panel in the pantry. He keyed himself into the system and then waited for me, his hand poised over the keypad.

I motioned for him to go ahead. "You should probably have the final say on all of that. Unlike my father, I'm not so good at wielding control. I make terrible decisions about everything."

Cotten dropped his hand and shook his head. "Let's do this in your father's office from the prime terminal."

I agreed and followed as he strode to Daddy's study, opening the solid wood door with his thumb swipe. "Not all of your decisions are so bad." He held the door for me as I entered the walnut-paneled room. "You hired me, didn't you?"

"Well, it seems Daddy actually did that, too." When I stepped inside, I froze for a minute, surprised that the room still held a hint of Daddy's smell. The combination of cedar and tobacco seemed to reach out from the gold silk drapes. Not a ghost, but a wish?

Cotten opened the top left drawer of Dad's desk and slid the false bottom back to reveal the touchpad controls. He stood at an angle as he fiddled with the log-in.

"You should sit down to do that," I suggested.

He hesitated as if it somehow usurped power to sit in Daddy's cowhide desk chair. I indicated it was okay, and he finally took a seat and went to work.

As he tapped away, my attention turned to the framed photos on Dad's credenza. The bigger one was a portrait of my mother, who I now realized resembled me more than I'd ever acknowledged. The smaller picture was taken of me at the age of three. I hung from the horn of one of the larger-than-life-sized bronze bull sculptures in Pioneer Plaza—the park across the street from the Petra offices.

The fierce creature was my favorite of the 49 longhorns; I'd named him Quincy. In the picture, I grinned from ear to ear, with freckles covering every inch of my face. I thought about how Daddy used to lift me enough to reach the horn. I would swing back and forth until my fingers couldn't hold anymore, and I'd slip to the ground. I remember begging Daddy not to let anyone else see the photo because it showed my ruffled panties.

But Dad always responded with a shake of the head. "You have to understand, Baby Girl. This is what I see when I look at you—no matter how grown up you get."

I stared at the three-year-old me, flashing my smile and my panties. Some things never changed. Cotten's voice startled me back to the moment.

"Do you want full run of the house or just your bedroom wing?" He looked up from the small screen with raised brows.

I thought for a second. This was my home, sort of—but not really. I had no intention of wandering the halls, no matter how secure the property might be. "I'll probably just stay in the bedroom area, but I might go hunting for snacks if I wake up hungry."

"I can handle that. Bedroom wing, with paths to the kitchen, laundry, and… where else?" He scrolled through a list.

"Can I get down to the basement?" I chose the word carefully—*basement* instead of the wine cellar.

"Yes. Anywhere else?"

With my most innocent shrug, I asked, "Are you staying overnight?"

"Is that all right with you?"

"I prefer it, thank you." I glanced around the office, exuding nonchalance. "In the guest suite?" It was across the hall from my room.

He shook his head. "I don't know if I'll need a bedroom. I thought I might just sack out in the hall outside your door."

"That's terrible. If this whole system is as good as you say, you don't have to sleep in the hallway."

Grimacing, he tilted his head to one side. "Using my work against me." He tapped on the keypad. "I'll stay in the guest room." He motioned for me to come to his side. "Let's update your passcode. It needs to be six numbers."

He shifted the keypad to me. I started to punch in a new code.

"Not your birthdate." He cleared his throat.

I deleted the numbers and started again.

"And not your father's birthdate. Or your mother's."

I exhaled loudly as I cleared the numbers again. This was going to be more challenging than I thought. Six numbers. I stared at the touchpad. Under each digit, from two to nine, were three or four letters. *Cotten* was six letters.

"Hmm." I tapped it in—2-6-8-8-3-6—and then a second time for verification.

"Something you won't forget?" he asked.

"I won't forget."

Cotten entered his passcode and logged out of the terminal. He shut the desk drawer and stood, glancing around the room. "Did you ever inventory your father's firearms?"

"Nope. I don't know anything about his guns. One of Dad's board members suggested I auction them, but I'm not ready yet. Selling his stuff. It's too soon. Too weird." It was true, but I also didn't know where Dad kept everything. Guns were not sentimental to me, but it felt strange to try to sell off one thing and not another. I needed some time. I needed to be more organized. And everything in this house screamed *Dad*.

"I understand that. And there's no rush to sell. I only wondered if you wanted to move them to a more secure place." Cotten gently touched the cabinet doors on each side of the credenza behind the desk.

I took a step closer. "More secure than bullet-proof glass doors and alarm-triggered locks?" I raised my brows. "I may not know much about the weapons, but I know they're secure where they are."

"And they're all here in this cabinet?" He knocked on the credenza top without opening a door or drawer.

"You probably know better than I do about things like that." I shrugged. "Maybe you can help me organize Daddy's stuff like that when all this is over." I leaned a little closer to him until I could feel the warmth of his body near mine. "If you want."

"I'd be happy to help. When you're ready." His tone was all business, but he kept a confident smile fixed on his mouth. A hint of a dimple formed on his right cheek. I hadn't noticed it before, but now I couldn't help but stare at it.

"So… I suppose we should go up to my room." I sighed in my most innocent fashion. "And you can make sure everything is secure up there."

A glimmer flashed in Cotten's eyes, and his dimple dug deeper into his smile. "Of course."

We turned off the lights in Daddy's office and walked to the back stairs off the kitchen. Cotten poked his head into every door along the way, ensuring we were the only ones in the house. We climbed the stairs side by side, his hand under my elbow. At the top step, he flipped open the cover on the security system panel and had me punch in my new code.

"Let's be sure you remember it." He averted his eyes.

I tapped 2-6-8-8-3-6 into the digital display, and a green light flashed. "I told you I could remember."

"Good." He led the way to my bedroom door as if he had visited it a hundred times.

I wasn't sure if that made me feel more secure or less. I stepped out of the way behind him as he opened the door and peered inside.

"Is everything okay?" I whispered as he paused in the doorway longer than I expected.

"How long has it been since you've been here?" He flicked on the light and gestured to my bed.

My heart slammed when I stepped into my room. The bed was not only unmade but the blankets and sheets were completely disheveled, nearly to the point of touching the floor on both sides. I almost swallowed my tongue.

"It's been several months since I was up here, and I certainly didn't leave it like this." I moved closer to the bed, but Cotten stopped me with a raised hand.

"Hang on." He approached the four-poster with caution. Dropping to one knee, he peered under the frame. He pulled back the comforter, the blanket, and then the sheets. Nothing. He rocked the six pillows forward and then back, one at a time, until he appeared satisfied. "I don't think it's been slept in. It looks like it was just mussed up a bit."

"Why would anyone do that? I mean, besides to scare me to death." I started pulling the cases off the pillows. I had no intention of sleeping on these sheets—maybe ever again.

"I think you may have answered your own question." Cotten stopped short when he saw my expression.

"You mean my stalker has been in this room?" My heart crashed against my ribs. I wanted to run.

He held up a hand to settle my wild imagination. "Or, more likely, one of the housekeepers came up to freshen the room and was interrupted. Maybe she never got back to it." He pulled a pillowcase from a pillow, held it to his nose, and inhaled. He shook his head. "I even thought maybe someone came up for a nap—or something else—but I don't think so. It smells like fabric softener. Still fresh."

Shaking my head, I said, "I don't care if Mr. Clean comes in here and scrubs the room from top to bottom. I'm not sleeping on these." I tossed the pillowcases into a pile by the door and began to pull the rest of the bedding off the mattress.

"I don't blame you." Cotten tossed the blanket toward the pile at the door and wrapped the comforter into a ball around his arm. He glanced around the room and then dropped it onto the armchair beside the far nightstand. "Where are the fresh linens? I'll help you put them on."

I took a deep breath and motioned toward the adjoining bath. I didn't want to go in until Cotten had cleared it. If someone had mussed my bed to scare me, I didn't want to see what they might have done to my bathroom.

He turned the light on in the white-marbled room and went inside. In a few seconds, he returned with my coral blush, 600 thread-count Egyptian cotton sheets. "These okay?"

I nodded. "Is everything all right in there?"

"Everything in place. All clean and sparkling. I really do think this was just a housekeeper interrupted." He sorted through the linens for the fitted sheet.

"I hope you're right." I wondered, though. Daddy's housekeepers were always top-notch. I'd never appreciated them until I was on my own. But I supposed everyone makes mistakes. Gets distracted.

We set straight into making the bed with the very tight sheets and over-plump pillows. Pulling. Stretching. Tugging. Bouncing. Not exactly the way I had hoped to spend ten breathless minutes in the bedroom with Cotten, but we both enjoyed the finished project. My bed looked magazine-perfect in shades of coral and turquoise. I finished the look with a linen throw pillow with the word *rest* scrawled from corner to corner in a wild script.

"Hah!" I punched at the pillow. "I'll rest when this is all over." I could still feel my heart pounding.

Cotten breathed heavily, too. "You and me both." He glanced around the room. "Anything else?"

"I dunno. What are you thinking?" I shot him my most seductive look, but between my wheezing and clutching at my side, I was pretty sure he didn't get that message.

"I'll take the laundry back down for you."

"Don't bother. I'll toss it into the chute. It's just outside the door." I grabbed the bundle of linens and went to the door. I peered out cautiously to show Cotten that I really was going to be careful. No one. I pulled down the hinged door and dropped the sheets into the darkness. Before I could turn around, Cotten was behind me in the hall.

"Now, to check the guest room." He motioned to the door across the hall. "You can settle into your room if you like."

I shook my head and said, "I'll come in with you. Just in case there was an interruption in there, too. Making beds is an excellent workout."

We turned on the light and made a quick sweep of the guest room. Nothing amiss. The bed appeared freshly made. We exchanged a glance, and I guessed he was as relieved as me that we didn't have to do more housekeeping.

"What now?" I asked, shifting my gaze from his face to the bed.

He cleared his throat and cocked his head toward me. "Why don't I escort you back to your room. I'll stay until you feel comfortable."

CHAPTER 10

The Past

BACK IN MY BEDROOM, he leaned against the door frame to the bath, looking suave with his hair just a bit disheveled. "You know, you're kind of remarkable."

"How do you figure that?" I tried to sound coy and posed casually on the opposite side of the door frame.

"I mean, you've been through a lot in your life. Growing up without a mother, the boyfriend thing, losing your father so unexpectedly, and now this lunatic stalker. And yet, you seem to just deal with it. You just forgive and move on. Remarkable." His eyes flashed with satisfied appraisal. He rocked forward on his feet, shifting himself half a step closer to me.

I decided not to mention that wine helped—this was going well, and I didn't want him to get judgey again. "My therapist always says that forgiveness is for you. That it always does more for the forgiver than for the other person.

He's completely right, too. I—" My brain sputtered to a stop as it processed his list of my injuries.

My mother, my father, and the stalker I understood. But what did he mean by *the boyfriend thing*? I'd never really had a boyfriend. Like, ever. In high school, I only dated a few times. In college, a few more. But I never had a third date with anyone. A first date, then a second, then nothing. No more calls, no Facebook or Insta.

Apparently, my face showed my confusion. Cotten tilted his head. "What is it?" He reached out and gently tucked a stray curl behind my ear.

"Nothing, I guess." I took a deep breath. I had to ask. "But what did you mean about the boyfriend thing? Are you talking about our conversation in the car? Because growing up, I never had a boyfriend."

"That's what I mean. How you forgave your father for interfering. How you put family first. A lot of young women would have cut ties for that. But, instead, you got a place of your own and went on with your life. Like it never happened." Cotten scratched at the scruff on his chin. "Had I been in your place, I don't think I'd have been as gracious."

I couldn't fake it any longer. "What on earth are you talking about? My father never hurt me. He never interfered with my life—not more than any other dad. Nothing to forgive."

"He didn't intentionally hurt you, no. But most other fathers wouldn't pay their daughter's boyfriends to disappear." He shoved his hands in his pockets. "I loved your father, too. But I told him this wasn't the way to keep you safe."

My mind was spinning now. What was he saying?

Standing there, looking beautiful from head to toe, he accused my beloved daddy of bribing young men not to date me. It was ridiculous. He was joking. He had to be joking. "You're making that up. He never paid anyone to not date me." He didn't laugh. I stiffened and took a step back.

"You know he did. He confessed." He mirrored my shift, and suddenly we weren't within reach of each other. "He swore to me that he told you."

I tried to maintain a stoic expression, but it was no use. Tears burned behind my eyes. "He never said anything. I don't believe you. He didn't do any such thing. He wouldn't."

For a split second, Cotten looked like a juggler who'd dropped all his bowling pins. "I can't believe he didn't tell you. He swore."

My hands trembled with anger. Not only was Cotten accusing my father of bribery but of lying as well. I took another step back from him. "How could you suggest something like that? You don't have any proof!"

Cotten shook his head a fraction of an inch, still maintaining eye contact. "Ben Kellman took five thousand dollars. Josh Deahl took five thousand. Zack Cooley took a thousand."

"Oh, good. I went on discount."

"It wasn't like that."

"No? Why don't you tell me what it was like."

Cotten swallowed hard. "I'm sorry, Veronica. I honestly thought you knew." He moved closer to me. "I shouldn't have brought it up. I never would have if I'd known."

"No. You can't just say oops and change the subject. How

do you know the names of the guys I dated? How do you know—"

"Because your father hired me to handle the transactions with them." Cotten paused as if speaking the words might cause some sort of explosion. After several seconds of silence, he continued. "I was your father's representative."

It was like being in a car accident. Everything sped up and slowed down at the same time. My heart thudded in my chest, and my breathing turned into a huff. I wanted to hit and cry and stomp and flail all at the same time. I wanted my daddy. I wanted someone to hold me and tell me everything would be okay. But my dad wasn't here for me anymore. And right now, even if he had been, I don't think I'd let him touch me.

A fire churned up from my gut. This man. The man I hired. The man I wanted so viscerally. He had betrayed me in the most hurtful way. Every ounce of energy in me turned into fury.

That's when I blew. "You... you... you're evil and horrible! You get out of here right now. You're fired. I never want to see you or speak to you again!" I stomped my feet and thrust my pointed finger toward the door.

He couldn't have looked more hurt if I'd actually slapped him. I refused to let myself consider his feelings, though.

He took a deep breath. "Please let me explain. Can't I make it up to you? I'm sorry. It was years ago." Each sentence throbbed with emotion.

I didn't want to hear it. I balled up my hands and nearly let them fly. "I don't want to hear any of it."

"Are you sure you want me to go?"

I wasn't sure of anything, but the fire pulsing through my veins took over. "Leave my house now."

Hurt settled heavy on his brow as Cotten shifted past me and into the hallway. "I am sorry," he whispered as I slammed the door in his face.

CHAPTER 11
The Night

STEAM ROSE from every pore in my body. My bones shook, and my vision blurred slightly. I forced a deep breath in and out several times before I could see clearly.

I stood in the middle of my room. By myself. Every inch of me ached, especially my heart. I'd spent the last decade believing I was a scab of a woman, unlovable and unloved. Maybe it was true. Maybe that was what I'd become. But I had to think that it was, at least in part, because of the scheme of two men. The one I loved and the one I lusted.

All I wanted was to throw myself onto my bed and cry. Well, it wasn't all I wanted. I could certainly use a bottle of bubbly to scrub away the last ten minutes. A trip to the wine cellar was in order.

I prayed he wasn't waiting for me in the hall. I'd fired him. Surely he had the decency to leave. I dropped to the floor to look under the door. The lowest five inches of hall space looked empty. I scooted on my stomach to adjust my view to see one direction and then the other. No shoes in sight.

I stood, took the doorknob in hand, and turned. It squeaked and clicked more loudly than I'd hoped. Frozen, I waited a few long seconds, hearing only the wheeze of my breathing through clenched teeth. I pushed open the door. A crack. A wider crack. I was alone.

I crept on tip-toes like a teenager trying to sneak out of the house and hurried to the little elevator at the end of the hall.

To most people, it looked like a closet door. It sat in the bend of the back stairs and serviced the main floor, second floor, and basement. It didn't go up to the third for two reasons.

First, the third floor was the housekeeper's quarters, and Daddy thought it would offer more privacy for the live-in staff. Second, a home elevator cost about the same whether it serviced two floors or three but jumped to double the price when a fourth floor was added.

Daddy wasn't a tightwad, but he never spent money unless he thought he was getting a good deal. I thought about that for a second. He paid a lot of money to at least three young men to leave me alone. Was that a good deal for him?

My stomach hurt.

The elevator car descended slowly to the basement. It didn't ding like elevators in public buildings. Instead, the requested floor number buttons flashed a few times and stayed lit until the door opened.

The *B* button flashed and glowed at me, casting a golden hue over the wood-paneled walls. I paused for a moment, letting my stomach settle, and then opened the door to the basement. I wasn't sure if I'd be alone. Cotten had restricted access to most of the house, but I didn't know if he'd check everything before he left.

He was going to leave. Maybe he already had. How was I supposed to know how to un-restrict access? I didn't know how to change security settings. I thought about asking someone at work, but Cotten was the at-work guy, too. Ugh.

I pressed the side of my face against the door, so I could open it only a crack and see. But the whole basement was dark. The smart lighting was on a motion sensor, but my tiny movement didn't trigger it. On the bright side, that meant nobody was down here except me.

Opening the door wide caused the overhead lights to click on in both directions. To the left was the wine cellar, and to the right was the media room. Straight ahead was the cater-er's pantry, complete with a fridge, freezer, sink, two dish-washers, and lots of storage. I'd be back.

Silently, I hurried to the wine cellar. I knew what I wanted. A nice bottle of Moscato—one I could drink quickly —usually took care of the loneliness. I found the cobalt blue bottle in the corner where Daddy kept his Italian collection. I considered grabbing two bottles, but I didn't want a full-blown hangover. The headache from this night would be bad enough.

One bottle. I gripped the neck securely. I walked back to the pantry, more confident that I was alone. I tugged open the freezer in the pantry and perused the glorious gold-rimmed pint cartons before me. What goes best with Moscato? Fudge Brownie? Tin Roof? No, both of those were more appropriately paired with reds. My eyes fixed on the carton in the middle of the row. Pecan Pralines and Cream, of course.

I snatched a tea towel from the countertop and wrapped it around the ice cream carton, tucking it under my elbow. Still holding the bottle in the opposite hand, I picked a spoon from the last drawer by the door. I was set for the night.

Hurrying to the elevator door, I looked in both directions, as much out of habit as fear. I set my bottle on the floor and closed the door. I punched 2 and picked up the wine again before the ascent began.

A noise, something like a low buzz, sounded outside the shaft. The higher I went, the louder the buzz. The elevator had never made this kind of noise before.

The 2 began blinking and then glowed. I hesitated. What was it? But before I had the chance to guess, the sound stopped.

Shifting everything to my left hand and arm, I opened the door to my hallway. Slow. Careful. I peeked but saw nothing. No one. No sound.

I was like a kid who's stayed up late watching horror movies, dashing to my bedroom door. I threw it open and slammed it closed in almost one motion.

I was finally alone in my bedroom. The bed was just as we left it, sadly unmussed by us. I set my snacks on the table by my reading chair and kicked off my shoes. With the slightest under-blouse acrobatics, I extricated myself from my bra, tossing the thing toward my bathroom door. Nope. I couldn't leave it there on the floor.

"Why can't I just leave well enough alone?" My voice hung in the apple-blossom-scented air of my room like a billboard for my life. I decided the question applied to everything lately. Everything.

As I picked up the bra and prepared for bedtime, I began my conversation. Aloud. To myself.

"Why did you even hire the man?"

Bathroom.

"Oh, I don't know. Because he's beautiful and smart and everything I like?"

Closet.

"Yes, and he could have stayed that way if I hadn't actually talked to him."

Sink. I brushed my teeth with ruthless vigor, fully aware that I would soon ruin them with wine and ice cream.

"Now I hate him, and he probably hates me."

Hair-brushing.

"Why should he hate me?"

Pajamas.

"I was mean to him."

Turning down the bed.

"He's the one who paid off my stupid boyfriends."

Prying off the ice cream lid.

"Well actually, that was Dad. And it happened ten years ago."

The conversation continued as I rechecked the hallway, locked the door, arranged a few magazines on my blankets, and placed the ice cream and wine next to my water glass on my nightstand. I found the corkscrew in the trinket box by my lamp and opened the bottle. I clicked on the TV at the same time I clicked off the lights.

The History Channel evening line-up was in full swing.

Good. I was ready to spend the night with a few aliens, ghosts, and mummies.

An hour passed. I was still talking to myself, but now I was also talking to the host archaeologist of the current show. "Maybe you should use the LiDAR thingy." He agreed.

I was finishing my third glass of Moscato and could just about see the bottom of the ice cream carton when it started again.

The buzzing.

CHAPTER 12
The Buzz

THE BUZZING SEEMED to be everywhere. Setting my wine bottle down, I mashed the TV remote, muting the Ancient Alien Theorist. I had to be sure the buzzing wasn't just inside my head.

ZZZZZZZZZZZ.

Nope. It was real.

I was still trying to figure out what was making the obnoxious sound when it went from bad to worse. The buzz changed from a steady hum to a blaring wail. It was like the alarm sound of a nuclear meltdown or a spaceship self-destruct warning in a movie. Though I wasn't in a spaceship or power plant, I was sure the alarm wasn't for something good.

My vision seemed to blur with each pulse of the siren. I picked up my phone to call Daddy. I slid through my apps for several seconds before I stopped with stunned realization. He wasn't there. I couldn't call him anymore. Who was I supposed to call when something like this happened?

The phone began ringing in my hand, and I screamed and dropped it on the bed. I couldn't take any more. The caller ID read All-Safe Security. I punched at the little green slider.

"Hello?"

"Is this Ms. Peters?" a woman's pleasant voice asked.

"Yes." My hands shook. The sound was loud enough that I could barely hear my own voice.

"Ms. Peters, this is Glenda with All-Safe. It seems the alarm at your father's estate has been triggered, and..." Glenda paused for a moment. "Ms. Peters, are you at the estate right now?"

"Yes. Please help me. Make this awful noise stop." I whined through tears. I pressed my phone against my ear. "Can you please help?" I thought I heard her whispering to someone.

"Ms. Peters, where are you in the house?"

I looked around. For some reason, I started to doubt my location. "Umm, I'm in my bedroom. Upstairs. My door is locked."

"Good. Okay. Does the room you're in have an adjacent bathroom with a lock on the door?"

"Yes."

"And is there a window in that bathroom?"

"No," I said, thankful that Glenda wasn't asking any hard questions.

"Ms. Peters, I need you to go into the bathroom and lock the door behind you."

My heart pounded in my ears, and I could feel my body

throbbing with the still-blaring alarm. I tucked my wine bottle under my arm and grabbed the almost-gone ice cream. I scanned the bed for one more thing, shifting into full-scale panic mode.

"Ms. Peters, are you in the bathroom yet? Did you lock the door?"

I searched but couldn't find it. My heart rate doubled. "I can't find it."

Glenda's tone remained calm, bless her. "What are you looking for?"

"I can't find my phone!"

"Ms. Peters. You need to calm down. Your phone is in your hand. You're speaking to me on it right now."

I froze in place. She was right. I forced a quick laugh and hurried into the bathroom, closing the door and locking it. "Silly of me."

"You'd be surprised how often that happens."

Glenda was a peach. She could be my best friend—absolutely was at the moment. I set my essentials on the vanity top and sat on my velvet dressing stool. "I'm in the bathroom. The door is locked."

"All right," she said in a very business-like tone. "I've called the police, and they have dispatched two units to your address. Our security liaison is also on his way to your location and will meet the officers there. You should stay where you are for now, and I will let you know when they've cleared the property."

"What happened?" I noticed the alarm was slightly less horrible inside the bathroom. "I mean, if you're allowed to tell me."

"Of course, I can tell you. You own the property."

I'd forgotten about that.

"Our records show that about an hour ago, we had a quick trigger. That means we showed an open gate to the back of the property. We reviewed the monitor, and it appeared to have been a false alarm. But then a few minutes ago, our system indicated a breach at the back door of the house. This time the monitor showed a man trying to enter the estate. When the pulse alarm sounded, he appeared to flee, going back through the gate. The police and the liaison will walk the property together to be sure you are safe. I've advised them of your location."

Glenda's professional tone calmed me right down. Maybe too much. I started to feel sleepy. I tried to concentrate on the moment to stay alert.

"Glenda, do I need to put on clothes?"

"Are you undressed, Ms. Peters?"

"Ronni."

"Pardon me?" Glenda was always so polite.

"My name is Ronni. You don't have to call me Mizz Peterssss." My voice sounded strange, like I had too much saliva in my mouth. I took a long sip from my bottle, finishing off the wine.

"Okay. Ronni, are you undressed?"

"I'm wearing my buzzy pajamas. Fuzzy, I mean."

Sometime during that sentence, the alarm stopped, and the quiet rushed in.

"Ronni, I just got word that the scene is clear. Hang on for one more second." She whispered to someone again. "Okay. They're telling me that the security liaison will be upstairs to speak with you in a few minutes. If you want to put on a robe, you can, but you don't have to get dressed unless you want to."

My heart swelled. I was safe. Glenda had saved me. "Thank you, Glenda. You're a lifesaver."

"My pleasure, Ms. Peters. I'm happy I could help."

"I feel like I should take you out for coffee or something. We've been through so much."

"No need. Just doing my job."

A soft knock sounded on my bedroom door. "Glenda, I have to go now, but you know you can call me anytime. I'm always heeeeere for you." I heard a click. Maybe we were cut off. Another knock.

"Hang on a minnnnnt." I slipped the empty wine bottle into the trash basket between the toilet and the sink. Nobody needed to know that I'd been drinking.

"Ms. Peters, are you okay?" The voice sounded familiar.

The doorframe bumped into me as I walked into the bedroom again. I said, "I'm alllllright. How're you?"

CHAPTER 13
The Return

"VERONICA, OPEN THE DOOR," came the voice again.

I fumbled with the lock for a second and then pulled open the bedroom door, almost swinging backward with it. Blinking, my vision finally focused on the man in the hall. Cotten.

"Hey, you came back."

"Of course I came back. Are you all right? Did you see anything?" He marched past me and looked around my room as if he'd never seen it before.

Shaking my head, I sighed and said, "I didn't see anything, but the noise was terrible. My friend, Glenda, called me, and we visited for a little while."

"Glenda?"

"Yeah, from the Safe Company." My dizziness was growing. I needed to sit down.

Cotten continued. "Glenda from All-Safe is your friend?"

I plopped onto the corner of my bed, grabbing the bedpost to keep from sliding off. "Umm, yeah. She's my best friend. We've been on the phone together all evening." I smiled. "We're getting coffee soon."

Cotten stopped his search of my room and stared at me with a severe expression. "You're drunk."

I started shaking my head again, but when I did, my stomach flipped over. "Not very. I'm mostly fine."

He made a sound like a growl. "Get dressed. I'm taking you somewhere safe."

"We came here because it's safe." There was something else I needed to tell him. What was it? "Oh, yeah. Glenda said she was calling the police and a security lays-son to come and talk to me. We'll have to wait for them."

Cotten rolled his eyes at me. "That's me, Ms. Peters. I'm the security liaison. I've already spoken to the police officers."

"Nuh-uh. Remember, I fired you." I knew he couldn't deny that one.

"Yes, but as far as they're concerned, I still work for you."

"That's just as well. I'm hiring you back."

"We'll talk about that later." Cotten stomped toward the door. "Get dressed." He studied me with a long slow glare. "Are you okay to dress yourself?"

I shrugged and slipped on a coy little smile. But at the last second, a tiny burp escaped between my teeth, ruining the moment.

"Whether you are or not, we're leaving in five minutes." He pulled the door open and turned back with another exasperated look.

He was angry, and I didn't know why. "Are you mad at me?"

Cotten blinked at me as though I'd spoken another

language. "Are you kidding?" He huffed and squinted. "Yes. Yes, I'm angry with you."

"But why?" I started to stand up, but the room was still a little crooked and blurry. "I'm not mad at you anymore."

He bowed his head for a few seconds, like he was praying or something, and then slowly raised his gaze to look me in the eye. "Because you're drunk."

"But…"

"I'm working my butt off to keep you safe. You do remember that there's someone out there—literally right out there." He pointed to my window. "And that someone wants to hurt you. You're not taking this seriously."

"I am." I was. That was why I hired him. Well, it wasn't exactly why I hired him. But it sort of worked out—until tonight.

"If you were taking this seriously, you'd stay alert. You wouldn't let yourself be compromised."

He paused for a moment, and I just sat staring at him. I wanted to say I was sorry. I wanted to confess I was wrong. But I was pretty sure that if I opened my mouth at all, I was gonna yark.

Cotten shook his head and waved a dismissive hand in my direction. "I don't know why I'm even arguing with you. You're not going to remember any of it in the morning." He took the doorknob in his hand and stepped into the hall. "Five minutes." He closed the door with a sharp crack.

He was wrong about me. Maybe some people forgot what happened to them when they were drunk. Maybe most people did; I wasn't sure. But not me. I kept my sloshy nights locked up in a little trunk in the corner of my mind, dragging them out in a parade of shame on the sober nights when sleep didn't come.

I relived stupid and embarrassing phone calls, texts, and online posts. I dove deep into the pitiful life of a girl who'd lost all her friends. Who'd never loved anyone but her father. Who was never loved by anyone but her father.

Tightening my stomach muscles, I launched myself from my bed, determined to pull myself together. I took careful steps to my bathroom and to my closet. I raked a brush through my hair, which felt good.

The light came on in my wardrobe, and I chose some old blue jeans and a t-shirt. I was going to put on sneakers, but that required bending over, and I didn't think I could. Flip-flops would do for now.

Back at the bathroom sink, I grabbed my toothbrush and paste and worked up a mouthful of minty foam. But before I could spit it out, my stomach lurched. I had to quickly shift to the toilet, and my bottle of wine and the pint of ice cream made an encore appearance.

They were much better the first time.

CHAPTER 14
The Other Woman

LEAVING Dad's house felt strange. It had never felt like a refuge, but once I was in Cotten's car, realizing how frightened I'd been, the castle transformed into a place of danger. As he drove out of the subdivision and back out into night traffic, we sat next to each other in silence.

He was still angry, and I didn't want to get into it. I was ready to forget all the mess. I wished it was that simple.

The highway lights glared brighter than usual. Maybe my eyes just ached from the tears of retching. My throat, too.

My thoughts from the day played over and over on a loop. Highlights, lowlights, and blooper reel. His eyes, his smile, his calm protection, his soft words. But then his harsh words flooded back. Scolding and scalding. But maybe I deserved it. He was doing the job I hired him for, and I *was* making it more difficult.

"You okay?" His voice startled me, and I gasped.

"Um, yeah. I guess." I took a deep breath and blew it out slowly. I wasn't okay.

"I'm gonna take you somewhere safe."

He wanted to talk? Sure, let's talk. "I thought I'd be safe at Daddy's house."

Without a glance in my direction, Cotten released a gravelly sigh. "I thought so too."

Did he want a formal apology? I didn't want to give him one. I wasn't quite ready for that. Maybe something more like a peace offering. "Thanks for coming back. I know you didn't have to—after I fired you. So, thanks."

"I guess you have no clue what my contract says, considering you didn't even know I worked for your company." He kept his eyes on the road as he spoke. Did he have to be so perfect at everything?

"Sorry, I don't." I supposed he'd tell me. I was the head of one of the biggest companies in America, and I didn't know anything about it. I knew the history. I knew the stuff Dad had told me. But I didn't know—really know—anything about how anything was done.

"I had an agreement with your father, and it's in writing, that he couldn't fire me, and I couldn't quit, in the middle of a job. I had to either finish the job or finish two weeks' more work—allowing time for a suitable replacement to be found. The only exceptions would be a mutual agreement between him and me, or if I'm arrested and charged with a felony." He smirked. "You fired me, but I still have two weeks to finish the job for which you hired me."

Shifting in my seat to face him, I drew a deep breath to start. "But I un-fired you. I want you back. Not just on my stalking case, but on everything. Petra needs you."

He tilted his head in my direction, rendering a quick pop in his shoulders. "I think maybe we should talk about this tomorrow. What if you get angry and fire me again?"

"Do you have any more horrific secrets?" I laughed insincerely. *Did* he have anything else to spring on me? I didn't really want to know.

"That's the problem, Ms. Peters. What if I do? If I say something else you don't like, will you just fire me again? Because I'm not going to work like that. I see every day the kind of havoc that secrets wreak on people's lives. I uncover secrets for a living. I don't live like that. I can't." His thumb thrummed on the leather steering wheel. "If you want me back in your employ, you'll have to give me permission to be honest with you. Whether you like it or not."

"And you'll do the same for me?"

"Absolutely."

"You want me to be completely honest with you? You'll accept anything I say without getting angry or leaving me?" I considered the idea. Could I tell him everything? Should I?

"Honesty is important, no matter what. Of course, that doesn't mean there aren't consequences for our words. Everything—every action, choice, thought, or word—has consequences. Nobody can escape that. We face the consequences now, or we face them later."

Consequences. Blah. I think he got that spiel from my dad. That was one of his favorite things to lecture me on. And what if Dad had told me about hiring Cotten to pay off my boyfriends? How would I have reacted? Not well, that's for sure. Probably a lot like I did earlier, blowing up in his face.

But I blew up in Cotten's face. Gah! Why did everything

have to be so hard? I decided that maybe just sitting in silence was better than talking.

Cotten must have agreed. The next half-hour was quiet.

When he finally turned the car into a residential area, I perked up. Little houses, at least fifty years old, lined both sides of the street. They were small, well-cared-for, but tired. Cotten pulled into a driveway at the end of a cul-de-sac and parked. The front porch light blinked on.

"Come on inside. I want you to meet someone." He got out of the car, looking back up the street as he came to my door. "Are you all right?" he asked, helping me out.

I was wobbly. The warm night air swirled around me, and my stomach started churning again. Cotten closed my car door behind me and opened the door to the back seat.

"I'll get your bag." He frowned when his gaze met mine. "You look a little green."

"I'm okay." I planned to say something cute and clever, but it stalled out in my throat. I wasn't going to make it inside. Nope. I took two more steps and un-swallowed right onto the hedge of roses that lined the walk to the front door.

Cotten stood patiently at my side, ensuring I didn't fall as I retched. He waited for the bile to stop. "It's okay. Take a breath. You'll be fine." His voice calmed my panic.

Still standing hunched over, hands on my knees, I gasped for breath and struggled to stop shaking. This was not okay. One breath, then two. Goosebumps spread over my skin, and sweat broke across my face and neck. I slowly straightened my back, feeling the tightness of my stomach gradually release and relax.

I wiped my nose and mouth with the tissue that Cotten handed me. I was ready to go inside.

"And who am I supposed to meet now?" My voice scratched.

As I spoke, the front door opened, and an older woman stepped out. She wore a pink-paisley house dress and settled her fisted hands on her hips. "Cotten Jameson Hammond, get in the house right now and bring your friend with you. I don't want my neighbors seeing this kind of spectacle in my yard."

"Veronica, this is my mother. Edna Hammond."

His mother. He took me to his mother's house. And I threw up on her roses. Perfect. What else could happen?

CHAPTER 15

The Mother

"COME ON IN. Veronica, your room is down this hall." She waved her hand through a dark archway. "First door on the right. The bathroom is directly across. Get yourself a nice hot shower and meet me in the kitchen after, okay?"

"Please call me Ronni."

Edna tucked her chin and appraised me from head to toe. "I'll call you Princess if you like. But first, you get cleaned up and settled."

In full panic mode, I shook my head. "You don't need to go to so much trouble. I probably should just go to bed."

Cotten shot me a grimace as he passed me, flicking on the hall light and carrying my bag to the guest room. I followed just a few paces behind.

"First off, it's only trouble if you *don't* let me make you some coffee. I get to know everybody over a cup of coffee before they spend the night in my house. Do you under-stand?" Edna was a woman accustomed to getting her way.

I thought I heard Cotten sniggering as he dropped my duffle onto the chair beside the full-sized bed.

I turned back to his mother and smiled. "Thank you, then. Coffee would be nice."

She seemed satisfied with my response. She turned and disappeared from view.

"Everything that happens in this house is strictly as per her orders," Cotten said under his breath. "She's a lot like your father in that way." He backed out of the bedroom and switched on the bathroom light across the hall. "And I'd suggest not to linger too long in the shower. Not just for her, but her water heater tank is on the small side."

I drew a deep breath and prayed for this night to end quickly. Cotten bowed slightly as he headed back down the hall after his mother.

"Let's just do what we gotta do," I whispered to myself. It wasn't much of a pep talk, but it would get the job done. I grabbed my toiletry case and pajamas and sojourned across the narrow hall.

The bathroom was in pristine condition and all original to the circa 1970 build. The wood vanity cabinet was stained dark, with a golden weave-pattern laminate countertop. The hardware and fixtures were antiqued brass, and the sink, toilet, and tub were all beige porcelain. Little blue butterflies were scattered over a wallpaper background of pink and yellow daisies.

The whole room reminded me of a 1972 TIME magazine I saw at a flea market a few years ago. The only thing that didn't appear to be fifty years old was the shower curtain. It was a transparent plastic sheet with a humongous blue butterfly in the center. I supposed that would cover all the essentials if someone were to walk in.

I turned the shower valve, and the water shot out in a hard, narrow stream. I brushed my teeth while I waited for the water to warm up. I undressed and noticed the first hint of steam forming at the mirror's edge.

Before I stepped over the tub's edge, I heard Cotten and his mother talking in the next room.

"You should have just let her go to bed. She's drunk, you know." Cotten's voice was soft, but his words felt like a slap. Truth hurts.

"I know she's drunk. Honey, I was married to your father for nearly thirty years. I have seen every shade of intoxication there is. I also know how to help her not have a debilitating hangover in the morning. You both just need to do as I say." Edna's voice trailed into an unintelligible mutter.

It was a punch to my gut. I'd thought Cotten had a holier-than-thou attitude about my drinking, but now I knew he only wanted to avoid a mess that was probably all too familiar.

I didn't want to hear any more. I got into the shower and let the water beat against my skull. No amount of soap could wash away all the dirt of the last few days, but I felt compelled to try. Another thought popped into my head. Was Cotten telling me he wasn't coming back to work for me? For Petra? Was he going to finish this job and then disappear?

My thoughts piled up like a heap of laundry I couldn't quite sort out. The alcohol still weighed down my brain, making it slow and stupid.

Before I could focus on what came next, the water turned ice-cold. I jumped back out of the stream so fast that I almost landed on my butt in the tub. Even out from under the showerhead, it took a few seconds for my skin to recognize the water as icy and not scalding.

As I hurried out of the tub, the plastic shower curtain clung to my leg, trying to pull me back in. Trying to kill me.

It took me two tries to get the faucet turned off while I freed myself from the giant butterfly. My teeth chattered as I patted dry and ruffled the small towel through my hair. I pulled on my pajamas once again. I thought that if I was quiet, I might make it across the hall and back to my room without being caught.

No such luck.

"Ronni! You're out, good. Now come in here and keep me comp'ny for a bit." Edna's tone was friendly, but I didn't dare say no.

I padded down the carpeted hall in my bare feet. As I turned toward the eat-in kitchen, I saw that Edna had pulled a chair out for me. There was a mug of coffee on the plastic placemat at the seat. She waited for me to sit before she took her place.

"Will Cotten join us?" I asked, wrapping my still-chilled fingers around the ceramic *world's best mee-maw* cup.

"Cotten left five minutes ago." Edna sipped slowly from a Fort Worth Zoo cup encircled with zebras.

"Oh, I didn't know he was dropping me off."

Her brown-black eyes stared through me without the slightest hint of a smile. I swallowed a big gulp of hot coffee, trying to hide behind my cup for a second.

"My son will be back. He said he had a few loose ends to tie up before tomorrow."

Subtle, but I noticed how she made sure I understood that

Cotten was her son, first and foremost, not my employee. I forced a yawn and covered it with an exaggerated sweep of my hand. "My gracious, I didn't realize I was so sleepy. I should probably get to bed soon."

She didn't yawn, and she didn't let a second tick by. "Then I s'pose we should get right to it. The sooner we chat, the sooner we can get you to sleep."

Trapped. "Yes, ma'am," was all I could say.

She set her cup on the table. Her long, bronzed fingers pushed it to the center of her placemat. Once it was precisely in the middle, her right hand relaxed beside it, and she began thrumming her pale pink fingernails against the side with a steady clickety-click.

"My son works for you. Has worked for your father, God rest him, for a decade now."

"Yes, ma'am."

"And you didn't even know it?"

A hot flush ran over me, chasing away whatever cold I may have felt. I dropped my head in shame. "Yes, ma'am. I mean no, ma'am."

"Your father knew everyone who worked for him."

"Yes, ma'am." Daddy seemed to know everybody in Dallas. I thought I should defend myself. To explain that I wasn't my dad. But Edna understood that all too well. That was her point. I stared into my coffee.

Edna sighed. "Dear heart, I'm not trying to make you feel terrible. You've had a tough year. I know that. But you still have some hard choices to make. You want to make your company a success, right?"

This was not where I thought this conversation was going.

I cleared my throat. "Petra is a great success. Daddy worked hard to make it so."

"That was *your father's* company. Now it's *your* company. If you want it to succeed, that's up to you now. He left you an example. Are you going to follow it?" Edna took another slow sip. "You need to get to know your people. Learn their names. Know what they do. Figure out what they need from you. And give it to them. That's what your father did. That's why his company is a success. And he left that to you."

I sat there, listening. She was right, of course. Though I hadn't thought much about running Dad's company since the funeral, I knew—somewhere in the back of my mind—it was something I had to do and possibly the one thing for which I was the least prepared. I thought about the people who worked for Petra. There were hundreds. Thousands. How could I even start?

I sipped another half-inch from the top of my coffee, and a thought popped into my mind. "I feel as though I've spent this last year working so hard not to fail. Maybe I need to start working just as hard to succeed."

Edna grinned at me. "That sounds like good advice to me. Where did you hear that?"

"My therapist," I spat out automatically. "He's very good."

Her lips pinched into a tight line, and her brows rose high. "I guess he is. Do you follow his advice or just repeat it?"

I blinked at her boldness. It surprised me so much that I set my mug down. "I try to follow it."

"Tell me something else he says."

I drew a deep breath and focused on today's episode. "He

often suggests that everyone on my side isn't really on my side."

A full laugh escaped her lips, and it startled me.

"Do you disagree?" I asked.

She shook her head and waved her hand at me as though she was shooing away her laughter. "No, Ronni. I don't disagree. He's absolutely right about that. You do have to be cautious about the people closest to you. Tell me something else your therapist tells you."

I stared hard at Edna. My brain was over-tired, and I couldn't decide if she was making fun of me, showing her disapproval of my need for a therapist, or if she might be sincerely interested. "Well, this one is my most difficult to process. I know he's right about it, but I just...." My voice seemed to give out.

"Hit me with it. Maybe I can help you out."

I wasn't sure how this stranger in a pink-paisley housedress would help me, but I had nothing to lose at this point. "My therapist says that my mission, my purpose, and my destiny are all tied to one thing—my gift. And that's the—"

Before I could finish my sentence, Edna guffawed, throwing her head back and clapping her hands together.

Yep. She was mocking me.

She finally composed herself, dabbed tears from the corners of her eyes with one hand, and fanned herself with the other. "Oh, Honey, I'm sorry. I tried not to laugh."

"I don't understand. You said you wanted to help me, but you're just making fun of me." I was somewhere between ashamed and furious, but the last of the alcohol still made me too slow to fight.

"Ronni, I do want to help, but you need to be honest with

me. You need to be honest with yourself. You need to tell me the name of your therapist." She leaned forward in her chair. She moved her coffee mug to the side, leaving a clear space between us.

"I don't understand. Why does it matter who he is?"

Edna lowered her chin and her voice. "Because he's stealing all of his best lines from Steve Harvey. Honey, I watch Steve Harvey every day. That's almost word-for-word Steve."

Busted. I tried to decide whether I could fake my way through. Should I act appalled that I was being ripped off by a fraud therapist, or come clean?

Cotten's mother didn't wait for me to decide. "You don't go to a therapist any more than I do. You spend a nice hour every morning listening to a smart man who makes you feel better. I do the same. Maybe you have to call it therapy for your friends. I won't tell anybody. But you have to be honest with yourself. And you need a few others who can stand to hear the truth, too."

Reluctantly, I admitted my secret. Steve Harvey was my only therapist; somehow, with Edna, I could be honest about it. She seemed to understand. At least she wasn't calling me a fool for watching his show.

We talked for another hour and a half over the rest of the pot of coffee. She told me about how the Diane Pawley-Peters Memorial Foundation provided financial assistance to her daughter, Betsy, when she was young and facing a rare condition that affected her ovaries. Edna explained that Betsy's treatment worked so well that Dad's foundation then paid for a dozen teaching hospitals around the country to have the training and equipment needed to help others facing the same health problems.

"Because of your father's generosity, I now have three grandchildren." Edna beamed.

It was nice to hear that people were blessed through the foundation. Daddy always reminded me that though we lost Mom, other folks received joy in her name. It felt good to hear a real story—to meet the real 'folks.'

Our coffee talk wandered in every direction. I told her how it was to grow up with everything I could ever want except a mother. I told her about how I'd only just discovered that my dad paid off would-be boyfriends. I left off the part about how Cotten had done the actual paying. I left off that I threw a fit and fired him, too.

Edna listened. She patted my hand a few times and muttered some choice words when appropriate. I wondered if this was what I had missed all these years.

When the carafe was empty, it was time for bed. Edna took the mugs and rinsed them in the sink. "Get on to bed. I thought Cotten might be back by now, but I expect he'll get in soon."

No arguing from me. Though we'd both downed more than our share of caffeine, I struggled to keep my eyes open. "G'night, Edna. And thanks."

I stopped in the bathroom on my way back to bed, turning off the light when I had finished. The little wall sconce in the foyer was the only light on in the house. Everything else was quiet.

I snuggled into the double bed and pulled the sheets and summer-weight coverlet to my chin. My eyes adjusted to the darkness, and I drifted off to sleep. Dipping in and out of consciousness, I became aware of a noise outside my window. Rattling. Keys.

The front door opened, and I bolted up and listened intently. A footstep. The door closed. A muffled voice from the other side of the house.

"It's just me, Mom." Cotten's voice whispered. "Don't get up. Everything's fine."

Thank goodness he was back. I sighed, realizing I had been holding my breath. I raked my fingers through my hair and turned to face my bedroom door, waiting for him to knock.

I could hear his footfalls approaching down the hall. But instead of a knock at my door, the bathroom door opened and closed. The sink faucet ran, the toilet flushed, and the shower came on. Okay, he's getting ready for bed, and then he'll check in on me.

The shower seemed to go on forever. I scooted back down under the covers. I waited a little longer, trying to stay awake, but Cotten never came.

CHAPTER 16
The Murder

SUMMER SUNLIGHT SLICED through the mini-blinds in my bedroom, striping the walls with its dazzle. I peeled open my eyes slowly, remembering that I'd drunk a whole bottle of wine the night before. The splitting headache I expected wasn't there. I waited. Nope, my head was clear. Weird.

I could hear whistling from somewhere else in the house, and the smell of coffee and bacon crept in under the door. My stomach growled.

I dressed quickly and hurried across the hall to use the bathroom. To my surprise, it was Cotten standing at the stove, whistling over a popping skillet.

"Good morning." I tried to sound cheerful.

"And good morning to you. Did you sleep well?"

"Yes." I scanned the kitchen, looking for a way to help, but the table was already set for three. Juice was poured. Napkins folded. "I heard you get back last night. I thought maybe you'd come in and talk to me."

Edna walked in, wearing the same pink ensemble as the night before. "Cot knows better than that. Don't you, Son?"

Cotten moved the skillet to an unused burner. "House rules. Men don't go into women's bedrooms without the appropriate jewelry."

"Jewelry?" I didn't understand.

Edna laughed. "They hafta have matching wedding bands, you know."

I laughed. "That's a cute rule."

Edna shook her head and grabbed her coffee mug. "Nothing cute about it." She pushed my cup across the table to me. "My house, my rules."

Cotten scooped a serving of scrambled eggs and two strips of bacon onto his mother's plate and then mine. "Nobody breaks her rules."

I took a sip of coffee. "Got it." I set my cup down. I almost picked up my fork but caught a warning glance from Cotten.

"I'll bless the meal," he said, with a dip of his chin toward his mother.

I bowed my head respectfully.

"Lord, we ask Your blessing on this breakfast and the day ahead. Guide and protect our steps. Thank You for Your love and mercy. Thank You for Jesus. It's in His holy name—" Cotten's reverent amen was interrupted by a pounding on the front door. "I'll get it. You two go ahead and eat before it gets cold."

Edna took her first bite and waited for me to do the same as Cotten went to the door. "I wonder who shows up this early. One of Cot's friends, I guess. My friends know better."

Swallowing a second big bite of eggs, I heard a voice I

recognized. Cotten took a step back and motioned for Detective Damon DuBois to enter.

"You know I can't come in. I need you to step outside for a moment," DuBois said, keeping his tone low.

I turned to see what was happening. Edna leaned in to look, too.

"Hey Damon, come on in and have a bite," she said, standing and waving her fork toward the detective. "How's your momma doing? I haven't seen her at the grocer's in a piece."

DuBois leaned in and flashed a nervous smile in Edna's direction. "I can't stay, Mrs. Hammond. I just need to talk to Cotten outside for a second. Uhm, but Momma said to tell you hello; next I saw you. She's well, thank you."

Something was definitely wrong. I was coming to realize how tough Edna was, but DuBois looked terrified.

"Please, Cot. Just come out onto the porch. Don't make this worse than it is."

Cotten's voice took on a quiver. "What are you talking about? What's going on?"

Edna and I both heard it. We hopped from the table and hurried to see what the trouble was.

"If you just come with me, I won't put the cuffs on you in front of your momma," DuBois whispered.

"What?" Cotten, Edna, and I said simultaneously.

"You're arresting me? What for?" Cotten crossed his arms over his chest, refusing to step out to the porch.

"Come on, man. You know what for."

Edna edged herself in front of Cotten. "Damon, I *know* you did *not* just say you were here to arrest my son. What would your dear mother say if she heard this?"

"What's going on?" I whispered to Cotten.

"I've no idea."

DuBois took a deep breath and shook his head. "I didn't want to do it like this, Cotten, but you're leaving me no choice. Please step outside now."

Cotten shot me a concerned glance and then leaned closer. "Take care of my mother. I'll call you as soon as I can. Y'all can handle getting my lawyer, right?"

"Of course."

Edna tried to push Cotten back inside, but he shook his head and stepped past her.

"It's better if I do what he says, Mom."

Detective DuBois stared at the ground as he pulled out his handcuffs. "Cotten Hammond, you're under arrest for the murder of Steven Wexler. You have the right to remain silent."

"What?!" Edna and I both gasped.

"Damon DuBois," Edna scolded. "You know good and well that Cot couldn't hurt a soul, let alone murder anyone."

DuBois continued to Mirandize Cotten.

"Wexler is dead?" I asked. DuBois never stopped.

When his speech ended, Cotten asked, "You're sure he's dead? How did he die?"

"He's on the coroner's table now, but six bullets to the head and chest are more than enough, don't you think?"

"I didn't kill him."

"C'mon, man, I can't talk to you about it. I've already said more than I'm supposed to." DuBois barely raised his gaze to meet Edna's. "Ma'am, Cotten will call you as soon as he's allowed. We'll probably need you two women to come in and give statements. Someone will call you soon."

Cotten looked over his shoulder as DuBois opened the car door. "Mom, if they send someone over to search your house, don't make trouble. Just let them do whatever they need to do. I didn't kill anyone. They won't find anything."

Edna clenched her jaw until her lips were quivering. Tears glistened at the corners of her eyes. I took hold of her arm as we watched the sedan drive away.

When the car was out of sight, Edna began muttering. I followed her inside, straining to make out precisely what she was saying—just in case she was speaking to me.

"World coming to... fire and brimstone... my own son feels like he has to tell me... I know he didn't... before breakfast even...."

Some of the words got buried under stomps and grunts. Every few seconds, she simply stopped talking and slapped the closest piece of furniture. I kept myself just out of arm's length. I didn't think she blamed me entirely, but if not for me, Cotten might never have heard of Steven Wexler.

Edna disappeared into her bedroom, so I cleared the table. I scraped the untouched food into the plastic containers I found in the cupboard by the stove. I rinsed the dishes and put them into the dishwasher.

Edna didn't blame me for Cotten's arrest, but I did.

I went into the bedroom and repacked my go-bag. In another ten minutes, I was ready for whatever came next. A rap at the front door.

Cotten's mother answered as I came down the hall.

"My son said you'd want to search. So you just go on and see what you find. There won't be nothin' at all, though. My son didn't do anything wrong." She directed two officers into her house. "Cot spent the night in the room at the end of the hall." She waved her hand past me. "But I s'pose you'll search everything."

"Yes, ma'am," the first officer said. He was tall and slim but kept his eyes down. Apparently, he'd been warned of Edna's fire before he arrived.

The other man was shorter by at least eight inches. He wasn't overweight, but he had a roundness that gave him a jolly appearance. Or maybe it was that the man smiled non-stop. "Mrs. Hammond, I know this must be upsetting for you. But if you and your friend could wait with Detective Oake in your front yard, we can get this all over in no time." He instructed, grinning from ear to ear.

I nodded to Jolly and led Edna out onto the front porch. Detective Oake, a younger man in a suit, was stooping over the hedge of roses where I had puked only a few hours ago.

"Ladies, you may want to stand back," he warned. "I'm afraid Mr. Hammond was sick here. It's not a pretty sight."

Almost laughing, I answered. "I was the one who vomited there last night. Had a little too much to drink, I'm afraid."

Oake lowered his sunglasses and scowled in my direction. "You don't seem hungover."

I shook my head. "No, I guess I didn't have enough alcohol left in me after that."

"And what is your name and relationship with Mr. Hammond?" Oake pulled a notepad from his inside jacket pocket.

"My name is Veronica Peters. I am Mr. Hammond's—"

"Hang on just one second," he said. His pen wasn't working. He squatted for a moment to drag the ballpoint across the black rubber sole of his shoe. "Okay. Got it. You're Hammond's girlfriend, did you say?"

"No, sir. I'm Mr. Hammond's boss."

A sudden smirk crossed Oake's lips. "You're his boss, but you slept here last night? After an evening of drinking. Is that right?"

The way he said it, the whole thing sounded ridiculous. I stuttered, trying to think how best to answer. Before I could, Edna spoke up. "My son's job is to protect this woman. He brought her here after her stalker tried to break into her home. And you have no right to make her feel bad for needing help. You know, she went to the police department first. Nothing your people could do to help her."

Oake stopped writing and held up his hands in surrender. I guessed Edna affected everyone that way. "Ma'am, I didn't mean to imply anything. I just want to get all the pertinent information."

"Yeah, just the facts," Edna sassed.

I decided it was my job to diffuse the situation. It definitely wouldn't do to have Edna in the cell next to Cotten. "Detective Oake, I'm happy to help you however I can. I know for certain that Cotten Hammond didn't touch Steven Wexler last night."

"Because you were with Hammond every second?"

"Well, no. Not every single second. But after Wexler broke into my father's house, the police came. I'm sorry, I didn't get their names. And after that, Cotten brought me here."

"And then he was with you the whole evening?"

"Well, not exactly." I thought about Cotten leaving and then coming back hours later. I thought about his long shower. I wondered how the hot water could have possibly held out so long for him when it lasted less than ten minutes for me. A thousand terrible suspicions sloshed in my head.

"Ma'am, you'd better come down to the station and give your full statement." Oake gestured to Edna with his pen. "You'd both better come in."

Edna sighed. "Can I go in and get my purse and the keys to the car?"

Oake acquiesced and turned his head to Cotten's sedan. "This is your car?"

"It belongs to Cotten." Edna sounded exhausted.

"Then go ahead and bring me the keys."

Edna hurried inside and returned with both her handbag and mine. A sense of dread came over me when I saw the look in Oake's eyes. He reached out for them and then called to Jolly. The two men whispered for a moment, and then Oake turned to face us again.

"Ladies, I'll take you to the station while they finish the search. Don't worry, Mrs. Hammond, they will lock everything up tight and bring you the keys when they're done." He pointed us toward his cruiser and tossed Cotten's keys to Jolly. "Thank you both for cooperating with our investigation. Your help is invaluable to our pursuit of the truth."

I wanted to be strong for Edna. I needed to be strong for myself. But my brain kept hammering over and over, *Cotten, what have you done?*

CHAPTER 17

The Station

DETECTIVE OAKE DROVE us to the station in downtown Dallas, where I'd given my previous statement.

Edna spoke up as we pulled into the parking lot. "Why are we in Dallas? I live in Garland."

Oake opened the door for Edna. "Yes, but jurisdiction belongs to wherever the crime takes place."

"Hmph," Edna muttered. "Not a crime when this known hoodlum follows a young lady around. Only when he gets bumped off does it become a crime."

Though I felt the same way, I knew that voicing those sentiments didn't help Cotten's situation. I started to say something, but Oake responded before I could.

"Mrs. Hammond, we're still looking into Ms. Peters' complaint. The two incidents may be connected. They probably are. Your son is key. He's the connecting agent in both. And even if he's not guilty of a crime, he may help us solve one or both of these cases. As I said before, your cooperation—"

But Edna didn't wait for him to finish. "Even if! Even if Cotten's not guilty. Of course, he's not guilty." She went on for another two or three minutes, with most of her tirade under her breath. Only a few intelligible words jumped out as we made our way through the metal detectors and up the steps to DuBois' office. "...justice...prison...murder...."

Passing Officer Green's desk, I took a second to make eye contact with her. I smiled, but she didn't return the expression. She only blinked once and then returned to her typing. Just as well. We weren't best friends, anyway.

DuBois stepped out of his glass office as we neared. "Oake, why don't you take Mrs. Hammond, and I'll take Ms. Peters."

"I thought you might want to—" Oake replied.

"Ms. Peters, come to my office and have a seat." DuBois directed me into his cubicle and shot a stern look at Oake.

I almost laughed. Everyone was afraid of Edna. Everyone. A wave of calm rushed over me. Whatever had happened, whatever was going to happen, we were going to be okay. Edna would see to that.

I could still hear Edna's muttering as DuBois closed the glass door, and I took a seat across the desk from him.

"Ms. Peters, I appreciate you coming down and answering a few questions. This will help our investigation."

I drew a deep breath and sat straight in the green vinyl chair. "I'm not sure how much help I can be to your investigation, but I'll do my best to answer your questions."

DuBois' huge, meaty hands fumbled with a pen and

notepad. "All I need is the truth. That's what Cotten needs from everyone right now."

"I don't lie," I said. And yes, that was a lie, but I had every intention of telling DuBois the truth from that point forward.

He fixed a patronizing grin on his face and continued. "How well did you know Steven Wexler?"

Oh, for Pete's sake. Was he serious? Was he trying to trick me? Or did he not even pay a nanosecond's attention to my complaint earlier this week? My brain felt squeezed in my skull as I tried to remain calm. I was not going to allow myself to explode.

"I never actually met Mr. Wexler." I did it. I stayed calm, and I told the truth. One down, a million to go.

He scratched out a few notes. "And so what was your relationship to him?"

My teeth ground together as I inhaled another slow one. "He was my stalker, as you may remember." I used my most polite tone. I exhaled, balled my hands into fists, and then flexed them open. I think I saw someone on Steve Harvey using this method to visualize releasing tension.

"And how long had Wexler been stalking you?"

"At least two weeks, of which I have documented proof." I made sure to remind DuBois that I did have proof of a crime against me. "But I'm not sure how long before that."

More scratches. "You can't give me a date when you first suspected Wexler was stalking you?"

"I called and hired Mr. Hammond on June 22nd, but I can't give you an exact date for my first suspicions. It wasn't an exact kind of thing." Still calm. Still true.

DuBois cleared his throat and twisted his lips from one

side to another. He raised his gaze from his paper to me and then back down.

"But Hammond already worked for you. This was not the first day of his employment." He posed both of these statements as questions.

"Correct. Cotten, Mr. Hammond, has worked continuously for Petra Resources for several years. My father hired him." Breathe in. Breathe out. "But this was the first time I had personally given him a specific assignment."

"I see."

What was that supposed to mean? Was he insinuating something? My heart pounded in my ears.

"And can you, Ms. Peters, in your own words, tell me what happened last night?" He looked at me again, raising his brows as he said *last night*.

"Yes, of course." I blinked hard, trying to figure out what *in your own words* was supposed to mean. Whose words did he think I would use? "I'm not sure where I should start, but I'll give it a go."

I explained that I'd gone to work, as usual, and that as I was leaving for lunch with an associate, I saw Wexler waiting for me outside my building. I told him that Cotten had come to my rescue. I gave him an abridged account of the rest of the afternoon and evening. How Cotten took me to my father's house and then about the attempted break-in. I told him about Cotten taking me to Edna's house, but he stopped me.

"At your father's house, what all did you do there?" He had his pen poised, as if he expected to hear something dramatic. I wasn't sure how much I was supposed to tell him.

"Well, we went inside and looked around to see if anyone else was there."

"Did you suspect someone had broken in? Or were you just being cautious?"

"Just cautious, I guess. We didn't have any reason to think there was an intruder. This is kind of a weird situation, but other people use the house. Nobody actually lives there except for a semi-live-in housekeeper, Celia. The house is like a company house since my father passed away." It was strange to me, and I was sure it sounded odd to others.

DuBois didn't show his opinion, one way or the other.

I continued. "The Board of Directors for Petra uses it for meetings, parties, hosting out-of-town business partners, and stuff like that. Many people have access to it, so we checked to ensure nobody was there."

"And nobody else was there?"

"Correct."

"And what about Celia?"

"She was not logged in to the security system, so we assumed she wasn't there. Probably at her home. We have a board meeting on Monday, and she usually takes the weekends off." I felt confident but then had a flash of doubt. "But I can't tell you for sure where she was. Just that we never saw her there."

DuBois scratched out a few more words. "And nobody was there?"

"Right. We went into Daddy's, my father's, office and set up the security system for me. I changed my password, and we tightened up the rest of the house."

"You went into your father's office at the house?"

Yeah, that's what I just said. "Yes, sir."

"And while you were in his office, did you or Cotten get out any of your father's firearms?" DuBois looked like he was trying to appear casual, but I could see he was going somewhere with this.

"No, sir. We discussed that his gun collection was secured and that when—in the future—I decided to sell some of Dad's guns, I would call Cotten to help me because I had no experience with that kind of thing."

"And you didn't arm yourself at that time?"

"I didn't arm myself at all."

DuBois leaned forward a fraction of an inch. "How about Cotten?"

"I have no idea about Cotten. I assume he carries, but I haven't seen a weapon in his possession." I paused to think over the last few days. "And he hasn't mentioned any."

"He didn't pick up one from your father's office?"

I shook my head. "No, sir."

"Not that you saw?"

"I didn't see him get one because he *didn't* get one. If he had taken one, I'd have seen him take it. It's not a big office. And the cabinet where Dad keeps his guns is locked up tight. You need a key and a password to access it." I didn't like this at all. My stomach tightened like I was being punched with each question.

"And all of your father's firearms are locked in the cabinet in his home office?" Punch.

"Yes," I said then, hesitating, added, "Wait, he did have a shotgun that he kept in his bedroom. He had a special hidden cubby for it behind his headboard. I honestly can't remember if it ever got locked up after he passed."

"Besides the shotgun, did he have weapons anywhere else?" DuBois put his pen down and leaned closer.

I stared at his hands again. What would it be like if they punched me? They were giant and muscular and couldn't possibly hit harder than his questions. "I don't think so. I'm not 100 percent sure, but I don't think so." I knew what he would ask next, and I prayed with all my heart he didn't.

"And who all has access to that gun cabinet?" Punch.

My heart sank. The pounding went from a deafening roar to a dead thud. "Myself and Cotten, I suppose."

"Nobody else?" Punch.

"No, sir."

"Not Celia?" Punch. Punch.

"No."

"None of the other board members?" Punch-punch-punch.

"No, sir."

He shook his head and resumed his notes. He looked up a couple of times but said nothing. Just a pitying grimace and then more notes.

"Cotten didn't take out any weapon. I'd have seen him do it."

"Because you were with him the whole time?" He paused from his writing as if he offered a glimmer of hope.

"We were together the whole time we were in my father's office."

He exhaled sharply and went back to writing. "But not the whole time you were in the house." He clicked his tongue as he wrote. One of those disappointed little sounds I've grown to recognize over the years.

"No, sir. Not every second." I watched him scratch out a

few more lines, trying to read his terrible handwriting. Upside down. It was impossible. A thought struck me. "But I think the security system at that house keeps a log of every lock that opens and every person who keys in. You can access that log. You'll be able to see the guy breaking into the backyard and when he tries to bust in through the back door. While checking that, you can see that Cotten didn't open the gun case."

"I have your consent to access that security log?"

"Of course. Please. Just help Cotten out of this mess. He didn't touch Wexler."

DuBois sighed. "I'm trying to help. But it doesn't look good. And Cot isn't helping his case any. If we only knew for sure where he was late last night. After he dropped you with his mother, can you tell me where he went?"

My shoulders ached now. I realized I had been drawing them up to my ears, anticipating the worst. I tried to let them drop, but they wouldn't relax. Everything hurt. What I wouldn't give for a random maniac to start yelling in the other room. A small part of me was afraid that I might throw a fit.

Looking up at DuBois with my saddest expression, I said, "I don't know. I was sick by then. Feeling awful. He might have told me, but I'm just not sure." Now I was lying again. I knew he hadn't told me where he was going, but I was pretty sure he said something about straightening everything out. It was too much.

With all my heart, I knew that Cotten didn't kill Wexler. He couldn't have because how could a man leave his mother's house, drive an hour to shoot a man to death, and then an hour back, only to wake up and fix breakfast for his mom the next morning? It couldn't happen. And even if some deranged psychopath could do something like that, Cotten couldn't. He was a good man. A good man only kills in self-defense or the defense of others. And even then, he calls the police immediately after. He doesn't kill someone in cold blood and then run away and hide. One shot—maybe two—to stop an attacker. Not unloading a weapon into someone's head and chest. I felt sick to my stomach.

DuBois asked me a few more questions, which I answered automatically. He assured me that the police would go through the security logs, but that if my situation had been going on for two weeks, Cotten might have picked up a pistol before he took me there last night. He had everything he needed from me.

My gut hurt, my shoulders hurt, my head hurt, and most of all, my heart hurt. I hadn't helped Cotten. I'd probably caused more damage.

All I knew was that my stalker had been shot dead, and they thought Cotten had done it. And, I surmised, they had reason to believe one of my father's pistols was the murder weapon.

Edna said she would arrange for Cotten's lawyer to come downtown to take care of the situation. I hoped they had better luck than me.

DuBois asked his last question. "What did Cotten say to you after he returned to his mother's house last night?"

I explained that we hadn't spoken until this morning, just a few moments before he arrived to arrest him.

I was floundering. "Are we finished?" I asked after DuBois had put his notes aside and sat staring at me for a long minute. "I'd like to speak to Cotten's lawyer and arrange for his bail."

DuBois smirked and leaned back in his chair. "We're done here, but I'm not sure the judge will grant Cotten bail."

His words were like another punch to my gut. I swallowed hard. "And why not? Whatever the amount, I'll pay it. I can arrange it this afternoon."

The giant detective grunted another little disappointed sound. "You're why not, Ms. Peters. Cotten works for you, and you could pay his bail with a personal check—probably without making special arrangements with your bank. That single fact makes him a flight risk. You could have him, and his mother, in South America by dinnertime. No, I'm afraid he won't get bail today."

Punch-punch-punch.

CHAPTER 18

The Lawyer

EDNA and her lawyer walked me down to the lobby at the street door. The summer heat baked the edges of the asphalt, mirrored off the building windows, and radiated over our skin from every direction.

"You should stay with us this afternoon." Edna stretched her hand toward mine. "If we hear anything about Cotten, you'll know right then."

How could I tell her that her son wouldn't get bail because of me? He sat in a cell with who knows who—accused of murder and not knowing what was coming next—because of me. For all intents and purposes, I'd wrecked his life. For no other reason than he was beautiful. How could I explain that to his mother—my new friend? I couldn't.

I forced a smile and shook my head. "I only live a few blocks from here. And I suppose if my stalker is, well, isn't stalking me anymore, I should be safe enough." A chill raced down my spine. Against the sweltering heat, the sensation almost made me sick to my stomach.

Cotten's mother took hold of my hand and held it tightly. I stared into her deep eyes and saw Cotten's compassion peeking back at me. "We don't know that for sure. And I'd feel better if you were with us." With her free hand, she grabbed her lawyer and pulled him into the conversation. "Marty, give her a good legal reason to stay with us."

Marty grimaced and held the door open for us. He followed us to the sidewalk, where the tar-lava smell permeated everything. "Edna, Ms. Peters should probably seek advice from her own counsel right now. Just because they haven't charged her with anything yet doesn't mean they won't. Technically, the firearm in question does belong to her."

Edna scoffed and turned away from Marty. "Ridiculous."

I wanted to amen, but I was sure that Marty was right. "Marty, what's the name of your firm?"

"Foreman, Todd, and Graham. I'm Foreman." He held out his right hand.

Hesitating, Edna released my hand so that I could shake Marty's. "Pleasure meeting you, Mr. Foreman. You're one of April Todd's partners?"

"Yes. Ms. Todd was your father's personal representative, correct?"

"Yes sir. And mine. Will there be a problem?"

Marty shook his head a fraction of an inch. "I'm sure we can work it out. Have you spoken to Ms. Todd yet?"

"Not yet, but I'll call her shortly."

Marty seemed to deflate. "We're heading to my office now. Why *don't* you come with us? I have a small conference room where you can wait until she's available. That is if she makes you wait at all."

"I don't mind waiting. It will give me a chance to check in with my office." I wasn't sure why I said that. I never checked in on the weekends unless someone requested it. But maybe I should call Celia and tell her about everything that had happened at the castle last night. Last night. It already felt like a week ago. As we walked to Marty's car, my stomach growled. Loudly.

Edna tucked her chin and raised her brows. "Hon, as soon as we're finished with the lawyers, let's you and me get something to eat. Neither one of us had more than a bite of breakfast."

Feeling the heat of a blush prickling my cheeks, I was grateful to be in the camouflage of the sun. "I'd like that—if it's not an imposition."

"Ronni, Hon, you're buying, so it's no imposition at all."

We drove the quarter-mile to the eight-story brick box with FT&G painted in a gold flourish on the glass double doors. I'd been there a dozen times since Dad passed. Each visit longer than the last. *Just one more thing*, Ms. Todd would say as she handed me another stack of papers.

Green flags marked where I needed to sign. Blue for initials. Pink to indicate choices I needed to make. The meetings always ended the same way. *Thank you. I'll take care of these right away. Sorry for your loss.*

Everyone was sorry. Of course, my loss had generated several thousands of dollars worth of paperwork for FT&G in the last twelve months, above their standard retainers and fees. Yeah, very sorry.

Striding through the glass doors, we were greeted with

the customary blast of conditioned air and a nod from a middle-aged man behind a massive desk.

Marty barely looked at him except to say, "Is Ms. Todd in? Veronica Peters wishes to see her."

"I think she's in a conference, but I'll let her know." The man reached for his computer mouse.

"She'll be waiting in Six-A." Marty led us to a bank of elevators without pausing. He turned to me. "I'll get you situated first."

We rode up to the sixth floor, and Edna and I chatted about what we might have for lunch. It occurred to me that this was not the Edna I'd spent time with last night. She seemed distracted, almost insistently so. I guessed she wanted to spend as little time as possible thinking about her son sitting in a jail cell.

I felt the same. Well, plus the guilt of putting him there.

We entered conference room A, and I went straight to the window. With a view of Reunion Tower and the Hunt Hill Bridge beyond, it was almost like being back in my own office. After the chaos of the last twenty-four hours, I craved something comfortable. Familiar.

"We'll be down the hall if you need us." Edna squeezed my shoulder, and that simple act gave me the boost I didn't know I needed.

Dad could always do that for me. Oh, how I missed him. "Thank you."

They were gone, and the room was quiet. After another minute at the window, I pulled my phone from my purse and sat down to wait.

I opened my email app and watched the number next to the envelope climb from six to thirty-four. A quick run-through sent more than half to the recycle bin. Left in the inbox were two interview requests, a shipment notice for a book I'd ordered last week, and a dozen reminders and reports from the Petra Board of Directors regarding Monday's Meeting.

"One more board meeting I'll have to miss," I muttered.

"You really shouldn't miss another meeting."

I flailed at the sound of April Todd's voice. I had no idea how long she'd been standing in the doorway. There was no recovering from a startle like that. At least, not one where I had any sense of dignity.

"I'm sorry about that. I didn't want to interrupt."

"That's okay; I'm just overtired. I guess my nerves are a little thin." I hopped up and shook her hand. "April, it's good to see you again."

"Likewise. Please have a seat. Did Marty offer you anything to drink?"

"I don't need anything, thank you." I settled back into my chair and slid my phone closer to my purse. I drew a deep breath and looked Ms. Todd up and down. I'd never been able to pin down her age. One moment she appeared to be no more than forty, and the next, she might be nearly sixty.

Her hair was slick and black, pinned into the same twist as always. Her thick tortoise-shell-framed glasses veiled round dark eyes. Her features were sharp and angular from the neck up and curvy from there down.

"Marty said you had some excitement last night. Don't worry. He's working on getting your man freed as soon as possible." She stared as if she expected me to crumble. "Your father respected Mr. Hammond a great deal. I'm sure he's above reproach in this situation."

"And I'll be happy to cover whatever fees he might incur. He was working for me when all this happened." I blinked hard, realizing how exhausted I was.

"We can talk about that later. So your pistol was used to kill Mr. Wexler? Did you give it to Mr. Hammond?" April tapped on her tablet

"No. I'm not sure how it was taken from Dad's house. He always kept his weapons locked up. I know that, legally, the gun is mine, but I've never even touched it. I'm not sure I've ever seen it." I paused for a breath. April hadn't shifted her stare away. "I don't even know why they think Cotten had anything to do with the shooting."

"They have circumstantial evidence, but it is compelling." April cleared her throat and again looked down at her tablet. "I'm sure we can manage your situation—and Mr. Hammond's—without scandal."

"Scandal?" I almost swallowed my tongue. "I don't care about a scandal. He's innocent. So am I. Wexler was the criminal."

She nodded again. "Yes, even innocent people can lose credibility and status in situations like this. I'm thinking of what it might mean to your company. Your board may not want to deal with it. They may not want to explain to share-holders what's happening. Stocks could plummet. Petra could take a big hit. That's why I advise you to go to the board meeting. Don't let them see you sweat. I'd also suggest you put a little distance between you and Hammond while we sort this out."

"I can't."

She grinned with a sly lawyer grin, if that's a thing. "I understand. And I'm not suggesting you cut ties. He's got a good reputation in the Metroplex. But you should consider the optics of this. He's an employee, and he should be seen as such. Publicly."

My brain churned through her words. "I don't see that as being better. I hired Cotten for an extra job—a personal situation—to discover who was stalking me. He did. And then suddenly the guy is dead, and Cotten is in jail for his murder. How can distancing myself help either of us? If anything, it only looks like I think he did it."

April looked deep in thought before adding, "*Or* like you hired him to get rid of your stalker, and now you're throwing him under the bus."

"I don't want anyone to think that. At all. For all the reasons." A heated flush ran over my skin. I hated getting angry in front of others. Even if she understood. I wanted to run. "Won't it look worse—like what you said—if I stay away?"

Setting her tablet flat on the table, April tucked her chin and inhaled. She squared her shoulders and narrowed her eyes. "All right, then let's own this. I have a couple of ideas we can roll out. I want you to come back here Monday afternoon. By then, Marty will have Hammond out. Bring him with you."

"The board meeting," I started, but she cut me off.

"Go to the board meeting. I'm serious. You take care of your business first." April tapped on her tablet. She studied something on it before raising a scolding glare. "Have you missed any other board meetings this year?" Her expression was severe.

"If I miss this one, it'll make for a clean sweep." I slipped my phone into my purse, ready to leave.

"You haven't attended any this year?" The urgency in April's voice scared me.

"No. But everyone understands. They tell me all the time that it's okay."

"Most definitely not okay. Have you studied Petra's bylaws? Missing all the board meetings in twelve consecutive months is grounds for removal from the board. You have to go."

I almost laughed. "I know the bylaws but doubt they'd remove me."

"Why? Because your father founded the company? Do you believe your father's death will keep them from taking it all away from you? Don't be naïve. In this kind of business, you cannot afford to be altruistic. You can't rely on the goodness of people. People aren't good. People are selfish and greedy. They may do good things to get what they want, but genuine goodness is rare." She took another breath and scooped up her tablet. "I'm a lawyer; I know."

A laugh burst out before I could stop it. I wasn't sure if I laughed because of the lawyer comment or because I was uncomfortable and completely self-conscious. Either way, I think April appreciated the outburst.

She smiled. "Don't worry. Go to the meeting. I've got some ideas. Come over after, and we'll get you fixed up." She started toward the door. "Oh, and then you can tell me the results of the company audit. I'll want to put a copy in your private records. What firm did you hire for the audit?"

"Oh, I think they just did an internal audit. That's what it said in the report. I can send it to you."

April stopped in her tracks and headed back to the table.

Though she said nothing, I could tell she wanted me to join her. "You have a copy of the audit?"

I scrolled through the emails. "Yes. Do you want me to forward it to you?"

"Please. Maybe send me copies of all the reports for this meeting."

Tapping each email in turn, I forwarded the lot to her. "Is there something I should be worried about?"

She looked up at me with pity in her expression. "Ronni, you can't be so trusting. Your father loved every person he worked with, but he didn't trust them a dollar."

I smiled, remembering Daddy using that idiom all the time. "So, what do I do?"

"You are the controlling shareholder. That puts a huge burden on you. But for the sake of all the others, you must request an independent audit." She held her gaze steady until I looked away.

My mind raced through a dozen worst-case scenarios. "I don't want anyone to think I suspect them of wrong-doing."

"That's why the bylaws are worded as they are. Audits are automatic upon the death of any board member. And when they are conducted independently, nobody has any reason to doubt anyone's motives. It takes everybody off the hook." She tapped as each email popped onto her screen. "Good. I'll look through these reports and message you immediately if I see anything else to address. In the mean-time, you need to secure the services of a good accountant. Do you have someone in mind?"

Accounting? I didn't know anyone who didn't work for Petra. I strained to think, and then a name—or rather a face—

floated to my mind. "I know one. But I can't have a full-fledged audit done before the meeting Monday."

"You only need to hire them by Monday. As the controlling shareholder, you have that authority."

I must have looked skeptical because April shook her head. "Don't let them walk all over you, Ronni. Act like your father expects you to. Act like you own the company."

A smile spread slowly over my face as I realized that I wouldn't be surprised or shocked if Greg Oberman requested an external audit. So why should anybody respond differently if I did it? I did sort of own the company, after all.

I shook April's hand again and thanked her. "See you Monday, ready for business."

She walked me to the door. "Get some rest. It's easy to lose your nerve when you're not feeling your best. Rest and eat well."

As if on cue, my stomach growled again. April smiled, and this time I wasn't embarrassed.

"I know just the place for a good lunch. And if I'm lucky, I'll have my accountant hired before dessert."

CHAPTER 19

The Accountant

AFTER LEAVING THE LAW OFFICE, Edna and I headed toward the bistro for lunch. I could see the worry lines deepening on her forehead with every step. Like a mantra, she repeated, "Marty is going to get Cotten out soon." I wasn't sure if it was for my benefit or hers.

Our destination was four blocks down and a street over, so we cut through mid-block on Stone Plaza beside the park with the humongous eyeball sculpture in the middle. I had a love-hate relationship with the thirty-foot monument. It was interesting, and the iris was a magnificent blue that seemed to watch over Main like an ever-alert sentry. But the red blood vessels that webbed the rest of the sphere grossed me out.

As we reached the sidewalk on Main, Edna looked over her shoulder at the eye. "Again, they did evil in the eyes of the Lord, and the Lord delivered them into the hands of their enemies."

"What was that?" I asked.

"A verse from the book of Judges in the Bible. Para-phrased a little. Still applies, though."

Smiling and nodding, I gestured down the street. "Dad's phrase was always *in a handbasket*. He said it a lot when he was downtown. He didn't like that I chose to live in the middle of it. I asked him why he put his office here. He'd laugh and mention the allure of the harlot."

"Your father was a wise man." She picked up her pace. "He made a few mistakes. What father hasn't? But he worked hard—harder than any man I know—to make sure you lacked for nothing."

"He was a great dad." I'd spent hundreds of hours this last year wondering if his over-zealous work ethic hadn't partly contributed to his heart attack. *I do all this for you,* he would say. Just one more reason to feel guilty.

"I'm sorry he's gone. Dallas—no, Texas lost a great man."

We walked in silence for the rest of the way. No words were spoken, but my thoughts were loud and jumbled. Dad was gone, and that wasn't fair. Cotten was in jail, and *that* wasn't fair. I had to keep going, and that wasn't fair, either.

When we reached the restaurant doors, Edna turned to face me as though she heard my thoughts. "We all just have to carry on. That's life."

Gavin greeted us in the vestibule with anxious energy. "Good afternoon, Ms. Peters. I'm glad to see you again, and with a guest. How delightful."

"This is Mr. Hammond's mother, Gavin." I gestured between them. "Edna, this is Gavin."

"Welcome, Edna. Please let me know what my staff or I can do to make your visit more pleasant."

Edna smiled and raised one brow. "Thank you, Gavin."

I leaned toward Gavin in a confidential stance. "Would it be possible for us to have our lunch in a private corner? We have quite a lot to discuss."

The man clapped his hands once and almost bowed. "It's my pleasure. I'll prepare the room your father used for his business luncheons."

He disappeared, and Edna shifted her purse from her shoulder to her elbow. "Well, I'll be. This place is a fair sight fancier than Chick-fil-a. I just hope the food is as good."

Still laughing when Gavin returned, we followed him to a quiet room with a small dining table.

"Will this be suitable?" Gavin pulled out a chair for Edna.

"Perfect." I waited for Edna to settle in and then for Gavin to inch out a chair for me. "Also, if it's not a problem, could you send Inez out to us? I'd like to visit with her for a second and thank her for her kindness."

He shook a disturbed expression from his face. "Inez? Of course, I will see if she is available. There's no problem. No problem at all. And Kevin will attend to your luncheon. He should be along any second."

Five minutes later, we had salads and iced teas, with eggplant parm on the way. We made exaggerated yummy sounds to avoid the awkward silence as we both wondered what terrible thing might happen next.

If Edna was worried enough to not talk to me, not to offer sage advice or even chit-chat, she must believe things were much worse than she let on. All of this was my fault. And if something happened to Cotten, well, that would be my fault, too.

When Inez joined us, relief swept over me in a wave.

"Inez, I'm so glad you could come. Inez Delgado, this is Edna Hammond. Edna, Inez."

"Nice to meet you," Edna said, reaching out for a hand squeeze, not even flinching at Inez's sugar-skull face tattoo.

"Pleasure." Inez reciprocated and turned to me with an obvious question in her eyes.

It took me a few seconds before I realized that Inez had no clue who I was beyond what Gavin may have said to prod her to speak to us.

"I'm not sure if you remember me, but I was in here the other night. I was the one who tripped and made a huge mess. And you helped me when I hid in the ladies' room."

A flash of recognition changed her face from confusion to amusement. "Oh, yeah. You had that delicious-looking man waiting for you in the hall."

I smiled and dipped my chin toward Edna. "Yes, and this is his mother."

Inez's face flushed bright red, but she recovered quickly. "Wow, that's embarrassing. Well, Mrs. Hammond, I'm a fan of your work."

Edna laughed, and I exhaled some of the tension I'd been suppressing. Inez was quick and clever. This gave me a little more confidence in my idea.

"Inez, please have a seat."

"I'm not supposed to."

Edna snorted and pushed out the empty chair between us with her foot. "It'll be fine. Ronni needs to tell you something, and I guess you already know that, with her, it's probably safer if you're sitting."

Inez twisted her lips from one side to another as she sat. "Okay."

I drew a deep breath. "First, thank you for talking me through my little panic attack the other night. If you hadn't been there, I might still be hiding."

"Not a problem." Inez leaned forward as if she was ready to go.

"Please." I urged her to stay. "It meant a great deal to me that you were willing to talk. And I listened. You were patient, and you made a difference. I appreciate you."

Inez looked uncomfortable. "Really, it was no big deal."

Edna tilted her head. "It was a big deal to Ronni."

"Okay, you're welcome. I'm glad I could help." Inez cut her eyes from Edna to me and back as if asking permission to be excused.

Another deep breath, and I was ready to ask. "Inez, you told me that you got your degree and certification in accounting. Is that correct?"

She almost rolled her eyes at my question. "I did. But what good is that now?" She traced over the inked eye socket and the rose on her cheek. "I blew that career."

"But you would pursue that job if it was an option?" I asked.

"Of course, but who would hire me?"

"I think I would."

"What?" Inez sat up straight. "Why? You don't even know me. You don't know if I'm even any good."

"Are you?" Edna asked before I could.

"Well, yeah. I was top of my class."

I smiled. "Are you wanted for any outstanding felony warrants?"

Before Inez could respond, Edna held up her hand.

"Maybe that's not the standard you should use, considering where Cotten is right now."

I laughed. "Right." I turned to Inez. "So, do you have any reason why I shouldn't hire you?"

The young woman squinted at me like I was a spot-the-mistake puzzle. "Why would you want to?"

I pushed my salad to the side and leaned forward, lowering my tone. "You see, I'm in a bad situation. Cotten, Edna's son, got arrested for murder this morning. And I have some tricky stuff with my business coming up in a few days."

Inez pushed her seat back an inch and shook her head. "No, no. This sounds wrong. You want me to do something illegal. I've seen this before. Hire the little Latina to throw under the bus when everything goes to hell in a handbasket. No way."

Edna and I stared at each other and grinned from ear to ear. *In a handbasket*. It was a sign.

Inez shook her head as she stood up and stepped back from the table. "Why are y'all smiling like that? I'm not going to jail for you or anyone. That's why my mom worked two jobs to put me through school. No streets and no jail for me."

I stood and held my palms up in surrender. "Nobody's going to jail."

"But your boyfriend?"

"No. He didn't kill anyone." I started to explain, but Inez cut me off.

"Right, they're always accidentally arresting good-looking rich boys."

Edna shook her head. "Miss Delgado, please sit down."

And like magic, Inez sat down. I still didn't understand how Edna had that kind of control over people.

I began again. "My company is Petra Energy Resources. Monday is a big quarterly board meeting, which also happens to be a deadline to request an independent audit on behalf of our shareholders. Of course, an examination can be requested at any time, but because of my father's death, this particular request would compel records to be turned over for review by the end of the month."

The young woman scowled. "And what company are you having conduct the audit?"

Shrugging, I asked, "What's your company's name?"

"Wait. You want me to run the audit?"

I bobbed my head. "I think you'd be perfect, so long as it's not too much for you. And you could hire whomever you like to help you. And charge us whatever is customary."

"But you don't even know me."

Edna tapped the table in front of Inez. "Seems to me that's an ideal arrangement. You'll be completely unbiased. No one can accuse anyone of impropriety."

Inez propped her elbows on the table and dropped her face into her hands. "Let me think about this. What's going on that you need an audit?"

"I have no idea. My lawyer thinks it's a good idea. And since you bring it up, the fact that I have no idea is, in itself, a pretty good reason to start one, don't you think?" Just saying those words gave me a slight sense of competence.

Inez pulled herself upright again and exhaled. "And there might not be anything weird going on at all?"

Good. She was coming around. "I sincerely hope there's not. I don't suspect anyone of doing anything underhanded. Our accounting department just completed an internal audit and didn't find anything amiss. At least that's what the report says."

"What report?"

"The one that will be presented at the meeting on Monday." I tried to sound unflappable. "If you agree, you can come with me to the meeting, and I can get you access to all the files you need by the end of the day."

I watched Inez process my words. Another head shake. "Nope. No. I can't come to the meeting."

"Why not?" I asked.

"Do you have a scheduling conflict?" Edna asked.

Inez stared at both of us like we had lost our minds. "Look at me. My face. I'll be laughed out of the boardroom. They're not going to hire me."

My unflappability held firm. I hoped. "It doesn't matter what anyone else in the room thinks. I'm the controlling shareholder. I decide if you get hired."

Edna worked her magic again. "But if you're scared of a few old men in suits...."

"I'm not scared. I just don't want this to be some kind of stunt. And I don't want Ronni's business to suffer on my account."

Kevin brought in our entrees, and we paused our conversation while he took away the salad bowls and refilled the tea. I gestured for him to wait. "Kevin, could you bring Inez something? Whatever she'd like."

The young woman furrowed her brow. "No, thank you. I've had lunch."

"Then some tea. Or whatever she prefers. And dessert for all of us. What's your favorite dessert here, Inez?"

She hesitated for a second. "You really shouldn't."

"What's good?" Edna asked.

Demurring, Inez finally answered. "I like the blackberry tart with ice cream."

"For three." I grinned at Kevin and waited for him to leave us. I turned to Inez. "I understand your hesitancy. I do. But I promise you this isn't a stunt. And if my career suffers, it will be because I've been floating along a river of self-pity and coddling, not because of you. If you agree to this, you might be saving my career. This is a big favor, and I beg you to help me."

"Can I think about it?"

It wasn't fair for me to say no, but I did need an answer soon. "How long? The meeting is on Monday, and I have to secure someone before then." That sounded so adult. But then I decided to impress her with how urgent my situation was. "And in the meantime, I have to help Edna get Cotten out of jail and figure out who framed him because that's probably the same person who hired the dead guy to stalk me."

As I heard the words coming out of my mouth, I wilted. I thought I sounded like a crazy woman. And by Inez's expression, she thought so, too.

She sat there staring at me, blinking every few seconds.

Kevin came in with the blackberry tarts. "Enjoy."

Still blinking like one of those old dolls that sleeps when you rock them back and forth, Inez picked up a fork and waved it in the air. "Oh, why not? I'm in."

CHAPTER 20
The Accident

WE LEFT Inez at the bistro, and Edna and I turned west down Main toward my apartment. The combination of heat and humidity always sent prickles up my spine, with a foreboding of tornadoes and other terrors that often wreaked havoc on north Texas.

"It's like it's raining up," Edna said. She poked at her wiry salt and pepper hair with one hand and fanned herself with the other. "I need to get myself back home."

I waved my phone in the air. "I'll call for my car—it's in a garage around the block. It won't take a minute to get to my place, and then I'll drive you home. If we're lucky, the valet will be waiting for us when we get there."

"Maybe I can freshen up before we set out into this mess?" Edna gestured to the heavy downtown traffic. "Does this ever let up? I feel like it will be a long drive to Garland."

As a herd of scooters flew past us, I shook my head. "Even Sundays are bustling these days."

I phoned the garage and asked for my car to be delivered to the Kirby's front door as soon as possible.

"Ten minutes?"

"That's perfect. Thank you." I wished I remembered the valet's name.

We approached the eyeball again, and Edna glared at it. "How far to your place?"

"It's at the end of this next block."

"I don't think I could stand to live near this thing." She frowned at all the people sitting in the grass around the sculpture. "Reminds me of the billboard with the eyes in *The Great Gatsby*. I surely wouldn't want to picnic next to it."

I laughed. "Just up here is a church with a pretty front. Maybe you'll like it better."

We hurried the thirty more steps to the little chapel. The facade was glass-front, topped with a mosaic tile mural of reds, golds, and blues. Edna paused to admire it for a second. "Yes, now this is art. Not like a grand cathedral, but somebody worked hard to make this an offering to the Lord."

Ahead, art-deco limestone carvings framed the entrance to my apartment. A flash of sweet familiarity swept through me, accompanied by a tinge of relief, knowing Wexler wasn't waiting for me in the vestibule. Despite all that had happened in the last few days, it was still my place. I knew Edna felt the same and just wanted to go home.

"Would you like me to stay at your house for a while and help you get it straightened back up? I'm sure the police won't get everything back in place, and I'm happy to help." I didn't want to be alone, and I was sure she didn't either.

She reached out and squeezed my hand. "Why don't you grab a change of clothes and stay another night? You can come to church with me in the morning. We can pray for Cot."

I swallowed hard at her invitation. Somehow she didn't blame me for the havoc I wreaked in her life. She was a mama bear protecting her own. And I now belonged to her.

Two days. Less than that. In these last few hours, Edna had become family. Maybe not a mother, exactly, but certainly a mentor. She raised a son into a good man. She plowed through pain and gleaned whatever lessons it brought. She didn't take grief from anyone, stayed calm, and knew exactly what to do. Like Dad.

And she wanted to take me to church. I hadn't been to church since Dad's funeral. The idea filled my stomach with rocks. But maybe being with another congregation would be different. Maybe.

"How can you live down here with all this noise?" Edna asked as honking cars and screeching tires filled the air.

"It's not always this bad."

As the squealing got louder, I heard screaming from people around us. I turned in time to see my car—my shiny red coupe—barreling down Main toward us.

People jumped out of the street and pressed against buildings as the people inside rushed out to see the chaos. Edna grabbed my arm and pulled me away when I leaned out to see why my car was out of control.

"Get back!" she yelled.

A pack of scooters whizzed by, trying to avoid being hit. Most of them made it, but the front bumper of my car clipped the last two. They shot forward, spinning wildly. One flew by me with a rush of air on my arm. The other careened into a parking sign on the other side of the street. The young man riding it tumbled off against a parked minivan.

I watched my car swerve violently. It missed a pedestrian as it jumped the curb and banged into the big tree at the edge of Pegasus Park. The airbags deployed with a pop, and smoke billowed from the engine.

The whole scene was straight out of a movie. My heart pounded, and I froze. Should I go to my car? Should I try to help the hurt guy on the scooter? I should call 9-1-1. I lifted my arm to reach into my purse and realized it had come off when Edna grabbed me.

Edna.

I looked around for her, but all I could see were the crowds huddling around the injured. I staggered a few steps toward my door, scanning a mound of people for Edna's hair or dress. And then I saw her.

She was sprawled out on the sidewalk, next to the scooter-rider who had buzzed by me. Both spattered with blood—both with their limbs at unnatural angles.

CHAPTER 21
The Talk

THERE WASN'T room in the ambulance, even if the police hadn't needed a statement from me. I wasn't driving, but my car caused injuries and at least two deaths. Edna clung to life, but barely.

"Is there family we can call?"

I nodded but didn't have answers beyond that. "Call Detective DuBois, please. He'll know."

When people say that someone is in shock, you think they just need a quiet place to calm down or something. That wasn't how I felt at all. I needed someone to talk to. I needed someone to tell me what had happened and what I needed to do about it. I needed my dad.

"Please sit down over here. It really will help." The police officer reached out gently to stop my pacing, and I recognized her as Officer Green.

"Do you remember me?" I asked. "I came in a few days ago. I had a stalker."

Green indicated she remembered and directed me inside my foyer to the marble staircase next to the elevators. The faint but ever-present old-building smell of sulfur filled my lungs. As much as I hated the odor, it had become my welcome home.

"Have a seat." Green pointed to the stairs.

I aimed for the third step, but as usual, I missed, and my butt landed hard on the second. "Someone is trying to kill me. And if Mrs. Hammond hadn't pulled me out of the way, I'd be the one hurt. It should have been me and not her. If she dies...." I couldn't finish.

"Ms. Peters, they're doing all they can for her."

"You can call me Ronni." I eased up to the third step. Marlowe, the cat, padded down the steps toward me as I spoke and climbed into my lap.

Green ignored the cat. "Why do you think that there's someone who wants you dead? It may have been an accident."

Marlowe's purring comforted me, and I released a deep, pained sigh; I began. "I had a stalker. I know I couldn't prove it at the time, but it was true. His name was Steven Wexler, remember? He even tried to break into my father's house in Turtle Creek. He's dead now, and Cotten Hammond is in jail for his murder."

Green raised her brows and jotted notes as I spoke. "I remember. But Wexler works for top-tier traffickers. What do you think he wanted with you?"

"Traffickers?"

"Yeah, drugs, weapons, women, kids, and all the corresponding porn." Green shook her head. "If you don't deal in any of that, you're not on his radar. You don't have anything to do with that stuff, do you?"

"No!" My head pounded in time with my pulse. "I've no idea why anyone would want to kill me."

"Besides the obvious?" Green tilted her head. "I mean, you're ridiculously rich and alone. But then they would just kidnap you, not kill you. At least not until they had your money."

"Are you kidding me?" I didn't take her pep-talk well. "First you say nobody wants to hurt me, then you say it's obvious why they do. May I speak with DuBois?"

Green shifted her right hip out and shot me a glance of exasperation. "DuBois is busy trying to get your boyfriend out of jail and up to the hospital to see his mother." She pointed the end of her pencil in my face. "You've got me."

She was telling me to get over myself—the nerve. I wanted to get right in her face and yell, *do you know who I am?* But of course, that was the *myself* I needed to get over. "He's not my boyfriend," I whispered instead. Marlowe nuzzled his understanding face against my hand for a pet.

Softening her stance, Green took a seat beside me on the step. "Look, I know this seems bad. But sometimes bad things happen. Sometimes a lot all at once."

"You think this is a coincidence?"

"You had a stalker, and suddenly that stalker is killed. If the guy you hired for protection didn't kill him, that's a pretty big coincidence, isn't it?" She pushed her notes aside and turned to face me. "Isn't it?"

I agreed. "But I called for my car, and then this? How can this all not be related? I saw the driver's face. He didn't look panicked. He looked like—I don't know what. Can't you talk to him?" Marlowe offered one last purr and retreated back up the stairs.

Green's radio crackled. "Give me a second," she said and walked to the other side of the lobby. She pulled out her phone and made a call. She asked questions and shook her head, but I couldn't make out anything she said. A minute later, she returned and leaned on the newel post. "Ms. Peters, DuBois wants to speak with you personally."

"What's happened?" A hundred worst-case scenarios flashed through my mind.

Her expression turned stoic. "He has some news."

CHAPTER 22
The Critical

OFFICER GREEN LED me to her car, and I spent the next fifteen minutes imagining what horrors DuBois would report when we arrived at the police station. But Green navigated away from the still-congested aftermath of the wreckage and turned east on Commerce toward the medical center.

"We're not going to the station?" I asked.

"DuBois will meet us at the hospital."

My gut tightened. Nothing good ever happened at a hospital. Not in my experience. The hospital was where people died. My mother, my aunt, my best friend's cousin—all gone in one quick trip to the hospital. And, of course, Dad.

When I left him at the office, he'd been fine, cheerful, even. The next thing I knew, my phone was ringing. A number I didn't recognize. Collapsed. He'd had a heart attack. They were doing all they could. I hurried, but by the time I arrived, he was gone. *So sorry for your loss, Ms. Peters.*

Over and over and over. What could I have done differently? I should have had lunch with him as he wanted. I should have been there for him. If I had been, I might have given him CPR right away. Or called 9-1-1 sooner. Or even just said goodbye.

"Come on." Green's voice shook me out of my loop.

"What?"

She held the car door open and stared at me as though I had lost my mind. Maybe I had. "We're here. Come on. DuBois is waiting for us."

I inhaled a lungful of heat radiating from the concrete and followed Green through the sliding glass doors. A guard acknowledged us, and Green marched us to the doors leading to the back. She tapped her badge as the attendant at the desk stood.

"We're here to see Edna Hammond."

"Yes, ma'am." The attendant pushed a button, and the doors opened.

The stabbing smell of antiseptic competed with the odors of bile and blood. We passed rooms partitioned with hospital green curtains. Monitors and machines beeped, buzzed, and hummed behind them. People moaned in pain and cried in grief from places I couldn't see. My pace slowed, and Officer Green walked steadily on.

I wondered how she could be so unaffected by all of this, but then she probably saw much worse every day.

She turned the corner, and I hurried to catch up. Green stood against the wall, motioning for me to do the same. A door opened, and an orderly emerged, pulling a gurney draped with a sheet.

My heart crumbled. Edna.

I pressed into the wall to keep from sinking to the floor.

My stomach lurched, and I was sure I'd be sick. Squeezing my eyes shut, I prayed, "Lord, give me strength."

Green tapped my shoulder. "That's not Mrs. Hammond. Come on."

We walked to the end of the hall, and as we arrived, DuBois stepped out to greet us. "Thanks, I've got it from here," he said.

She turned on her heel, nodded once, and walked down the hall, leaving me with DuBois. Standing next to the mountain of a man, I began to shake, my nerves no longer able to fake it.

He reached out and took hold of my elbow. "Don't lose it now. She wants to see you."

"Edna's okay?" My voice rasped from breathing through my mouth.

DuBois shook his head. "No, she's hurt pretty badly. She has fractures all over and has already gotten a few dozen stitches. Don't touch her. And she really can't talk yet. But she wants to see you. She wants to make sure you're okay. I told her, but she doesn't believe me."

"You did arrest her son."

"She'll never forgive me for that." DuBois stepped to the side of the door. "Listen, I'm sorry. We're going to dig a little deeper into your case. This thing with your car, well, it's given us some leads. For now, though, please don't get her worked up. She needs rest. Just let her know you're fine. The doc said they'd move her to a private room as soon as they get her wrist and knee set."

"Thank you, Detective. Officer Green said there were fatalities?" Just saying the word made my heart pound.

"Yes, ma'am." He dropped his chin. "The young woman

who crashed the scooter into Edna and the man driving your car." DuBois's Adam's apple jumped as he swallowed hard. "And the other scooterist who was hit is in critical condition."

Tears stung my eyes. "Will you please let the families know their hospital and funeral expenses will be covered? I know I can't bring back their loved ones, but I want to help."

"That's very generous of you."

"No, it isn't. It's my fault they're in this situation." I glanced toward Edna's door. "But she's going to make it, right?"

DuBois furrowed his brow. "If you know Edna, you know she's too tough to die."

A chuckle burst from my lips before I could stifle it.

"And don't you dare tell her I called her Edna," he whispered. DuBois pushed open the door and gestured for me to go inside. "I'll be around if you need me."

I took a timid step into the dimly lit room, unsure of what I was about to see. The foot of Edna's bed was fitted with a contraption to keep her legs immobile. I took another two steps in and saw her swollen face looking in my direction. Her eyes lit up, and her cheeks rose slightly into a pained grin.

Tears broke like a dam and flooded down my cheeks as I hurried to the chair at her side. "I'm here. And DuBois says you're going to be just fine. You're even getting a nice quiet room to yourself in a little while." My words blubbered between sobs.

"Here," a voice whispered from behind me.

I turned to face a hand with a box of tissue. Following the arm up, I found myself looking into the smoky, smiling eyes of Cotten.

CHAPTER 23

The Job

MY MOUTH GAPED, and I struggled to shake away the fog to be sure my eyes weren't playing tricks. "You're really here," someone stammered. Seconds later, I realized it was my voice.

"So are you," Cotten rasped.

I hopped to my feet and threw my arms around him, squeezing as if my life depended on it. The tissue box hit the floor as his arms tightened around my waist. As I relaxed my grip, he cinched me closer. A shudder rolled over his spine, and his face burrowed at my neck. He needed me as much as I needed him.

"I'm not dead yet!" Edna's voice called.

We jumped apart like teenagers caught in the backseat of a car.

I tried to catch a glimpse of Cotten's face, but he reached past me to pick up the tissues and then moved closer to his mother.

"Hey, Mama, you're awake." He settled into the bedside chair.

Edna's voice scratched. "Been awake for a minute or two. The doctors tell me it's serious. Your friend must think so, too, if he's pulling strings to get you outta jail."

"Mama, it is serious. You need to rest. Don't get worked up." Cotten leaned closer. "They still have to set your fractures, but your stitches look good."

The older woman frowned and winced as the movement pulled against her swollen cheeks. "I have no intention of dying, so you can just get that thought out of your head. I certainly won't be done in by one of those little scooter contraptions. It's ridiculous."

Trying to stifle a laugh, I pressed my curled fingers against my lips. The tiny hiss that escaped drew Edna's attention to me.

"And you, Ronnie? You're not hurt bad, are you?"

I stepped toward her bed, directly behind Cotten's chair. "No, ma'am. You saved my life. I'm so very sorry you were hurt in the process. I am forever in your debt."

"See there, Cotten? I'm not gonna die now. She's in my debt, and she's rich."

Cotten and I guffawed, and Edna's eyes smiled in our direction. "Thank the Lord! I didn't know how much more it'd take to get you two to smile." She looked down at her broken body. "So, we're all good now, right?"

Cotten shot a glance over his shoulder to me, and I shrugged.

"What do you mean, Mama?"

I let my fingertips rest on Cotten's shoulders, waiting for Edna's explanation.

"I'd have sworn you were smarter than this, Cot. You're not only out of jail to watch me die, right? DuBois got you out clean?"

"What?" I asked, still unsure about where this was going.

Edna drew a deep breath, obviously struggling with bruises all over her body. "It's a simple question. If the doctors come back here and say I'll be fine, DuBois isn't gonna haul your butt back to jail, is he?"

Cotten shook his head. "No. He talked to the judge on my behalf. I'm out on bail. You not dying doesn't send me back."

"Good. Then y'all can go." She dismissed us like a queen to her court.

"No." Cotten shook his head. "We're not leaving your side. I'm glad you're feeling better. But you have a tough road ahead, and I want to be here for you."

"Mrs. Hammond, you shouldn't be alone. We'll stay here and ensure you have whatever you need." I patted Cotten's shoulder, and he reached up for my hand. His fingers were icy against mine.

Another long sigh from Edna. "And what if I need some quiet time to rest?"

Cotten squeezed the bed railing until his knuckles blanched. "You do. And we'll be right down the hall in the family waiting room, where we're just a minute away. But while you're awake, we'll stay with you."

The door creaked open behind us as a man in a white jacket rapped it softly. "Mrs. Hammond, I'm Dr. Willingham."

He strode across the dim room without acknowledging Cotten or me. When he reached the far side of Edna's bed, he flipped a switch that triggered the light on the wall above the bed to flicker on. Only then did he seem to notice us.

"Are you family?" he asked, directing his gaze to me.

Before I could explain my connection, I felt Cotten's hand squeeze mine. "Yes, she's our mother."

"Good." The doctor squinted at the clipboard in his hand. "Then you're Betsy and Colten?"

Cotten shook his head. "It's Cotten. And I'll be calling my sister Betsy soon."

Edna interrupted. "She's already been called and is on her way."

"Why, Mom? Betsy doesn't need to come down. I said before, I can stay."

The doctor's attention volleyed between Edna and Cotten, and I decided to keep quiet.

Edna's voice held a tremor. "I want her here with me."

"But if it's not life-threatening…." Cotten turned to the doctor. "Her injuries are not life-threatening, are they?"

"No, I expect her to make a full recovery—or nearly so. Of course, much will depend on how she does with physical therapy, but she won't start that for a while." He turned his head back to Edna. "For now, we just need to get your wrist and knees set. You broke them clean. The good news is you only have a hairline fracture on two ribs. All the rest is just scrapes and bruises."

"See, you don't need Betsy. I can handle this." Cotten's voice suddenly matched her tremor. That worried me.

Please don't cry. I can't handle it if you start to cry.

Edna turned her gaze to meet Cotten's. She might as well have her hands on her hips with her toe tapping impatiently. "Cotten Jameson Hammond. I will not argue with you right now. I'm your mother, and you'll do as I say. You have a job to do, and you know it."

"But you…" he started, but she cut him off.

"But nothing. This handsome doctor's come to fetch me to put my casts on. Betsy will likely be here before they put me in my private room. You and Ronni get out and finish your job. That will help me more than anything else right now, do you understand?"

Edna's magic worked again. Calling Cotten by his full name let him know who was in charge. Calling the doctor handsome turned him to putty in her hands.

My turn. "What do you need us to do for you, Mama?" I asked, gently inching closer.

She softened her laser glare and almost smiled at me. "Honey, take him on out so I can talk to the doctor privately. I'd surely appreciate it. You two get a little work done before your big meeting tomorrow. Betsy will call with updates, so you won't have to worry. And maybe," her voice dropped to a whisper, "you could bring me a hamburger and a Coke later. Betsy likes hers without onions."

"Of course." I suppressed a chuckle.

Dr. Willingham grimaced. "I *do* need to visit with her for a second, and then I'll send her upstairs." He glanced at his watch and then back to Cotten. "It may be a couple of hours before she's in her room. I'll text you when she's settled."

Cotten's expression twisted from confusion to anger and frustration. "Mom?"

Edna's face flinched a fraction of an inch. "Cotten, come close so I can tell you something."

His brow furrowed, and he leaned his ear over his mother's lips. I couldn't hear what she whispered, but his response was, "I will, Mama."

He stood straight and reached over the bed to shake the

doctor's hand. "If you need anything, I can be here in minutes."

"I'll take good care of your mother," Willingham said.

Cotten turned to me and slipped his hand around my back, leading me into the hall.

"We'll see you soon," I threw over my shoulder as we shuffled out of the room.

DuBois waited for us at the end of the corridor. "How is she?"

"Stubborn as always." Cotten sighed. "She'll be fine. Thanks, Damon. For everything."

"Listen, Cot, I'm gonna post an officer outside her room. And your mom had me call Betsy. I'll stay until she gets here."

I stood in awe of these men. At odds on occasion but friends through it all. More than that. Family. And at that moment, I felt included.

We walked back through the maze of halls and out to Cotten's car, and my body started to recover from the tension and fear that flooded every inch of the hospital.

"She loves you, you know. Of course, you do. That's probably what she whispered in your ear, right?" I fixed a sympathetic smile on my lips.

Cotten chuffed. "You wanna know what she said?"

I nodded as he helped me into his car. "Sure. If it's not too personal."

He closed my door and rounded the front, taking his time to get inside. He turned to face me, deadly serious. "She said that whoever wanted to hurt you nearly killed her. And she told me I had to find him and make him pay."

CHAPTER 24
The Adult

THE MUSCLES in Cotten's jaw flexed and released in the same rhythm as his fingers, gripping the steering wheel tighter and stretching out toward the windshield. Just watching it made me nervous.

"So now you're on a mission from God?" I turned away from him to look up at the purpling sky.

He sighed. "No more than yesterday. We have to get you to a safe place to figure out who wants you out of the way."

The other cars on the street rushed ahead, intent on their purpose—busy ants in a bustling line. I felt as though we were wandering in circles. That reckless little misguided one, cut off from the others, unable to find the way.

Our way. My way. But someone did want me out of their way. "What do you think I'm standing in the way of?"

"What?"

I faced Cotten squarely, the seatbelt cutting across my shoulder into my neck. "You said that someone wants me out of the way. Whose way am I in?" It didn't sound right when I asked the question, but from the look on his face, Cotten understood. I could see the wheels in his brain turning.

"Do you have any ideas?" His eyes stared straight ahead, cutting only to me for a second.

"I don't have a clue." But then thought again. "Actually, I might. Something April said this morning."

"Who is April?"

"April Todd is my lawyer. She was Daddy's lawyer. I inherited her; now she's mine."

His cheeks rose, forming tiny creases at the side of his eyes, but his lips didn't curl. "And why did you speak to your lawyer today?"

"Well," I drew a deep breath before explaining. "Your mother and I went to see your lawyer this morning to get you out. It just so happens that my lawyer, April, and your lawyer, Marty, are partners at the same firm. So while your mom met with Marty, I spoke to April."

"And what did she say?"

"She asked about Petra—business stuff, you know. And about the board meetings. She told me I absolutely, positively had to go to the next meeting. But—I mean, with everything like it is now—maybe not."

"Why did she say absolutely, positively?" He steered the car around a corner, pointing us back downtown.

"Those might be my words. But she was adamant. April said that if I missed four quarterly meetings in a row, the rest of the board could vote me off. But under the circumstances, they wouldn't do that."

"Why not? And why have you missed all the other meetings this year?" Cotten's tone remained urgent but not overly bossy.

I didn't feel the need to defend myself to him. Maybe I did. Why did he not simply understand? "I missed the one just before Dad passed because I didn't have anything to report. Being the historian for the company is not a big deal. I mean, everybody else knows what's happened as well as I do. And then, Daddy died. I was just...."

The emotions of the whole stress-filled mess-of-a-day came crashing in, and tears spilled over my cheeks without warning.

Cotten pulled the car to the curb, parked for a moment, and faced me. "Hey, I didn't mean to make you cry."

Digging through my purse, I found a tissue and began blotting black mascara blobs from my cheeks.

"It's not you. It's everything. I didn't go to that next one because Daddy died, and everyone told me to take as long as I needed. They were all sad, too. So I did." The words spilled out, piling up in a heap. "And the next meeting came along, and I still missed him. The thought of sitting at that long table with all the others staring at me and not having him there to wink at me or even just nod in my direction—it made me feel like I couldn't go. Like I never wanted to go to another meeting without him again."

He handed me a fresh tissue from the pack in my lap. "And the one after that?"

"Kinda the same. But everyone was so nice to me. They always tell me to take whatever time I need. They won't vote me off. I don't think."

Cotten leveled his chin with mine. "Are you still grieving?"

"I miss Daddy every single day."

"I know. I feel the same way. But I'm doing my best for him now. Honoring him by living up to the standard he always set. It's part grieving—a smaller part these days—and part growing. You're doing the same." His voice trailed off on a higher note as if he was going to finish a thought but then decided not to.

"But I've grieved more and grown less," I finished for him.

"That's not what I said."

"But it's what you meant." I shifted away from him. It was too much. I didn't want to think about it. Too much truth to take in. Daddy had sheltered me my whole life. That shelter had been ripped away without so much as a stumble or even a cough. I had to grow up now. A year. Almost a year. It was time, and he knew it. I knew it. I straightened, folding my hands in my lap.

He patted my hand. "Look, grieving works differently for everybody. I shouldn't have said anything. Your father took care of you the best he could." Cotten again stopped short.

"He babied me. Kept me a child instead of growing me into an adult. So now I'm nearly thirty years old, making terrible, childish decisions, unable to go to a meeting without Daddy holding my hand." My voice crashed hard in my ears. "I don't know what I'm supposed to do. I don't know the rules."

Cotten chuffed. "Rules? There aren't as many rules as you think. At least, that's how it feels to me. Every morning I wake up and wonder what would happen if I didn't do my job. What if I just drove to the lake and spent a week fishing? Or up to the mountains? Or just plain didn't get out of bed?"

I grinned. "Your mother would tan your hide, wouldn't she? You're too big to be spanked, but I bet she'd figure out a way to take you to the proverbial woodshed."

He chuckled. "Yes, ma'am, she would." He relaxed into his seat. "I guess I'm saying that our only rules are those we take upon ourselves. We want an income, so we go to work and follow the rules of our job. We want to be good people and please our parents, so we follow the values they instilled in us. I watched my father—he rarely followed any rules—and after so many years of living a selfish, man-child's life, it killed him. I don't want that for myself, and I certainly don't want that for my family."

"So I gotta go to the board meeting."

"I won't tell you what to do. But Ms. Todd is right; you don't want them to vote you off."

"But can they really do that? I'm the controlling shareholder." Ugh, the words coming out of my mouth sounded so smug. I was a spoiled child. It was past time for me to grow up.

"As the controlling shareholder, it's even more important to have a say in the company's direction and well-being."

I'd never thought that. Of course, that's how Dad would have seen it. April's was Dad's voice now. "I should ensure the company is acting responsibly for the other shareholders' investments."

"Something like that." He pulled back into traffic.

The sky overhead turned a deep eggplant, but the city's lights kept the streets and sidewalks bright.

"Have you decided where is safe?"

"I'll run by your place for a few things. We can figure it out from there, I guess."

Cotten turned onto Main, down the block from my place. Just a few hours ago, this road had been a disaster. Crunched cars, glass, and scooters. Broken people. As we pulled to the curb, I stole a glance across the street, where my car had slammed into a tree at Pegasus Park. There was a low dent in the tree where the bark was bare. The parking sign nearby tilted at an angle. No other signs of the wreck were visible.

Cotten came around and opened my door, reaching for my hand. His gaze was laser-focused on me, and I wondered if he dared to look for where his mother had been hit.

We shuffled upstairs silently, and when we got inside my apartment, he locked the door.

"Do you think this will be safe for tonight?"

He shook his head. "We won't stay here. It's not secure."

"Okay." I waited while he swept through the place. My bedroom, closet, bathroom, kitchen, and back to the living room. "All clear?"

Cotten gestured toward the bathroom. "Everything's fine. Why don't you run in and do whatever you need to while we're here? Get another bag together, and I'll decide where to go."

"Help yourself to whatever's in the fridge." I hurried into the bathroom. I took care of some much-needed business and then brushed through my hair. I opened my drawer to find a barrette, and a thought struck me. "I think someone was here."

Not sure if Cotten had heard me, I opened the bathroom door. He was standing there, ready for anything. "Why do you say that? What did you see?"

"Nothing now," I explained. "But the other night, when

DROP DEAD DALLAS   179

we were going out. You know that barrette I had—the one with the tracker?"

"Yes."

"I think someone broke in and planted it."

A relieved expression settled on his face. "Well, that's a possibility, but it's as likely that the tracker was attached while you were out in a crowd. It was small and magnetic. It wouldn't have taken two seconds for someone to get close enough to stick it to your barrette and disappear. Maybe a bump at the grocery store or passing in an elevator."

I shrugged and then shook my head. "Maybe, but that afternoon, when I put it on, I remember thinking I had lost it. I'd been looking for it for weeks. And then that day, I opened the drawer, and there it was, on top of all the others."

He looked as though he might play devil's advocate, but then he looked into my drawer at the dozens of barrettes, hundreds of bobby pins, and the tangle of miscellaneous hair ties. He knew as well as I did that a lost barrette does not magically float to the top of that kind of mess.

"Show me where it was when you found it."

I placed the green crystal hair clip precisely as it was a few days before. It had been perched on the top, in the middle of the sectioned drawer divider. "I couldn't have missed it if I'd tried. And I'd searched for at least two weeks."

Worry spread over his face. "Okay, grab what you absolutely need and leave the rest. For good measure, let me scan everything before you pack. No sense taking another tracker with us."

"Good idea." I went to my dresser and pulled out fresh underwear, now acutely aware that I was handing my undies to the man I had a crush on for him to inspect. I made my selections based on style, condition, and what matched. Unsure of how many days I might be away, I thought of his go-bag instructions from before and chose enough for three days. I could always purchase more if necessary.

Cotten, always the gentleman, went over each piece carefully. He then folded my things and placed them into a neat stack. Once I'd chosen two outfits and shoes, he assessed them. I found another overnight case, which he also went over with a fine-toothed comb before adding my things to it.

"My toothbrush is at your mom's house, with my other stuff."

"I have an extra at my apartment."

"That's where we're going?"

He slung my bag over his shoulder. "I think it's the safest for now—and still close to the hospital, just in case."

"Do you think it's safe to take my laptop? April wanted me to read through the agenda and reports for the board meeting. And I promised Inez I would email her the financials."

He assured me it would be, and I handed him the computer. He scanned it and gave it back.

"Who is Inez?" Cotten snapped off the lights as we left the apartment.

I scanned the hall for Marlowe or any other neighbors but saw no one. "She's the girl from the Bistro the other night. The one from the ladies' room, remember? She's the independent accountant I hired today."

He looked at me as though I had lost my mind. "You hired a woman from the ladies' room to be Petra's accountant?"

"Yes, but it's not like it sounds. She's the one with the face tattoo. I know her. Inez Delgado, I think. Or Del Rio." *Don't second-guess yourself, girl.* "No, I'm sure it's Delgado."

"And how long have you known her?" He tossed my stuff into the back seat of his car, and I slipped the laptop under my purse at my feet.

"I met her that night. You know, when I fell."

"And you think sending her financial reports for your company is safe?" He started his car and gave me a raised-eyebrow glare.

"Okay, if you want to run a background check on her before I send the email, that will be fine." I rolled my eyes at his semi-judgey attitude. "She's really nice. And I needed someone independent. That's what April said."

At the light, Cotten paused again, wearing a severe expression. "Why don't you tell me everything that Ms. Todd said?"

"I think I've told you everything now. She said I needed to go to the meeting so I didn't lose my seat on the board, though who else would want to be the historian, I couldn't say. And then, she said that I needed to request an independent audit of our financials on behalf of the shareholders. She seemed shocked that the board had only conducted an internal one." I thought about the meeting, and another pang of dread crept into my mind.

"There was an internal audit done? Why?" he asked.

"Rules. No matter the circumstances, an audit must be conducted within twelve months if any board member dies. The board voted to keep it simple and ordered one in-house. April said it needed to be independent, and I—as the controlling shareholder—needed to request one."

"What if the board votes no?"

That thought hadn't entered my mind. "Can they do that?"

He chuffed. "No. If the shareholders ask for one, they have to do it. But you need to be ready for pushback. You can't back down; it's not just you. You have to take care of all your investors now."

My stomach flipped. I wanted to ask Cotten to attend the meeting with me, but that would probably not show much growing up. The worry must have shown on my face.

"Maybe this will help. My mom has shares in Petra. Just take care of her interests in there."

At first, I wasn't sure if that would help or not. But as Cotten drove into the parking garage of his place, a phrase formed in the back of my mind.

What would Edna do?

CHAPTER 25
The Confession

WE DRAGGED my stuff inside the Adolphus Tower, down the block and catty-corner from my apartment. His office suite was at the far end of the second floor. When I'd walked the corridor earlier this week, it had seemed like a quick little adventure. But at the moment, we were both exhausted. It transformed into a hall from a movie where the pan-and-zoom effect makes the end of the hall race farther and farther away.

"What are we getting from your office?"

"A good night's sleep." Cotten unlocked the door and pushed it open, peering inside and back down the hall.

"At your office?"

"It's also my home." He got me and my stuff inside and then went through the place to be sure it was secure. "We're clear." He returned to the front room and flipped on the lights.

I scanned the room, which had been perfectly tidy only

days ago. I noticed open drawers, doors, and files piled up on the desk blotter. "What in the world happened?"

"Police search." He picked up my bag and disappeared through the door behind his desk.

I ambled toward the desk and saw the black finger-printing powder on a few things. "What were they looking for?"

"Checking to see who all's been here," he said. "This isn't too bad, really."

"Too bad?" I repeated. "This is a mess. Did they say when they're going to clean it up?"

My question must have been hilarious because Cotten guffawed. "They're not going to clean it up. I'll clean it up."

"But..." I stopped. I sounded childish again. Of course, the police weren't coming back to clean. I thought about Edna's house—the police searched there, too. "I'll help you get it straightened. And when we get a chance, we'll clean your mom's house."

His laughter had settled. "You don't need to worry about that. I'll take care of it."

My exhaustion had turned to determination. "All of this," I gestured to the mess, "is my fault. If you hadn't been working for me, there'd be no reason to search your place. Someone set you up because of me."

Cotten went to his desk and began closing file folders and sorting them into alphabetical order. I went to the credenza and started shutting the cabinet doors and pushing in drawers.

"You know, they weren't setting *me* up. They're setting *you* up." He frowned at the black powder spreading across his hands. "This stuff is everywhere. I'll grab some towels before we make it worse."

He left and returned, armed with a roll of towels and a bottle of cleaner. He sprayed a couple of towels and handed one to me. "Use it for the cabinet knobs. And be careful not to get any on you."

"Why do you think they were setting me up, not you?" I wiped the towel over the first knob, shocked by how much black powder had come off. "Yuck! I'll need a lot more cleaner. This stuff is everywhere."

Cotten laughed again. "The pistol used to kill Wexler was your father's. Yours now. Whoever killed him wiped it clean of prints. But they didn't pick up the brass. They left the shell casings and didn't wipe them clean. A couple still had my fingerprints on them from when I loaded the weapon for your father."

"DuBois told you all this?"

"He didn't spell it out. But between what he told me and what Marty said, I figured out that much. You should be glad they found my prints. Otherwise, you'd have gone to jail." Cotten handed me a freshly spritzed towel.

The idea soaked through my mind, saturating every thought. "Who wants me in jail? Why would anyone want me in jail?" A hundred more thoughts stewed and bubbled up. "If DuBois had arrested me, your mother wouldn't be in the hospital right now, and the others who died this afternoon would still be alive."

A tremor raced through my arms and legs, and my vision blurred. I needed a place to sit down. Now.

"Okay, Ronni, take it easy." Cotten's arms were around

me before I knew it. "Let's sit you down and get you something to drink."

He walked me into the other room and helped me onto his couch in his private office. This wasn't a habit I liked. "Do you have any wine?"

"How about some water?" He hesitated in front of me for a moment, ready to prop me up if I started to tip over. Once he looked satisfied that I was somewhat stable, he hurried to his refrigerator for a bottle of water, opening it as he returned. "I'll fix something to eat in a few minutes."

"But I'm right." I gulped down one swallow of cold water after another, feeling the icy sensation trickle to my stomach. "Someone is so bent on getting rid of me that they're willing to commit murder. What have I done? How can I hurt someone so badly and not know it?"

Cotten knelt in front of me, taking the water bottle from me and holding my clammy hands. "Murderers aren't right in the head. You didn't necessarily do anything at all. There's something wrong with them. You can't take the blame for that."

But I couldn't shake it. I tried to think of something—anything terrible I'd done. Something I'd said without thinking? Maybe I caused a fit of road rage that got out of control. I was a blank. I hadn't even made any major business decisions since Daddy had died. Maybe someone was angry because of my lack of action? Is that why they wanted to get me off the board? Could someone be trying to prevent me from attending this meeting in the hopes that the board would vote me off? It sounded ridiculous in my head. "I've got to think."

"Not about that." Cotten left me for a second and came

back with my laptop. "Why don't you check your email and run through your notes for Monday's meeting?"

Monday's meeting. Would it be safe to go? Would it be safe not to go? Edna needed me to be there. And then I remembered Inez. I had promised to send her meeting notes. When was that? Yesterday? Two days ago? No. It was this afternoon at lunch. So much had happened since then.

"I need to email Inez. Where's my purse?" I looked around the room but didn't see any of my things.

"I'll get it for you." Cotten went through the door in the corner behind me, leaving it open. I watched him flip the lights on and walk to the bed, where my purse was perched on the corner. He scooped it up and brought it back to me. "Do you carry?" he asked, holding my bag by the shoulder strap.

"I carry lots of stuff in there. What specifically?" I dug for my phone.

Cotten laughed. "A sidearm. Do you have a gun?"

"No." I almost laughed this time. "I think you'd know if I did."

"I thought so, too. But your purse weighs a ton. If you don't have a pistol in there, what's so heavy?" He raised and lowered my bag as if he was lifting a dumbbell. "Do you see a chiropractor regularly? You should."

At the exact moment I retrieved my phone, it rang. Inez Delgado flashed on my screen. I took my purse from Cotten and dismissed him with a wave. "Hello, Inez."

"Hi, Ronni. I wanted to call and see if you had changed your mind. I checked my email and didn't find anything from you yet. If you did change your mind, I understand."

"I didn't change my mind at all. I was just about to

forward the reports to you. We had an accident this morning, which set me back quite a bit."

Her voice seemed hesitant. "An accident? Are you okay?"

"I'm fine. Edna is in the hospital, but she'll be fine, too. Thank you for being patient with me." I opened my laptop and pulled up the folder with all the reports for the meeting. "I'm sending you the files now. And tomorrow, I'll access the main office files. You'll need those to do anything."

"Yes, I will, but the reports for the meeting will be a good start." Inez sounded relieved. "And where is this board meeting happening? At your main office?"

I attached the document to my email and hit send. "Actually, no. The meeting will be at my father's home in Turtle Creek. I'll text you the address. It's gated, but your name will be on the list. So you won't have any trouble." I paused for a second as five- or six-dozen emails filled my inbox. Mostly junk, but a few I flagged to check in the morning. "I just sent the email. Let me know when you get it. And if you have any questions about anything at all, just call. If I don't know the answer, I can find out."

"Oh great," she said. "The email just came through. And the files are here." She was silent for a second, and I could hear her typing. "No problem opening the files, either. I'll get to work on these right away."

"Thank you, Inez. You don't know how grateful I am for agreeing to do this for me."

"No, thank you, Ms. Peters. I appreciate the opportunity."

Cotten returned as I finished up with Inez. "You can call me Ronni. And I'll check in with you tomorrow to see if you need anything. Thanks, and have a great evening." I clicked off and set the phone on the table beside me.

Smiling like the Cheshire Cat, Cotten shook his head. "You sound like your father."

"I do?" Nobody had ever told me that before. Dad always said I reminded him of my mother.

"Your telephone manners are right out of a textbook— gracious, grateful, putting people at ease. There's no way you hurt anyone intentionally."

"I'm telling you, I didn't. I would never hurt anyone intentionally."

He gestured to the bottle of water. "Are you feeling okay now?"

"Yes, much better, thanks." I started to stand up, but he held up his hands and shook his head.

"Stay right there. I've about got everything straightened in the office. You relax and take care of your business while I fix dinner." He started back out but spun around in the doorway. "Spaghetti okay with you?"

"I'll eat whatever you make."

"Brave woman," he said over his shoulder as he retreated to the kitchen.

Culling through my email folders, I deleted the junk, flagged the Petra-specific, and started on the personal memos. Most were quick check-ins. *How are you getting along? If there's anything we can do... We hope you'll visit soon. And a few announcements. Mary-Claire turns two next week! Jess got a promotion, and we're moving to Lisbon.*

Quick responses in return. *I'm well; thank you for your sweet note. I appreciate your concern. Looking forward to seeing you then. Isn't she precious? Congratulations, and bon voyage!*

That finished, I turned to the Petra emails. Typical requests for investment, a few résumés, and then the ones marked BoD. The Meeting. Just thinking about it raised goosebumps on my arms.

First was the roll call. Thomas Curry wouldn't be attending because he would be somewhere over the Atlantic on his way to Cairo. Besides Curry, I appeared to be the only one who hadn't responded in the affirmative. I checked that off the list with a short, *Looking forward to it!* email.

Financial report for review—eleven pages. Minutes from the last meeting—four pages. Overseas divisions—nine countries at three pages each. The Diane Pawley-Peters Women's Foundation report—five pages. New technologies report, labeled Horizons—ten pages. Three other reports—another ten pages. This was going to be a lot of reading tomorrow. All that was missing was the historian's report. That would be next on the agenda. Wait, where was the agenda for the meeting?

Typing into the search feature on my inbox, I found the email containing the tentative agenda with the subject line: *a call for new business.* I opened it and scanned. I nearly swallowed my tongue when I saw the first item under New Business: *Review and Reinforcing Meeting Attendance in the Bylaws.* The item in question was called for by VP of Dallas Operations, Beverly Muncy.

Bev.

"Cotten?" I called to the other room.

"What is it?" He leaned back into the room.

"I may have found something. What do you know about Bev Muncy? She's…"

"I know who she is." Cotten sounded as though he had a bitter taste in his mouth. "She is, in the most polite way to put it, a cougar. And it's a pity, too, because I understand she's got a sharp business sense."

"I'd always thought she was all talk. She's always very friendly. But you think it's more than talk?"

He glanced down at the dishtowel in his hands. "Talk doesn't squeeze your butt in the elevator."

I gasped. "That's harassment. Did you tell anyone?"

An embarrassed grimace settled on his face. "Tell someone she got light-headed and reached out to keep herself from falling and that my backside saved her? Because that's how she explained it."

"Hmph. A man would have been fired for that kind of thing."

"No, my dear. Men have been getting away with that for hundreds of years," Cotten scoffed. "And before that, their bad behavior didn't require an explanation."

"Well, it's still disgraceful."

Cotten nodded with raised eyebrows. "It is. But why were you asking about Bev in the first place?" He peered over his shoulder toward the kitchen for a moment. "What are you thinking?"

"She's the one asking for a review of the meeting attendance bylaws." I gestured to the laptop screen as if he could see the copy of the agenda.

"And so you think she's the one trying to remove you from the board? Interesting. If your lawyer hadn't told you to attend, would you have even looked at the agenda?" His attention quickly shifted to the beeping oven. He held up an index finger. "Hold your thoughts for just a second."

While he disappeared to take care of dinner, I thought about his question. I was ashamed to say that I wouldn't have opened the email until after the meeting was over, and then only if someone had asked me something specific about it. I'd been failing my father. I'd been failing his company. And it might have cost me everything.

I didn't want to wait for him to come back. This was something I needed to own. I was going to get in front of it from here on out.

Joining Cotten in his kitchen, I found him trying to balance the pan of boiled noodles in one hand while trying to drain the water off without losing the spaghetti into the sink. "Let me help you. Do you have a colander or a strainer I can hold?"

Cotten shook his head. "Melted in the dishwasher. Can you just hold the noodles back with a spoon for me?"

Grabbing the spoon from the jar on the countertop, I looped my arm under his and positioned the flat of the spoon against the pasta. He poured off the water and carefully placed the pan back on the stovetop.

"That was fun." He smiled at me for a second and then turned to pour the smaller pan of sauce over the noodles. "I haven't made spaghetti since I threw out my strainer. Completely forgot."

He took the spoon from my hand, letting his fingers linger over mine.

"Now I know what to get you for Christmas." I inhaled the sweet scent of roasted garlic and basil. "But that's still a ways off. When is your birthday?"

"August seventh."

"That's better. It will be an early birthday gift. I don't want to wait six months for more pasta."

His eyebrows shot up. "And how often will I be cooking

for you now?" He gestured to the stack of plates on the shelf behind me.

"I suppose that depends on how everything tastes." I inhaled another luscious breath. "But chances are pretty good that it will be quite often."

I laughed and set the plates onto the two placemats on his small round dining table and straightened the forks on the paper napkins. "I'm so exhausted I may fall asleep in my dinner."

"Don't do that. The bed is more comfortable than the table."

He said it out loud. I tried not to think about it—our sleeping arrangements. For weeks I'd imagined a romantic evening with him. Witty banter over wine, gourmet dinner, maybe dessert. And then? That had all been in my imagination. Not now. This was real. I felt like a giant neon arrow flashed over my head: *You are here.* And all I could think was that if I blinked too long, I might fall asleep.

We sat and ate and chatted about tomorrow and the meeting on Monday. Given the implications of the hours looming immediately before us, tomorrow seemed easier to think about. Combing through emails, looking for clues or hints—especially Bev's missives—would keep us busy.

After dinner, we moved back to the couch so I could put away my computer. By then, my head was swimming with detached thoughts. Would he kiss me? What was I going to wear to the meeting? Was I going to be murdered before the meeting? Was I going crazy?

"Can I confess something to you?" Cotten asked once all my gear was closed and organized into a neat stack on his coffee table. "Will you promise not to fire me again if I tell you something?"

I might have laughed if I wasn't nearly dozing off already. "I'm too tired to fire you, so go right ahead."

He turned his shoulders square with mine, and I could see the faint worry in his eyes. That alone sparked my focus.

"You hired me to follow you to see if you had a stalker." Though his voice trailed off, his stare remained intent.

My heart pounded in my ears. This was it. Cotten was about to tell me that he knew I had lied. It was over. I could feel it. "I know." I couldn't think of any other response short of pouring out *my* confession and begging for forgiveness.

He didn't blink. "It wasn't the first time I'd worked as your bodyguard."

I squinted, trying to understand.

He continued. "After your father sent me to… dispatch… your suitors, he hired me to occasionally watch over you. To keep you safe."

"What do you mean?"

"A few trips overseas and a girls' weekend with your college friends." He laced his fingers together in his lap. "I was there, watching from a distance, to ensure you were safe."

"Okay," I replied. "Dad hired you for stuff like that. He was overprotective. I get that now." Why was this a confession?

His gaze broke off, and he stared at his hands. "But after he passed away," he started again. "I was worried… concerned that you needed… I'm not sure what." He took a long, deep breath. "About once a month, I took it upon myself to check in on you. To make sure you were okay."

"You followed me?" My brain was finally sorting it out. "Without asking?"

Cotten slumped his shoulders. "When you called to hire me, I thought maybe you had seen me—not well enough to identify me, but enough to realize you were being followed. I was scared. So scared, I thought maybe I wouldn't take your case."

"But you did take it." My thoughts started falling together in images I didn't want to imagine. "Did you hire Wexler to follow me to keep me from suspecting you?"

He flinched as though I had lunged at him. "No. Absolutely not. I'd never do anything like that."

The expression on his face told me plainly that I'd hurt him. Instinctively, I reached for his hands. "But then, what exactly are you confessing?"

He looked confused. "I'm confessing that I almost didn't take your case because of my past actions. I hate to think of what might have happened to you if I hadn't. *And* I'm confessing to following you when I had no right to do so."

My pulse calmed slightly, but my curiosity was piqued. "So why did you follow me? Why did you care? Was it just a habit? Did you think you were honoring my father's wishes and carrying on his overprotective practices?" I almost laughed just saying the words. But Cotten didn't. He looked as though I was making fun of him.

"Because I had grown to care for you. I get it; it's crazy. I didn't even know you. But somehow, I cared, and not just from your father's point of view." He inched away from me slightly. "And don't worry, I'm aware it's inappropriate. You're my boss. I have no business caring."

He continued for another minute, sputtering about why

he had no right to expect anything from me. But I didn't hear any of that. All I heard was, 'I cared," and it buzzed in my mind and melded with the beat of my heart.

I cared. I cared. Thump-thump. I cared.

When I finally regained my mind, he was still going on about how he would respect my wishes about something or other and that he hoped we could remain friends. I couldn't stand it any longer. It was just too much.

So I threw my arms around his neck and kissed him. That shut him up.

CHAPTER 26

The Office

THE RICH AROMA of sizzling bacon woke my nose before the rest of me. Sitting up in Cotten's mussed bed, I tried to recall the events of last evening. I remembered sending emails, reading reports, enjoying spaghetti, talking, and then a kiss. And then another. I remember resting his head on his shoulder. And then I couldn't recall.

I was fully clothed except for my shoes. I supposed that answered that question.

Rolling out of bed, I turned toward the sizzle. I poked my head around the corner and found Cotten dressed in Wranglers and a black tee. His feet were bare, and his hair was still damp from showering. He stood at the stove, poking at a skillet. He tilted his chin in my direction when he noticed me. "You're up."

"Do I have time for a quick shower?"

He waved his spatula over the pan. "Go on. I'll keep your breakfast hot."

"Yes," I heard my voice saying, though my brain was screaming something else. I hurried to the bathroom, scooping up my bag on the way.

I achieved a new personal best time for showering and dressing and was back in the kitchen before Cotten had the food ready to plate. He waved his tongs from my coral jersey dress to my floral-print sneaks. "Cute."

"Everything smells delicious," I said, setting the juice glasses on the table. I debated whether to ask about the previous evening but decided that it might be desirable to keep a certain level of plausible deniability for the sake of future conversations with Edna.

As if he read my mind, Cotten said, "I called the hospital this morning. My mother is well—already asking about us. We can visit her in an hour. Does that fit into your plan?"

"You tell me." I sat down when he gestured, and he followed. "You're in charge."

He bowed his head for a moment, and when I realized he was blessing the meal, I did, too. After another second of silence, he continued. "Hardly in charge." He took a bite of his bacon. "What do you need to do before your meeting tomorrow?"

The bacon was crisp and savory, and I chewed while checking my mental to-do list. I swallowed and sipped my orange juice; I had a few ideas. "After we see your mother, can we run by my office? My navy skirt suit is still there from the dry-cleaners, and I could send Inez a few files from my desktop computer, too. That one has all my saved passwords for the main storage files."

"Please tell me you don't have your computer auto-fill your passwords," Cotten said between juice gulps.

"Only for the office files. And everyone there has the same access. So it's not a big deal."

"Says the boss to her head of security."

"Fine, you can watch me change my passwords while we're there. Will that make you happy?" I waved my fork in his direction.

"Nothing would make me happier."

"That so?"

"No. That's a lie. But I would feel better if you keep your passwords up here." He tapped on his right temple.

I laughed. "If I could keep them in your brain, it wouldn't be a problem. It's my brain that forgets."

We finished our breakfast and straightened his apartment before leaving for the day.

Spending an hour with Edna was harder for Cotten than I expected. While she looked much better—more color, more comfortable with her casts—he looked worse.

"You're going to be fine," he repeated a dozen times until it was evident that it was more for his own peace of mind and less for hers.

"Betsy got in last night," Edna told us. "She's coming shortly. It's been forever since she's been down. You should take her to dinner before she goes back. I think she'd enjoy meeting Ronni."

Cotten held his mother's hand as he spoke to her, both nodding in my direction every few minutes. I tried to be supportive, but all I could think was that I should have been in that hospital bed, not her.

When the hour was over, Cotten kissed her forehead and then spoke for a minute to the nurse. I waited in the hallway, scanning both directions for anyone staring too long or making too much effort not to look at all. Everything seemed normal.

"The doctor will be in later this afternoon, and he's supposed to call me after. The nurse says she's doing fine." Cotten's assurances were again for himself.

"She's strong." I squeezed his arm. Edna had looked good, but I was a little discouraged that she hadn't scolded or even bossed us except to suggest we take Cotten's sister to dinner. Maybe she was in worse condition than I thought.

We drove to the Petra offices in silence. I wanted to tell him to turn around and return to the hospital, knowing that if I had one more day to spend with my father, I would give up everything I had. He needed her as much as she needed him. Maybe more. But Edna had spoken on that matter, and Cotten was his mother's son. He was on the job.

At the Petra office, Cotten parked in the spot I'd inherited from Dad, and we took the executive elevator up to twelve, keying in my passcode. Still no witty banter or even a *here we are* when the elevator car arrived on our floor. I led the way to my office and unlocked the glass door while Cotten scanned the corridor.

"There shouldn't be anyone up here on a Sunday," I whispered. My voice sounded loud and echoed in the relative quiet. "The cleaners won't even come in until four o'clock."

Cotten moved past me and checked the room before I could step inside. He studied all around my desk and then my credenza. He checked the closet and my private bathroom. His index finger led his eyes over my bookshelves. He swiveled out the wall-mounted television to scan the back of it before returning it to its place. He pulled back my drapes, looked behind them, and then down to the street below. The view of Reunion Tower was incidental at the moment.

"See anything?" I dropped my purse onto my desk.

"Everything looks all right." He inhaled deeply. "I need to run downstairs to the security room and check the system logs. Will you mind if I leave you alone for a minute or two?"

"Just make sure you come back." I picked up my keys again. "And I'll lock the door behind you."

"Good idea." Cotten stepped into the hall and waited until I'd turned the key in the lock before turning back to the elevators.

Sunlight flooded the room, so I didn't bother turning on the overhead lights. I sat down at my desk and switched on my computer as if it was Monday morning. I opened my email and ran through it again before starting anything else.

I plugged in my phone to sync contacts, and within seconds Inez was added to my digital address book. I opened the Petra cloud files—letting my computer auto-fill one last time—and then scoured through the folders to pull up the financials for the previous thirty-six months. I copied them to Inez's email and also added the records for the women's foundation. For good measure, I browsed through the files one more time to see if anything else might be helpful to her. I found a list of employees and positions, updated to last month. It included all the contact information in case she had questions for anyone.

Another minute to run the email through encryption and a quick send. After unplugging my phone, I texted Inez with the code to open it. She immediately texted back with a thumbs-up.

My next message to her included the address for the castle

and the start and end times for the meeting. I added her to the gate access list and the guest list for the castle. I ensured the whole thing was responsive to being added to her calendar, address book, and GPS all at once.

She replied with a smiley and TY.

My business with Inez—done.

I pulled out my navy skirt suit from my armoire. It was still in the dry cleaning bag, which I pulled into a cowl around the hanger's neck. I inspected it to ensure the gravy stain was banished from the sleeve.

I had worn it last at Daddy's memorial service. He'd always said he didn't want me to wear black. Black was for formal events. Stuffy. Uptight. Sad. Navy was his go-to. I remember choosing the suit after looking through pictures of Dad at Mom's funeral. He wore navy. I wore navy.

To protect it from whatever dangers lay ahead, I shimmied the clear plastic bag down and tied the excess in a little knot at the bottom. I draped the package over my Eames chair and went into the bathroom to freshen up before Cotten returned.

As I washed my hands, I thought I heard him tapping on my glass door. Coming out of the bathroom, I flipped the overhead lights on, and the tapping stopped. I went around the corner to find the hallway in front of my office door empty.

I glanced in both directions but could see nothing. Maybe I was hearing things.

I grabbed my phone and messaged Cotten.

Did you just knock on my office door?

No. Was someone knocking?

Yes. Probably nothing.

I'm coming back up.

I'm fine.

Almost there.

Seconds later, I heard the faint ding of the elevator. Another second, and I saw Cotten hurrying toward my door. I turned the key until the bolt retracted with a clunk. He flipped it back into the lock position and began his questions.

"What exactly did it sound like?"

"Well, I was in the powder room with the water running. But it sounded like tapping on the glass. I turned on the lights, and it stopped. But when I looked, there was nobody. I really thought it was you. And now—I'm not sure I really heard anything at all." I felt embarrassed. What if I had imagined the sound?

Cotten appeared concerned and maybe unsure how to proceed when the sound of a door closing down the hall made us both jump. "That wasn't your imagination."

We both hurried to the door. "I'm coming with you."

"You should stay here."

I shook my head. "Maybe I should, but I'm not going to."

He exhaled but didn't argue. "Okay, but stay behind me. I'm armed; you're not."

I agreed and tucked myself behind him. I locked my office door from the outside and worked my keys outward between my fingers, just in case I had to hit someone. I hoped I didn't have to hit anyone.

We crept quietly down the hall toward my father's former office, on the east side, opposite corner from mine. The sounds grew louder. Banging and muttering. We saw a light glowing beneath the door to the documents room.

My fist tightened around my key fob until my knuckles

melded with my keys to create a formidable weapon. I watched Cotten's right hand hovering just above the back of his waistband, ready to draw his sidearm if needed. I instinctively stayed back as we approached the door, allowing Cotten to lead the way inside.

"Shh," I heard him whisper.

I held my breath.

He pushed the door open and stepped into the room, yelling, "Hands in the air!"

"Ahh! My great-stars-a-mighty!" Karen Richter screamed as she collapsed into a huddled mass on the floor in front of the copy machine.

As soon as I heard her voice, I raced into the room and waved Cotten down. Thankfully, he hadn't fully drawn his pistol.

"Stop, Cotten. It's only Karen. She's my secretary—the one I inherited from Dad. She's okay." Though I was pretty sure she was *not* okay. The 55-year-old woman trembled significantly, with one arm up in surrender and the other clutching at her heart. She was dressed in a pink linen dress and pearls, her matching block-heel shoes left empty next to her stockinged feet.

"Please don't kill me," she pleaded, not hearing or recognizing me through her panic. "I don't have any money."

Dropping to my knees beside her, I wrapped my arm around her shoulder, and Cotten stepped back. "Karen, it's okay. It's me, Ronni. We just ran up to grab a few things before the meeting. We heard noises. We didn't know it was you. What are you doing up here on a Sunday?"

Karen seemed to calm down. I helped her to her feet and then to the small task chair beside the copy machine. She fanned her hand in front of her face. "Oh, my. You two scared the life out of me. I thought you had left half an hour ago. I hope in my fright I didn't say anything vulgar. On a Sunday, too. Oh, my."

Cotten's mouth twisted into a faint grin, and he turned away from us and looked back out into the hallway.

"We're so sorry to frighten you. But what were you doing up here? We heard you talking to someone."

She drew a deep breath that seemed to expand her bosom to the total capacity of her dress seams. As she spoke, the whole upper portion of her body deflated. "Well, I saw last night that you had replied to the roll-call email for the meeting, and I had already made up all the attendee packets, as I do every Friday afternoon before Monday meetings. But you didn't respond until Saturday night."

I understood clearly that this was a gentle reprimand toward me.

"So after church this morning, I had to come up here to put together your packet for the meeting. I was just talking to myself, coaxing the copier to do its job. It makes 100 copies perfectly without a glitch, but it hates to make singles. The paper jams nearly every time, you know." The tremor in her voice had nearly vanished at this point, and her complexion was regaining color.

"I am sorry. For scaring you and for not responding on Friday. I will certainly do better next time." I ventured to ask one more question. "Karen, did you tap on my office door a few minutes ago? Maybe as you walked by?"

She shook her head. "No, I came the other way 'round from the elevators. I didn't go past your office."

Nodding, I smiled. "I think I was just hearing things. Old buildings make noises, don't they?"

Karen grimaced and wrung her hands around each other a few times. "Did you find what you were looking for?" she asked.

"What do you mean?" I exchanged a quick glance with Cotten.

"In your father's office?" She inhaled and exhaled. "When I first arrived, I walked by your father's office. His desk lamp was on, and I could hear you shuffling through things. I heard his filing cabinet close. The middle drawer squeaks, you know, as it shuts. Did you find whatever it was you needed?"

"When was this?" Cotten's tone sounded urgent.

Glancing at her wristwatch, Karen sniffed. "Maybe 45 minutes ago? And then everything got quiet, and I thought you had left."

Cotten and I exchanged a worried look.

"You didn't see who it was?" I could feel the trembling shift from Karen's fingers to mine.

"But wasn't it you?" she answered with another question. "Who else would it be? The office door was locked. No one else has a key but you and myself."

Cotten shook his head and turned to the hall. "I'll make a quick loop of the floor and check things out. You both stay here until I get back. I won't take five minutes."

He left us alone in the copier room. Karen went back to her business. I waited in the task chair. As she'd said, the machine made a dozen copies without a hitch, but when she flipped the original over to make just one duplicate, the red light flashed, and an alarm began beeping.

She squinted her eyes in determination. "Ridiculous machine." She muttered something unintelligible as she opened the paper tray and slammed it closed again. "Oh yes, your email mentioned something about your historian's report and something else about a shareholder request? Do I need to make copies of those?"

"No, ma'am," I replied, still feeling remorseful. "I'll deliver those items at the meeting. Don't worry about that."

A few seconds later, Cotten returned, shaking his head. "I didn't see or hear anyone. Nothing out of place in your father's office, either. Whoever it was is gone now. I can log in from home and see if any cameras picked up a face."

Karen shot me a glance, not even acknowledging Cotten. "All right then. Now I still have another half-hour at my desk revising the agenda, sending out that email, and then adding the revisions to the packets of all the attendees."

Cotten stepped into the conversation. "Then we'll leave you to it and be on our way. That is if you feel okay to be alone."

She blinked, and her expression turned to exasperation. "I don't mind at all being alone. And I prefer it to being scared half to death."

I repressed the urge to laugh, and in another ten minutes, we were stowing my suit into the back seat of Cotten's car.

"Let's grab some lunch." Cotten started the engine. "I want to check on something before we go back to my place."

CHAPTER 27
The Park

COTTEN DROVE us to the sandwich shop at the end of the block, down from the Tower Business Suites. He paid the parking fee from his phone, and we went inside. Before we got in line to order, he sent a quick text message.

"Something wrong?" I noticed he stood back from the storefront window a few feet and focused on the street traffic.

"Just checking to see if anyone's following us." His phone buzzed and lit up. A smile crossed his lips. "One minute more," he said under his breath.

A few seconds later, a black and white rolled by at a snail's pace. As soon as it had passed, a gray coupe pulled out from across the street and sped away. In another minute, the patrol car returned, and this time the officer in the passenger seat gave Cotten a thumbs-up before driving on.

"What was that? Someone was following us?" My jaw hung open. "Did you get the license plate number?"

Cotten directed me to the line to order. "I think we can leave that up to the police, don't you?"

"I suppose they can do more than we can, anyway." My stomach growled as I was talking. The scent of sourdough bread sharpened my appetite. "What's good here?"

Cotten rolled his eyes. "You live right there. Not a hundred steps away. You've never been here?"

"I keep thinking I'll try it, but I just—I don't know. It seems easier to eat at home when I'm by myself."

He shook his head. "Do you trust me to order for you?"

"Yes. I'll get a table." I left him in the line and scouted a table at the window within view of his car. When he joined me, I stood again. "I'm going to wash my hands."

A quick trip to the ladies' room, and I returned to find a bright blue basket loaded with a half-sub sandwich and a pickle spear. Cotten's basket matched precisely, except that his also included a short cup of sliced jalapenos. Two tall glasses of lemonade, garnished with fruit slices, cherries, and mint sprigs, flanked the baskets.

"This looks yummy." I sat, and Cotten hopped to his feet.

He gestured toward the restrooms. "I'll wash mine, too."

While he was away, I inspected my lunch. Sourdough, stacked with thin-shaved turkey and ham, balanced with a creamy layer of gouda. A slice of tomato, minced black olives, baby spinach, dressed with Thousand Island. Nice.

I sipped my lemonade and had to wipe the condensation from the glass before I felt confident taking another. I didn't like to think about how many times I'd dropped a full glass all over everything.

Cotten motioned to the car as he sat down. "See anything interesting out there?"

"Sorry, I didn't know I was supposed to be watching."

He chuckled and moved a paper napkin to his lap.

Waiting for his silent blessing, I lowered my eyes until I heard a soft, "Amen."

I picked up my sandwich, careful not to squeeze the insides out, and leaned in for a large bite. The bread was delightfully chewy, holding the dressing and cheese and meat and veggies all in place. It was a savory combination of sweet and salty, and as I set the sandwich back in the basket, I heard an ecstatic moan escape my lips.

An amused grin spread over Cotten's mouth as he held out the jalapeno cup. "I was going to ask if you wanted any of these, but it sounds like you're enjoying it as is."

My face warmed as I felt a full blush rising from my core. So much for trying to impress him. "Thank you, it's delicious."

He leaned back in his chair and took a long draw of his lemonade. Something between contentment and concern settled into his expression.

Swallowing another bite, I asked, "Are you all right?"

He bobbed his head a fraction of an inch and jawed at his lunch without another word.

My thoughts danced from one anxiety to another. Were we in danger? Who was following us? What was Cotten thinking? Was this technically our third date, or was this all one long—whatever it was? Was I just a job to him? What would happen when all this was over?

We finished up and got back into the car. Cotten stared back at the Tower. "Why don't we spend some time outdoors?"

"Okay with me." I started to reopen my door, but he

stopped me.

"Let's take a walk through Pioneer Plaza."

"Daddy's favorite place downtown. He always took me there when the weather was nice. Of course, today would be warm for his taste, but there's a nice breeze."

As we drove to the park, I thought about Daddy. The walks we would take when I was a kid. The massive bronze sculptures of longhorn cattle being driven down a stream by bronze cowboys on bronze horseback scared me a little at first. But as I got older, I considered the hulking bovines my friends. I thought about the picture on Daddy's desk. With me swinging from a bronze horn as if I were on a trapeze.

We parked on the plaza's west side and took the path up to the cemetery. The parking area steps were steep and still covered with mud from last week's rain, and Cotten took my hand to steady me. He didn't let go, and for the first time in my life, I thought I knew what those couples felt—the ones you see in parks and on the streets, holding hands for no reason other than love. Why did I have to think about that word? My heart pounded loudly in my ears. Maybe from fear, but mostly from something else. Something new.

I glanced up at the Petra building across the street from the park. The afternoon sunlight reflected in blue-white strips of window glass stacked between the tan brick and cut stone corners. Being downtown always made me feel like I was near Dad.

"You know this is why your father chose the southeast corner office, don't you?" Cotten pointed up to the windows in Dad's office.

We stopped for a moment to look around the park. I drew a deep breath. "Yes, he said the cemetery reminded him of all the men and women who had struggled to make Texas what it is today, and then the cattle sculpture inspired him to keep driving to make it better tomorrow."

"That's what he told me, too." Cotten led us off the path and through the gravesites shaded by hundred-year-old trees. "Your father was a dyed-in-the-wool Texan. He once told me he was related to Davy Crockett. Is that true?"

I scoffed. "I think we may have been related through marriage, a cousin, or something. That didn't matter to Daddy, though. Crockett was his hero." I glanced up at Cotten and saw a mist in his eyes. "Are you okay?"

He nodded quickly at first, then inhaled a deep breath. "I don't know, Ronni."

He called me Ronni! Squeezing his hand, I tried to assure him. "Your momma's gonna be okay. She's the strongest woman I've ever known."

His lips twisted for a split second, trying to form a smile. "She is."

"But?"

"This whole last year, I've been missing your dad. Maybe more than I missed my own." He hesitated. "That's not easy for me to admit. I loved my father, but he had a tough time just being a good man, let alone a good father."

"My dad wasn't perfect, you know."

"I know he wasn't." Cotten's grip was firm. "But even all the dumb stuff he did was because he adored you."

There was no denying that. I could feel another confession building, expecting something terrible to spill out of Cotten's lips. I squeezed his hands, hoping that would keep him silent. I didn't know if I could take any more.

We ambled into the middle of the herd of longhorns, and

Cotten leaned against the limestone retaining wall hemming in the sculpture, mimicking canyon walls and riverbanks.

I reached out and rubbed the nose of the longhorn posed in front of us. "I named this one Quincy."

"Anyway," he chuffed and continued. "I've spent all this time mourning your father, believing I knew exactly how you felt. Like we had this connection because of it." He paused again as if he wanted me to say something, but I had no words that fit here, and he went on. "I was wrong. I had no idea how much you were hurting. Not until this week. Not until Damon came to the jail to take me to the hospital. All I could think from the moment he told me about the accident— that you were all right, but that she might not make it—was that if I lost her, I would be alone." A shimmer formed beneath his eyes. "And it wasn't until then that I understood how you might feel. Ronni, I was scared to death."

I reached around his waist and pulled him into a hug. We both needed it. After several seconds we loosened our embrace, and I rested my head on his shoulder. "But she's going to be fine. She'll need you a little extra for a while, and your sister, too. But she's going to be just fine."

"I know." It was an automatic reaction.

"And I'll be there for you. I won't let you be alone," I heard myself saying. The words sounded bold in my ears. Like someone else, someone much stronger than me had said them.

And just like that, I felt grown up. Not like a kid playing pretend. Not that I had any delusions of being wholly self-sufficient or able to handle whatever came my way, but I could see the direction I needed to go. And know that I didn't have to walk there alone.

CHAPTER 28

The Warning

WHEN THE SUN reached its apex, it seemed to stay there an unnaturally long time, baking everything below. Even the park's green space became too hot for us, and Cotten and I retreated to his car. We endured a few moments of leather-scented sauna until the AC brought the interior climate into the 80-degree range.

Cotten drove us to the hospital again, where we found that Edna was being bathed and unable to receive visitors. I met Betsy for the first time and invited her to dinner with us.

The tiny young brunette declined politely, asking Cotten for a rain check. "I'm just exhausted. I know Mom will be fine, but I can't help but worry when I'm not with her. If I can get a night or two of measurable rest, I'd love to catch up over dinner. For now, I'd be pretty poor company."

Cotten kissed his sister on the cheek. "I understand. Tell Mom we came by, and give us a call if you want us to pick up something to eat."

Betsy assured him she would. "Oh, I almost forgot. Mom wanted me to ask you if you've found him yet. I'm not sure who she means."

"I do, but no—we haven't yet. Tell her I'll call Damon and see if he's heard anything."

An amused grin spread over Betsy's face. "He came by about an hour ago. He only poked his head into the room and saw I was here." She tilted her head and blinked. "He ducked back into the hall without saying a word. He doesn't know I saw him." She almost laughed. "When you talk to him, tell him he doesn't have to be afraid of me, okay?"

Cotten agreed and suppressed a little laugh, too. "I will."

As we left the hospital parking lot, I couldn't resist. "Why is Detective DuBois afraid of Betsy?"

He chuckled to himself. "They dated in high school, broke up during college, and both of them think they completely broke the other one's heart. I don't know. Maybe they did. Now, whenever they're in the same town, they spend most of the time avoiding each other."

I tried to create a mental image of petite Betsy on the arm of a house-sized DuBois. "Wow, I don't think I'd have ever guessed that." I wondered for a second about what kind of relationship they might have had. "Maybe they each have a bad case of the what-ifs."

"Do you get those?" he asked.

"You mean like, *what if my dad hadn't paid off my boyfriends?*"

Cotten nodded and added, "Or, *what if my boyfriends had thought more of me than money?*"

"Ouch!" I directed a severe scowl in his direction. That was the exact what-if I had played through my mind's eye since the horrible revelation. "Am I really so easily discarded?"

"They were boys. They couldn't see past the next prom or whatever." Cotten rested his hand next to mine on the armrest. "Those guys didn't bother getting to know you." His pinky finger gently hooked over mine.

It was a tiny movement, but my body responded as if he had bent me back into a dip and kissed me. I tried to play it cool. "And you know me?" My voice may have cracked as I asked the question.

The creases at the corners of his eyes deepened. "A little bit. I know you love to write stories but aren't comfortable letting others read them. That this book you're writing about Petra has you stretched far beyond your comfort zone." He shot a glance in my direction, and I felt a blush rise on my cheeks.

"My dad probably told you that."

"I know your feet can't help but move when music plays. Any music." He let a smile cross his lips. "I know you not only aren't afraid of flying but that you enjoy it—unlike your father. I know you like your steaks cooked medium, preferably mesquite-grilled."

"And so you really *are* the one who's been stalking me?"

"If by stalking you mean am I the one watching from across the room at the Women's Foundation Galas, or pretending not to listen to the speaker-phone conversations you had with your father, or watching you during monthly Petra meetings? Yes. I'm that stalker. I'm the one who is entirely mesmerized by your presence whenever we're in the same room."

I wasn't sure how to react. Was he serious? I laughed. "You're kidding, right?"

He pulled into the parking garage at his apartment. "The morning you called to hire me—to see if you had a stalker—I was scared, like I said. You thought you might be imagining it. I thought you had caught me watching over you. Or maybe had just noticed me staring too long or something. It wasn't until I saw Wexler following you, literally everywhere, that I started to almost relax. But then I couldn't because then you were in real danger."

My body warmed with every word, and it wasn't from the car or the weather. He got out and came around to open my door, giving me a moment to sort out my next question. When he took my hand, I asked, "If you were so interested in me, why didn't you ever call me? You have the contact information for every person who works at Petra. You certainly had mine."

As we walked into the building, he scoffed. "Sure. I could have just called you. Maybe left a voicemail. Hello, is this Veronica Peters? Yes, hi, my name is Cotten Hammond, and I work for your father. Yes, well, I've been secretly in love with you for the last seven years, and I wanted to know if I could take you to dinner sometime. Press one for yes and two for no."

What? My brain wasn't processing correctly. Did he really confess to liking me, loving me, for seven years? No, this was just something silly he was saying. But everything else? It was true. Could it be?

My breath quickened, and I felt light-headed. Maybe it was the conversation. Perhaps it was the sudden blast of air conditioning after being so warm. I didn't know. I didn't know anything.

Before I had the chance to get clarification, heavy footfalls sounded behind us in the hall. Spinning to confront the threat head-on, Cotten swished me behind him. "Stay where you are," he ordered in a solid, confident tone.

"Whoa-whoa-whoa, cowboy," DuBois' voice sounded. "It's me."

Cotten's shoulders eased when he saw him. "Damon, you scared us to death. Come in, and I'll get you some iced tea."

The police detective followed us in, and both men checked the whole suite thoroughly before we relaxed.

"I have news about your case, Ms. Peters." DuBois gestured to the leather couch in Cotten's office. I sat, and he pulled a chair to face me. "I just got the preliminary lab report for your car."

"My car?" Why would they run a lab report on my car?

Cotten came in with three tall glasses of tea. "What did you get off her car?"

DuBois held the glass in one hand and let the condensation run over his fingers. He switched his grip and slipped the damp hand over the back of his neck. "We had several witnesses say the driver acted like he couldn't stop. So we checked the brakes. Your line had been punctured, not cut outright. The longer the car was on the street, the less the brakes worked. But that's not the crazy part."

I gulped at the cold liquid, hoping for my brain to start working. "What's the crazy part?"

"The K-9 unit went over the car; it's routine. And got a hit. Our dog went nuts over your steering wheel. Lab says it was coated with Lucy X. It's the street name for a designer drug, a kind of liquid LSD suspended in oil. Super potent and skin-permeable. Let's just say that driver didn't feel a thing when he hit that tree." DuBois shook his head. "Our guys are at your father's house, testing all the vehicles in his garage now." He shot a glance at Cotten. "We'll post a guard specifically to watch your car tonight."

My hands trembled as I set my glass back on the tray. I tried to release a breath I didn't know I was holding. It came out as a shuddered hiss. "I don't understand."

DuBois leveled his eyes with mine. "Ms. Peters, I can't say this in plainer terms: Someone wants you dead."

CHAPTER 29

The Theory

WHATEVER ROMANCE HAD HEATED between us got pushed to the back burner for the rest of the night. DuBois gave us the routine assurances, including that he was doubling the guard at the hospital, too. Just in case.

Cotten and I spent the rest of the evening pacing, brainstorming, peering out his bedroom window—the only window with a good street view—and poring over business emails from the last six months. My phone rang at 9:45, startling me so badly that I let out a shrill scream that probably woke anyone already asleep in the adjacent Adolphus Hotel.

My screen showed it was Bev Muncy. "Hello," I answered with a rattle in my voice.

Bev paused for a second before responding. "Oh, hi, Ronni. It's Bev." Another pause. "I didn't expect you to answer this late; I thought I'd get your voicemail."

A weird excitement settled over me, and I put my phone on speaker and set it beside me on the couch. "Well, it's actu-

DROP DEAD DALLAS 221

ally me. What can I do for you on a Sunday night?" What would Edna do?

"Uh, it's good to hear your voice. I just got off a call from Greg. He said he saw a piece on the news about an accident in front of Pegasus Park and that it looked like your car. I know you live right there, and it got me worried for you. But it sounds like you're all right. I'm glad it wasn't you." Bev spoke even faster than usual.

Trying to psychoanalyze her with merely a high school-level psychology course proved less challenging than one might guess. Her tone registered a slightly higher pitch. Definitely nervous, possibly deceptive. I exchanged a glance at Cotten, who took a seat without making a sound.

"Well, my car was in the wreck, but I wasn't driving. I'm fine." I waited for a moment to see if she responded. Just her breathing, maybe fumbling for something. I continued. "There were people killed in the accident and a few others seriously injured. It was terrible."

Again, Bev seemed to be searching for something to say. Dad had always told me that if I was ever unsure of someone's motives, to let them dangle in silence for a few seconds and see what happened. "Okay, well, I'm glad you weren't hurt. I'll let you go. See you tomorrow." She clicked off.

"What was that?" I asked after a few more seconds.

"In my professional opinion as a detective," Cotten began, "I believe it was an alibi call."

"Kinda what I was thinking," I agreed. "Or maybe to check to be sure I was dead. She'd have been less surprised if a police officer had answered."

"Maybe you should have recorded the call." Cotten stood

again and reached for his phone. "I'm going to shoot a quick message to Damon. Let him know about it anyway."

"I've always liked Bev. And I thought she liked me." I pushed my cell to the far end of the coffee table after lowering the ringer volume. "This is making me crazy."

Cotton finished his text and set his phone next to mine. "Are you hungry?"

I frowned. "Even if I was, I doubt I could eat."

He sat next to me on the couch. "We can't jump to conclusions. She said that Greg Oberman had called her and that they were worried. Maybe that's all it was."

"You said it sounded like an alibi call. That's what it sounded like to me, too." I pondered how many seasons of forensic shows I'd watched over the years. Thousands of hours. I knew this kind of thing happened, but always to other people. Other women. Other single women. Other single Texas heiresses. Oh my word, I was in my own episode!

"You need to get some sleep. You have a big day tomorrow." Cotton took my hand in his. "We'll figure this out soon enough. You hired the right guy for this job."

Barely hearing him, I rambled, "I'll bet Greg didn't even call her. I'll bet it *was* an alibi call to me. And just for good measure, I'll bet even more she's with Greg now. Probably having dinner. She knows he's one of the most respected businessmen in town. She needs someone to say, 'She couldn't have done it; she was with me all evening.'"

"But we're not jumping to conclusions, right?" He shot a goofy smile in my direction. "And isn't Greg Oberman married?"

I was on a roll. "All the more weight will be given to his

testimony if he comes forward for her. Who would jeopardize a marriage for someone who's guilty? Nobody. 'But Your Honor, she can't have done it. Would I come forward if I believed that for one second?' Oh, it's going to be a big production."

It took Cotten another half-hour to talk me down to the point I could doze in his bed while he kept watch. Every time I started to drift off, I heard Bev's voice whispering.

I didn't expect you to answer.

CHAPTER 30
The Flats

ANXIETY HELD me in a fitful state all night. Strange noises rose from inside Cotten's bedroom and beyond the window. Every car revving, door slamming, or bird squawking pushed my eyes open to the blue-black darkness, and I'd have to console myself back to sleep. *Cotten is keeping watch. The police are on alert. Nobody can get to you.*

But then I felt it. The searing heat of fiery fingers clutched my left arm above my wrist. I tried to pull free, but I was paralyzed. Struggling against the hot hand, I attempted a scream, but no sound came. Well, I wasn't going down without a fight. I tried kicking and punching, but the paralysis persisted. I could feel sweat forming on my brow and upper lip. And then the light.

I realized my eyes were closed, but light flooded the room, casting a bright orange glow through my sticking eyelids. I roused slowly from my sleep and forced my eyes to open, if only into slits. Alone in the room, I discovered the sizzling finger grip on my arm was nothing more than the sunlight striping over the bed and me from the wood blinds.

The sweat was real. The rest was illusion.

Hopping from the bed as if it had been a trap, I hurried to the bathroom without looking for Cotten. My daily routine grounded me and gave my body something useful to do as my brain processed worst-case scenarios for the meeting.

Would the board vote me off like an episode of Survivor? Would someone try to kill me during the meeting? How? A gun under the table? A cyanide pellet in my sweet tea? Or maybe someone would drop that hideous bronze egret statue from the ledge over the dining room door on me. What a horrible way to go, skewered by the beak of a waterfowl art piece. Yuck.

Using the blow dryer, I drove away the crazy thoughts as I fluffed my natural waves around my ears. Nothing was going to happen to me. I was a big girl, and I could handle a meeting in my dad's—in my own—house.

"How's it going in there?" Cotten asked through the door as I was finishing my lipstick.

"Almost done." I realized I'd been hogging the only bathroom in his little apartment. I rushed to get my blouse and skirt on and carried the jacket and my shoes out with me.

Cotten edged into the bathroom as I slipped out, giving me a quick *thanks* and a wink as we passed.

Gathering my things for the meeting and organizing them into my purse and tote, I started feeling more confident. I took my stuff to the table by the office door and saw that Cotten had the dining table set with a biscuits-and-gravy breakfast spread. I sat and checked my phone while waiting for him to join me.

A few emails—mostly junk. A notification for a new 'like' on a photo I'd posted a few weeks ago. A text from April Todd: *Change of plans. I will see you this morning at the meeting.*

Good. If April was by my side, probably nobody would try to kill me. I was clutching at straws, but I needed everything I could get. I replied with a thumbs-up.

Another text, this one from Celia: *I'm at the grocery for fresh mint and fruit.* Can you think of anything else we may want for the drinks or snack trays?

Dad had always insisted on serving pistachios at the meetings. Did anyone else eat them, or were they just for him? *Remember the pistachios,* I messaged back. She replied with a smiley.

I was deep into a memory of Daddy and a pile of nutshells when I felt a kiss fall gently on the top of my head.

"Good morning." Cotten sat across from me and blessed the food in a whisper. "Did you get any sleep at all?" he asked.

"I slept a little." I inhaled over the coffee cup in my hand before taking a slow sip. "Weird dreams."

"Yes, I know." He sliced open his biscuits and drowned them with the steamy white sauce. "I think I checked on you a dozen times. You were tossing and turning—sometimes talking. You've been through it these last two weeks. You should take some time off soon."

"Like a vacation?" The thought hadn't occurred to me. Dad had always arranged travel, and even then, trips were as much business as pleasure.

"Exactly like a vacation." He took a bite, and I watched him chew and swallow, enjoying his creation. "And you should go someplace nice where you don't have anything to do. Just rest on the beach or by a pool or enjoy a mountain view. Something like that. Where do you like to go best?"

My mind was blank. I had never planned a vacation for myself. I had been on three girls' weekend escapes, but none of those had been organized by me. We'd gone to Vegas, Myrtle Beach, and San Diego. Plenty of fun, but I had no interest in going back. I thought for a moment. Considering what Cotten had confessed about guarding me when I traveled, I felt sure he had been on those excursions, too.

I shook my head. "I think I'd like to go someplace new."

"After the meeting, why don't we do a little research on a few places?" He took another bite.

"Yes," I agreed. "After the meeting." I worked my way through my first biscuit and into my second, and then my phone rang. I jumped at the sound. "Sorry. I meant to put it in my purse before we ate."

He shot me a don't-worry-about-it smile and gestured for me to answer the call.

"Hello?" I said as the caller ID name registered in my mind.

"Hi, Ronni, this is Inez."

"Yes, Inez. How are you this morning?"

Her voice sounded weary. "Well, not so good. I was getting ready for the meeting, and when I took my satchel out to my car, I discovered I had four flat tires. They got slashed overnight."

My heart pounded, and my stomach flopped. "Oh, no." I swallowed hard, not sure what to say next. I thought I might send a car, but I didn't want to risk it after Saturday's fiasco. I looked at Cotten, and his expression reassured me. "Okay, so we'll leave now and come to get you."

"No, that's too much trouble. I'll get an Uber or something. I just wanted to let you know that I might be a little late."

Cotten shook his head and began clearing the table. "We'll pick her up."

"We're already on our way. Don't give it a second thought." I didn't want to scare her by sharing the details of the last 48 hours. "Just be ready to jump in as we swing past your door." I tried to force a little laugh as I said it, but humor was the last emotion I was feeling. I punched in the address from my contact card for her. "GPS has us there in nine minutes. We'll all be on time."

I clicked off and grabbed my gear. "Someone is trying to keep her away, too. Tires slashed."

Cotten picked up his keys as we flew out the door. "I'm just glad it was her tires and not her."

That was precisely what I had been thinking.

Traffic was crazy most Monday mornings, but today seemed worse than expected. Cotten wove through cars like a shark through a school of fish. I kept trying to tell myself that maybe the tire-slashing had been a kid's prank or a gang thing—still horrible, but not necessarily a murderer's message. But Inez's neighborhood showed no signs of gang activity or mayhem. Her car sat sadly at the curb, resting on the rims.

'Y'all didn't have to go out of your way to pick me up." She got into the back seat and slid her case across the middle to rest against mine. "I could've called a car."

"No worries," Cotten said, not waiting for me to respond. "It's not an imposition to accompany two women to a meeting."

I turned back to face her and noticed she had skipped her cat-eye contacts. Her dark brown eyes were stunning. "I'm nervous. Are you nervous?" I thought sharing nerves might lessen them for both of us.

"On the one hand, yes." Inez raised her brow, putting a slight crease into the flower tattooed on her forehead. "I've never been to a business meeting of more than four people before, and at that time, the net income for the company was only about $150,000 annually. Your company currently nets more than that in a week." Inez took a deep breath. "That's quite a leap for me. But on the other hand, I know what I'm doing and am prepared for everything. So, in that respect, I'm not nervous at all."

Her confidence bolstered me. She was ready. I was ready —somewhat ready. I could be self-assured and independent. I could handle the board meeting. And I could make sure I was never standing beneath the egret sculpture.

Cotten took the rest of the drive to Turtle Creek as if he had a police escort. I offered a wave and a smile to the gate attendant as we sailed past his station. Pulling into the long drive, I quickly inventoried the cars. And yep, we were the last to arrive.

April Todd waited for us at the front door, looking at her watch as we approached. "You're still in the ten-minute window. But get in there now."

"C'mon," I urged Inez as we climbed the front steps and bustled through the foyer to the dining room doors. Watching her eyes devour the grandeur of the house, I said, "I'll give you a tour after the meeting."

April held the doors for us as we entered the meeting room. The others sat around the fourteen-foot table, chatting about the weather and baseball. And, of course, our seats were at the far end, so our entrance became the sudden topic of conversation. Whispers of *She's actually here* and *Who is that and what's on her face* surrounded us. I felt terrible for subjecting Inez to that kind of criticism, but when I turned to her and gestured to her seat, she appeared to have heard nothing. She was poised and placid and smiled as she sat.

With April on my left side and Inez on my right, I regarded Cotten as he closed the doors to the room. I could do this.

CHAPTER 31

The Board

ACTING PRESIDENT GREG OBERMAN called the meeting to order as Karen took minutes. A quick roll call followed, and we were off to the races.

Greg went through agenda items without pause, and I guessed he was trying to make up the six minutes my tardiness had cost him. He asked everyone to skim through last quarter's meeting minutes, but before anyone could get through the first paragraph, Bev Muncy had made a motion to accept the minutes as presented.

I'd reviewed the minutes from the last three meetings yesterday and had nothing to add, so I poured a glass of water for myself and offered another to Inez.

George Lovett immediately spoke up, starting a wave of eye-rolls from one end of the table to the other. He objected to using the word 'tribute' regarding a new scholarship for the Women's Foundation and suggested that the word should be 'memorial' instead. Greg objected, stating that they had discussed this ad nauseam last time and that they should use a different descriptor because the foundation was already a memorial.

I was never so glad to have missed a meeting in my life. George Lovett quickly turned to face me. "Why don't we ask Ronni? It's her father we're honoring with the funds."

Letting my eyes squint into a smile, I tilted my head toward Lovett. "Why can't it just be called the Alexander Peters Scholarship or something simple like that? Does it have to be specifically named as a memorial?"

April almost seemed to be hiding a laugh behind her fingers. "You go," she whispered.

The other board members seemed to brighten and thus commenced a quick lecture on Robert's Rules of Order. After a few rounds of withdrawals, amendments, and more discussion, the minutes were officially revised and accepted. A lot of fuss over one word.

The meeting trudged on. Bradley Dunne gave his report about the overseas operations, along with a formal request to begin an equipment inspection and appraisal, as some of the gear had depreciated out and needed replacing. More motions, seconds, discussions, and votes.

Bev delivered her report on domestic operations. She provided the stats on each energy sector with a slide presentation comparing fossil fuel production to wind, solar, and nuclear segments. She showed technological advancements in each field and upcoming regulations that might affect production and scaling. Her slides were in brilliant primary colors mirroring the confidence Bev naturally exuded.

Bev didn't ask for anything. No motions made. No votes required. Refreshing.

Around the table we went until it was at last time for the historian's report. I was in the spotlight. I rose from my swivel chair and directed everyone to find their copy of my handout. I had no slideshow. Only the mock-up of the book jacket for *Petra Resources, A Quarter Century of Energy Excellence*, and a table of contents. "We're in the final round of edits. The release date is set for September 1st," I explained.

"I thought it was supposed to come out mid-August," George Lovett said, using his copy to fan his face.

"Yes, it was supposed to, but when my father passed, I made a few changes to the manuscript, and that went through editing again, and so forth." I couldn't understand why a two-week delay in the release should worry anyone. The publisher was expediting the release as it was.

George Lovett seemed dissatisfied. "Is there anything in this company that wasn't affected by the old man's death?"

The words burned my ears, and I sank back into my seat. I thought I heard a collective gasp from the others, but it may have simply been my breath escaping my lungs. Greg responded to Lovett harshly.

"That's uncalled for. Ronni has suffered beyond any of the rest of us. Her father was much more than a job to her. He was her whole life. Remarks like that will not be tolerated."

Lovett didn't back down. "Oh, I see. At any other meeting, I can say what I want. You've all made similar comments. But when the princess deigns to honor us with her presence, we must mind our manners?"

Inez reached out with a supportive squeeze to my wrist. April stood and shook her head. She looked like she might explode, but Greg rose and marched to Lovett's chair.

"Are you drunk?" he asked.

Lovett rumbled. "Not yet, but I've got a good mind to get there. This is a farce."

The doors to the foyer opened, and Cotten stepped into the room. Shooting a sharp glance at Greg and Lovett, he asked, "What can I do to help?"

Greg grimaced. "Lovett needs some fresh air. He can come back in when he's cooled off." He then turned to the others. "Why don't we all take a break? We'll resume the meeting in fifteen minutes." He rapped his knuckles on the table like a gavel.

Karen looked at her watch and noted the time in her records.

I sat frozen in my chair while most of the board left the room. April and Inez stayed at my side, offering encouraging words I could barely hear, let alone comprehend. What had I done? How could I have abandoned Daddy's life's work to these people? They were supposed to be his partners and his friends. They didn't care. To them, Dad's death had meant nothing more than a step up the ladder. To me, it was a push into an abyss.

"It's good to see you back here," Celia said, patting my shoulder. She poured fresh ice water into my glass and wiped the condensation off the pitcher. Celia's voice soothed my nerves like no others could. "I sure wish you'd move back into this house. It needs you."

I smiled automatically, and the tears that had been standing in my eyes spilled over my cheeks.

"Now, don't do that, Ronni." Celia pushed a tissue from her pocket into my hand. "I didn't mean to upset you."

"You weren't the one to upset her," April said.

I dabbed at my face with the tissue. "Thank you, Celia. It

is good to be back here. It's good to see you. You always take such good care of me."

Celia worked her way around the long pecan table, wiping pitchers and refilling crystal bowls with hard candy. "I mean it, you know. The house needs you. It knows when it's empty. And anyway, the devil lives in the city. Your father always said it. And it's true."

Inez leaned close to my ear. "My mother says the same thing."

"If you moved back in, I could take care of you like I used to. Like I took care of your father." Celia's head bobbed with each step. "I think I'll bring the fruit tray now and save the cookies for after lunch. Is that all right with you?"

"That's great," I said without thinking. Somehow, doing the automatic seemed to bring me back to calm.

April shuffled through a short stack of papers resting on an open folder. "The financials are up next. Are you good? If you need me to explain the audit, just say the word, and I'll introduce Inez and take it from there."

Yes, that would work. April could do it. After all, my most mundane historian's report caused an eruption. What would happen if I said something that might actually cause someone problems?

As I settled into that decision, an echo sounded softly in the back of my mind. *What would Edna do?* I almost laughed.

"No," I mumbled to April, still unsure I had the nerve to carry out my task. "Thanks, but I have to do it. My dad would want me to. And the shareholders need me to do it." I took a deep breath and felt stronger. "I need to do it."

"If you can do it, I can do it. You introduce me, and I can tell them what I need." Inez stood and adjusted the jade-green scarf at her neck. She pulled out her business cards and circuited the table, placing a card above each board member's folder.

April nodded and examined the card Inez handed to her, then held it out for me to see. The card was white with green lettering, with a sugar-skull logo that matched Inez's face tattoo.

I chuffed. "Talk about making lemonade."

Inez chuckled. "I considered having it removed, but when I thought about how much it hurt to get the tattoo in the first place, and that was when I was drunk out of my mind, I decided I would just roll with it. After all, nobody's gonna forget me."

Cotten came in through the kitchen door as a few others stood in the doorway to the foyer. "Lovett just drove away. I don't think he'll be back today." He gestured toward the others. "I heard it was a full-fledged blow-up. Are you all right?"

I glanced at Inez and April. "I'm gonna be just fine."

"I called DuBois and gave him Lovett's vehicle info. Just in case." Cotten gave me a reassuring nod and gestured toward Celia, now setting out the trays on the sideboard. "This angel is going to make us all fat." His voice was loud enough for her to hear. "She forced me to test the cookies fresh from the oven." Rolling his eyes as if in ecstasy, he added, "They're terrible. You won't like them at all. Especially the lemon bars."

"Right." I pointed to the foyer. "You should get back out there and be ready for the next round. We haven't even gotten to the exciting stuff yet."

Cotten saluted and exited to the foyer as Karen herded the others back into the dining room.

"The meeting will resume in ninety seconds," she called out.

They filed past the buffet spread and filled the crystal snack plates with fruit, crackers, and cheese cubes. I watched as everyone returned to their seats, leaving only one seat vacant. That was fine with me.

Karen poised her fingers above her laptop and nodded to Greg.

"Let's get back to it, then," he said. "Ronni, did you have anything more to add to your report, or should we go on?"

I swallowed hard and stood up again. "I don't have anything more to add, but if anyone has questions, I'd be happy to answer them." Forcing a smile, I let my gaze go around the table, making eye contact with each person before moving to the next. Nobody had a question. Nobody had a comment. I tilted up my chin with a contented expression before taking my seat. They needed to know I was back. In every way.

"No questions? Then let's go over the financials and get to the old business." Greg tapped his pen on his notepad.

Everyone pulled out the financial statements, and Stewart Jeffries read through each line. Everything added up. Every dollar. Every penny. Nothing to discuss. Greg moved on.

"Bev, you wanted to revisit the bylaws about meeting attendance. You brought that up at the last meeting, and we had to table it because of time constraints. What exactly did you want to discuss?"

Bev looked at her notes and then looked around the table; her penciled brows rose high as she looked at the empty chair, then at me, and then back to Greg. "Um, I suppose my concern is a moot point now. I..." She shook her head. "I guess I'd like to keep it tabled for a future meeting."

Greg furrowed his brow and shot a grimace toward Karen. "Ms. Muncy, Lovett may not be present, but we have a quorum. So if you have a motion to make, the board can hear it today."

The woman looked like a mouse trapped in a maze. I could see the perspiration on her forehead, and I thought I noticed a tremble in her hands. "No. It's not necessary." She looked paranoid and avoided eye contact with me. "I'm not feeling well. I have to go."

"Bev?" Greg got up. "Can I get you a car? Why don't you go up to one of the guest rooms and rest? Maybe you shouldn't be driving."

"I'll be fine." She gathered her folder and purse and hurried toward the door.

"Can I help?" I asked, reaching out.

"NO!" she practically screamed. She slammed the door, and we could hear a muffled exchange between Bev and Cotten. A few seconds more and the front door slammed.

Greg released a deep sigh. "All right. Was there any other old business?"

"No, sir," Karen stated without hesitation.

If it wasn't on the agenda, it didn't exist.

"Then on to new business." Greg shuffled a few pages. "Bradley Dunne, you requested time for addressing a matter about the conference room at the office?"

"Yes, sir." Dunne stood and gestured to the room. "While this venue is beautiful and quite useful for our more enter-taining events and hosting new contractors, it seems impractical to use it for our board meetings like today, when we could do an inexpensive renovation at the downtown office and stay on site. Let's face it, some days, it takes longer to drive over and back than it does to hold the meeting. With that in mind, I put together a bid from a local design-build firm, with sketches for everyone to review. They're in the back of the packets."

Everyone flipped open the stapled pages, and a general chattering began.

Dunne continued, "I'm not suggesting we make a decision today, but I'd like the board to consider it and hold a vote before the next quarterly. Perhaps in a special meeting."

Greg gave him a thumbs-up. "Excellent proposal, Dunne. But before we discuss this, we might ask Ronni her opinion, considering this house is technically hers, and we've been meeting here by her graces." He turned to face me. "What say you, kid?"

My thoughts jumped through hoops. While Dunne made his presentation, I weighed the option of using the office versus the Castle. Dad had this place explicitly designed to host meetings and large gatherings. The dining table could extend to seat up to thirty. The great room and parlor could open to create a ballroom suitable for sixty. This was Daddy's dream. But, as I was so rudely reminded, Daddy wasn't here anymore.

The office was a company asset. Meetings there would be more convenient. When people stormed out—however often that happened—they could just go to their office to sulk. Easy for everyone.

I smirked at Greg, not thrilled he'd called me *kid* in front of everyone. Condescending. Undermining. Maybe he didn't mean to, but still. I cleared my throat. "Thanks, Mr. Ober-man." I secretly hoped I made him feel old. "But I have no strong feelings one way or the other on meeting space. What-ever consensus you all come to will suit me fine."

Greg raised his brow as if he expected something more complicated. "Great. Then I'd advise you to review the sketches and the bids, and we will call a special meeting if necessary. If you'll direct questions through Karen, she can make sure everyone is heard." He and Karen exchanged an efficient glance. "Thanks, Dunne."

Dunne grinned and took his seat.

"And now, Ronni, you have the last agenda item?" Greg took a sip of his tea. "Proceed at your leisure."

"Thank you." I stood and gestured to the women on either side of me. "I'd like to introduce my associates." April stood. "This is Ms. Todd, my lawyer. She will help me better transi-tion into my father's former position and be my primary advisor regarding my father's assets. I want to assure everyone that I will always keep Petra before me as I make decisions regarding his estate."

April took her seat. Putting my hand on the back of Inez's chair, I continued, and she stood. "And this is Ms. Delgado. She represents the accounting firm I've hired for Petra's inde-pendent audit on behalf of the shareholders."

As a low murmur rose, I noticed Inez's shoulders hunch-ing, and I gave her a quick don't-you-dare glance.

Greg chuckled. "I understand you want to do things right, Ronni. We all do. And maybe you didn't realize it—being out of commission lately—but Petra ran an audit already. We went over it in the financials. All wrapped up. It was strictly procedural."

"Oh, I do understand." I leaned toward Stewart Jeffries. "I'm sure the audit was managed perfectly. I do not doubt that in the slightest." I took a deep breath, trying to quell the deafening pounding of my heart in my ears. "But I would be remiss in my obligations to the other shareholders if I didn't request an independent audit. And what assurance it will be if we provide them with double the proof that they have made a prudent investment in Petra, don't you agree?"

While most offered affirmation, Jeffries and Greg seemed annoyed.

"Why don't you consider waiting for another six to twelve months? I'm concerned that doubling up on audits may signal doubts to our investors. I'd hate to do that, not to mention the added expense." Greg clicked his pen and flipped his file folder closed.

April started to stand, but I blinked an I've-got-this in her direction. "Ms. Todd has assured me it is within my rights as the controlling shareholder to order the audit. In fact, the review is already underway. I do not require any motions or even permission. I am only asking that if Ms. Delgado requests any information, you will give her your time and cooperation." I aimed my gaze back around the table. "As if the request came directly from my father or me."

I pressed my fingers into the table in front of Inez, indicating it was her turn.

She squared her shoulders. "I've provided my business card to each of you and hope you'll add me to your contacts. Though my firm is young, we employ state-of-the-art software to spot anomalies and troubleshoot potential problems before they happen. I may reach out to each department if I have any questions, concerns, or an item I need to clarify. I thank you all for your cooperation."

She sat again, and it felt like a mic-drop moment.

"Does anyone have any questions for my associates or for me?" I leaned a fraction of an inch forward, but no one else moved. I let a broad smile spread over my lips. "All right then, Greg. I'll let you wrap up this meeting."

"I su-suppose, then," Greg stuttered, "if there is no further business, I'll adjourn."

The room hummed, and Karen directed everyone toward the patio. "Celia has lunch for us all in the back."

The room emptied, and April gathered her things and shook my hand. "You did just fine. Your dad would be proud of you." She shook Inez's hand, too. "And please let me know if you find anything I need to look into, Ms. Delgado."

"I will. Thank you." Inez leaned back in her chair, and we watched April leave.

Cotten entered the dining room as the last board members left. I waved a finger toward him as I exhaled, trying to settle my heart rate.

"How did it go?" he asked.

Inez sat up straight and sighed. "She did great."

I patted the table in front of her. "You did, too." We scraped our papers together into our bags. "We all did."

We stood, and Cotten pushed our chairs in, motioning toward the door. "Good. Ms. Muncy was a wreck when she left. I sent DuBois a heads-up on her as well."

"I'd never seen her like that." I side-stepped toward the staircase, trying to avoid being directly below the bronze egret, and when I did, I suddenly remembered something. I found myself frozen in place as I thought about it.

Without a word from me, Cotten seemed to read my mind. He took my bag and directed me to the wing chairs in the alcove formed by the curved stairs.

We all sat down, and I must have looked green or pale or some other shade of terrible because Inez asked, "What happened? Are you okay?"

Dropping my head into my hands for a second, I skimmed through the last couple of hours in my mind. Who said what? Were there any hints I should have caught? Clues I missed?

"I just don't know. I was so nervous about the meeting that I forgot to pay attention." I ran my fingers through my hair, trying to concentrate.

"It's okay; we'll figure it out." Cotten's voice calmed me. "We'll go through it again. Step by step. Don't worry."

Inez dropped her head beside mine. "What is it? Can I help?"

Raising my eyes to meet hers, I whispered, "I almost forgot about my situation."

"Situation?"

Waving my hand toward the patio, I answered, "One of these people wants me dead."

CHAPTER 32
The Plan

INEZ STARED with her mouth agape. "Someone is trying to kill you?" Her words came out in a half-whisper-half-squeak.

I exhaled my confession. "Yes, we're pretty sure."

The color drained from her face, making the skull tattoo more pronounced. "And that's why my tires were slashed this morning? I'm close to you, so I'm a target, too?"

I opened my mouth to explain, but no words came. My whole body began to tremble.

Cotten shook his head toward both of us. "Ronni is the target. And yeah, that's probably the reason your car was sabotaged. But I don't think you're in danger. Whoever is doing this just wants to keep Ronni out of the way."

"And slashing my tires does that?"

"They're trying to scare me." I dropped my head back into my hands. "They started out with a stalker, maybe tried to kidnap me. Then they were tracking me. Then whoever it was tried to frame me for murder." My voice bounced from the curved walls around us. "Then, they drugged my car."

"Drugged your car?" Inez inched away as if I babbled nonsense. "I'm sorry, but I really don't understand. And I'm not sure this is where I should be right now." She picked up her bag and started to stand up.

"Please wait," Cotten and I said at the same time.

"Wait? For someone to kill me?" She shook her head. "Listen, there's not enough money in the world for this."

Reaching out for her wrist, I begged, "Please. Let me explain, and then if you want to leave, that's fine. I'll get your car fixed either way. And I'll pay for the work you've already done. No hard feelings."

Some of the board members began filtering back inside after their lunch. Cotten gestured to the stairway. "Why don't we talk as we walk. I'm sure Inez would enjoy a tour, and I need to look the place over. We can start at the top."

Inez hesitated, then looked around and agreed, so we started up to the second floor. "But I'm not sure what you think will persuade me."

"I understand. If I had a choice, I'd be out of it, too. I suppose I do. I could resign from my dad's company, sell my shares, and be done with it all. Short of that, I'm stuck." We reached the long, narrow loft that overlooked the foyer. "See, I believe I wouldn't have had much to worry about if only I'd stayed home from today's meeting. I think they would have voted me off the board—it's in the bylaws that you can't miss four consecutive quarterly meetings and keep your place."

Looking at the portraits of my father and mother on the loft wall, Inez narrowed her eyes and turned to me. "So that's what the fuss was about with Ms. Muncy? They were removing you, but then you showed up. Nasty." She shifted her gaze between my mother's painting and me. "You do look like her. She was pretty."

"Thanks." I continued, leading us to the game room. We circled the pool table and passed the wet bar. I opened the French doors to the deck that overlooked the backyard. "Maybe slashing your tires was a warning—or a last-ditch effort to keep me away. I don't know."

As Inez and I talked, Cotten scoured every inch of the room, inside and out. He seemed to listen to us with one ear and to the stragglers in the yard with the other.

"But I don't get it." Inez kept her voice low. "I haven't even seen a hint of a misstep in the financial statements. Everything I've looked through seems square. So besides getting you off the board—which I assume will leave more control for someone else—why would anyone want you dead?"

"I really don't know. I've always been a spoiled brat to most of them. But I never had ambitions to take over the company. At least, not until the last couple of days."

We moved back inside and through the seating area in the same room until we were back in the loft. Inez and Cotten followed me down the hall to the bedroom wing. I opened the doors to all four bedrooms, but we only went inside my bedroom at the end.

"So the real question is, who knew I was coming? My name wasn't on the agenda of the meeting. I checked." Inez roamed through my bedroom, looking at my senior photo and the snapshots of my dad and me. She studied the books on my shelves and looked out to the yard. "Whoever had my name slashed my tires."

I pondered the question. That's the tidbit that had been scratching the back of my brain since she called this morning. "I don't think I gave anyone your name. Possibly April, but she's been our family lawyer for years. And she's the one who insisted I attend the meeting when I said I wouldn't."

Suddenly Cotten perked up and joined our conversation. "Ronni, you inherited all your dad's assets when he passed. Who gets yours?"

"Yeah," Inez said. "Follow the money. Isn't that what they say in the movies?"

I laughed. "Yeah, but right now, my will leaves everything to my mother's foundation. April knows this. She set it up."

Cotten leaned closer. "Does anyone else know this?"

My mind flipped through memories like an old photo album. "I don't know. I remember we had to have it witnessed, but I can't think who it was for the life of me."

"But you could call April. She could look that up." Inez held her palms up.

"Yeah." I followed Cotten back to the hall. "But if April is the one trying to get me out of the way—which I don't believe for one second—she would then know we were on to her. So she'd most likely just put a hit on me right then and there."

Cotten pushed the elevator button and opened the door when the carriage dinged. "Let's visit the basement."

Inez raised her brows. "An elevator?"

"Dad liked gadgets." When we were all inside, I hit the 'B' button. "He said it would be a great investment when he was too old to take the stairs." As we descended, I thought about the night last week when the buzzing had signaled an intruder. I remembered the last time I had ridden with Dad down to watch a movie in the basement. "Casablanca," I heard myself say without realizing it.

"What about it?" Cotten asked.

"Oh, it was the last movie Dad and I watched together. Sorry, I didn't mean to say it out loud."

Cotten and Inez exchanged glances, and I suddenly felt like that lady on the street corner mumbling to a plastic doll about what the cereal box had told her. I was losing my mind, and I knew it.

We stepped out into the basement, across from the pantry, and I led the way to the wine room. I swung open the antique gate that guarded the entrance. "This came out of a French chateau from the thirteenth century. Dad had new hinges made for it so it wouldn't scream down the whole neighborhood." I entered the room with a bit of trepidation. It was stocked with the wine I drank the last time I'd been blotto. The wine I threw up on Edna's roses. I never wanted to be like that again. I looked at Inez—her sugar-skulled face—and wondered how she felt at the moment. My gaze wandered to Cotten's expression. I thought about how many times his father had come home drunk. How he'd hurt Edna and Cotten.

We all stood there for a moment in silence. Were we all thinking the same thing?

I directed our group to the movie room, flipping the switch that lowered the screen over the painting of a field of sunflowers. The lights automatically dimmed as my memories fired up.

"Whoa," Inez gasped. "Your own private theater?"

"Dad's other splurge." I gestured to the reclining seats. "This was where we spent our family nights."

Saying the word squeezed my heart. Dad was my family. My family was gone.

The projector hummed, and the screen lit up with the local news. The redheaded anchor my dad loved reported on a tech giant that had been hacked, temporarily knocking out their mail servers and making their search engines worthless. She delivered the news piece with flashing green eyes and a permanently glossed smile.

Cotten shook his head and muted the reporter as we strolled past the classic movie posters to the table-top popcorn maker.

Inez looked around the room, and I noticed a pained expression in her eyes. "And someone is trying to *kill you*? I don't understand. You're like Bambi, with your big eyes and little voice. You're nervous just giving a report about the release of a book. So how are you a threat to anyone?"

Cotten ran his fingers around the frames of the wall art. "This is what we're all trying to figure out. Even the police aren't sure. I think someone is getting away with something illegal right now, and they think that Ronni will uncover and stop it."

Inez's face changed from pained to determined. "And if it's money-related, I could help expose it?"

Hearing her say it, I realized I was asking her to risk her life for me. "You're right. I have no business putting you in danger. I'm sorry I dragged you into this. It's not fair to you."

She shook her head. "No, it's not fair that you're in this position. This company is yours. This home is yours. Your father worked hard to give this to you." She settled her fists on her hips. "If you'll take me home, I'll get to work." And she barely waited for us. She marched resolutely to the elevator.

The tour was over before we had the chance to run through the main floor again. As we headed to the front door, Celia stopped us. "Wait. You three didn't get lunch. I have your plates ready in the kitchen."

Cotten shook his head. "Celia, you're an angel, but we have an urgent situation that has come up."

"At least take some cookies, Mr. Hammond. I know you like them."

He leaned close to her ear. "If you'll save some for us, I promised to come back tonight."

The petite woman smiled. "Oh, your face. I can never say no to your face." She looked at me over his shoulder. "He does have such a pleasant face."

I chuckled. "Yes, he does."

"Then, you go and do what you need to do." Celia looked at me. "And tonight, I'll make your favorites."

We got our things and hurried out to Cotten's sedan. As he pulled out of the drive, he sighed. "Let's take Inez home, and then we should run by the hospital for a moment before going to the office. I can touch base with DuBois as needed."

Inez scribbled something in her pocket notebook. "My cousin wrote a computer program for a fantasy football website that compiles every stat on every player on every team. It extrapolates minute by minute to create the best team for the user." She paused for a second to finish a note, then snapped the book closed and dropped it into her bag. "He asked me last week if I would try it out—well, a modified version of his program—for accounting. It will scan all the bookkeeping for repeated entries and trends. It can do hundreds of entries in a matter of seconds."

Cotten glanced into the rearview mirror as he drove through the heavy noon traffic funneling through town. "So if you find anything, call us immediately." He paused at an intersection. "Thinking about your car tires, is there someplace more secure I can take you than your house?"

"I have my laptop, so I can work from anywhere, but I have to get the software installed from my cousin, so I need to go home for that," Inez said. "If I'd realized the danger, I'd have grabbed it from him yesterday."

Before she could say another word, I gently slapped Cotten's arm. "Turn around. Go back to the castle." I shifted to face Inez. "Call your cousin and ask him to take the day off and meet you at my father's house. Cotten can make sure you're safe there. You can set up in the basement if you like, and I'll ask Celia to take care of whatever you need."

Inez pursed her lips and shifted them from side to side. "You would do that for me?"

"Of course, and you can stay as long as you like. Just ask your cousin not to tell anyone where he's going, okay? We don't know who knows what." I grabbed my phone. "I'll message Celia right now."

Tapping on her phone, Inez began her message to her cousin. "And how will he get through the gate?"

"I'll tell the gatehouse as we go back."

Cotten was almost back to Turtle Creek when he said, "We'll run through every option to figure out who knew you were the accounting firm Ronni hired. I'll do my best to keep you out of danger."

My phone buzzed in my hand, and I read the message.

"Celia says the last person just left the house. Go around the back to the castle so we don't pass anyone on the way in."

Cotten stopped for a moment at the gatehouse and left Inez's cousin's name with the guard. As soon as we cleared the gate, he drove to the left instead of the right. We took the long way around the boulevard to the castle.

After messaging and emailing furiously, I clicked my lock screen and dropped my phone into my purse. "Celia will take care of everything, Inez. She'll tell you where your cousin should park and get you whatever you need. I just emailed you a link into my cloud so that you can access whatever accounting information you need, along with the contacts for every department head at Petra."

Before I'd finished talking, my phone buzzed. Mail-system Delivery Failure. Ugh.

"Sorry," I apologized. "I must have typed your email wrong. It says it didn't send. I'll try again."

Inez shook her head and stared at her phone. "No, I just got it."

"That's weird. It says that it failed to send and will try again. Maybe it wasn't for the email I sent to you." I opened my mail app and read the notification. "Hmph. It says the email I sent Victor19 at Steele Mail dot com didn't go through. Whoa, I have six of the same message. All to the same email. What's going on?"

Cotten furrowed his brow. "That means you sent a message to someone using Steele for their email. I think that's what was on the TV in your basement. Their server got hacked. It's not a big deal. It will try again and probably go through in a while." He parked his car and gestured to the house. "Was your email time-sensitive?"

"It's not that," I said as we all got out of the car. I waved my phone at him. "I never sent any emails to that address. I don't know anyone named Victor."

Inez frowned. "It's probably not a Victor at all. Lots of people use Steele for vanity emails. You know, like Luvs2-Dance at Steele Mail dot com or something like that. You most likely have their name in your contacts and have never paid attention to the email address. I do it all the time."

That wasn't it; I knew it. My stomach flopped. "But I know all the emails I've sent today." I mentally scanned through all my emails for the last couple of days. "And yesterday. Most of them were business—Petra dot com." We went back into the castle, and I stood there, staring at my screen. Mail-system Delivery Failure. "Have *I* been hacked?"

Cotten shot a nervous glance in my direction, and I knew I must have looked bewildered.

"Well," Cotten said, his voice tense, "I suppose we have a good place to start our search."

CHAPTER 33
The Discovery

COTTEN and I rushed back to the Petra offices, finally with a hint of where to look for evidence. We hurried through the lobby at a clipped pace, scanning the faces of everyone we passed on our way to the elevators. Employees and clients alike greeted us with smiles and *good-afternoons*.

Stepping into the elevator car, Cotten mashed the '10' button with the side of his fist.

"You missed. I'm on 12, you know." I reached out to press '12', and Cotten caught my hand in his.

"Yes, but the executive IT is on 10."

I raised my brow but didn't argue. I enjoyed his touch as he laced his fingers through mine. "Executive IT? Is there a regular IT?" Everyone I knew seemed to toss around the word *executive* as though it was the hottest new designer label.

He clucked at my question. "I'm glad we're alone in here right now. Yes, the top three floors have their own IT department. You really should know this. You have your own servers and security—the works. Corporate espionage is rampant in the US, especially in companies that do as much research and technology development as Petra. Executives want to protect trade secrets. Lower-level employees have less company loyalty and are more easily enticed to sell secrets to other companies for money, favors, or higher positions. Thus the top tier has extra security to keep their secrets safe." Cotten stared into my eyes. "Your father never explained this to you?"

"He probably did, but I spent much of my life thinking that none of this would ever apply to me. It's like algebra." The elevator dinged, and I slipped my hand free of Cotten's to preserve the illusion of a purely professional relationship. I wasn't sure what was an illusion and what was real, but I was sure about how I wanted things to be.

We stepped out of the car, and I looked to Cotten to lead the way to our destination.

At the end of the hall, we found Merle Cleeton—at least that was the name on the brass plate—sitting at his desk, staring at a bank of three monitors. He had a headset around his neck and an earbud in his right ear. He quickly pulled it out when he saw us approach.

"Good afternoon, Ms. Peters. Good afternoon, Mr. Hammond."

"Afternoon," we responded automatically.

"Are you experiencing computer troubles, Ms. Peters? I'm happy to help however I can." Cleeton showed bright white teeth through a wide professional grin.

I forced a matching smile and shot a glance at Cotten. He returned a you've-got-this smile. "I need to check on my email. I'm getting an email message about a delivery failure."

Cleeton seemed to relax for a second. "Yes, ma'am. That's happening a lot today. Is it a Steele Mail address? Their system got hacked, but it should be up again within the hour, according to the news."

Cotten acknowledged his statement. "Yes, we're aware, but this is something else—something more. Ms. Peters is getting this delivery failure notification for an address—it is a Steele address—that she hasn't intentionally emailed. She'd like you to check her email logs."

"Oh, sure. I can do that." Cleeton swiveled his chair to face the far right screen and wove his fingers together. He flipped his palms outward and flexed, causing a cacophony of knuckle cracks and pops. "Let me just log in to your account."

I furrowed my brow. "You can log in to my account? From here?"

"Sure," Cleeton replied. "Technically, anyone with Admin can log in from anywhere. But only five of us in Exec IT have Admin rights. Of course, anyone with the right passwords can log in to individual accounts. You should keep your passwords locked and change them often."

"And not use auto-fill programs." Cotten winked at me.

I was a schoolgirl getting a mild scolding for doing something practically harmless. But I didn't mind the scolding if it was followed with a wink from Cotten. His eyes could turn me into a puddle.

"Never use the auto-fill option. I wish it wasn't even a thing. If you have auto-fill, anyone can get into your accounts." Cleeton typed without looking up. "Okay, I'm in.

Yes, you do have several delivery failures—all to the same address." He glanced up at me and smiled. "And you didn't send any emails to this person?"

Shaking my head, I responded, "No, I don't even know who that person is."

Cleeton scrolled through a screen filled with letters and numbers. "Hmm. It looks like you've been emailing them for months."

Cotten rounded the end of Cleeton's desk for a better look. "When was her first email to that address?"

Cleeton typed again. "Almost a year ago. Here. This one." He pointed to a line on the monitor, and Cotten bent closer to read it.

"The week your father passed." Cotten took a step back. "Sorry, didn't mean to invade your space."

"No problem. But look at this." Cleeton pointed to one line and then ran his finger down a column. "This address is getting copied on all of her emails." Cleeton glanced up and shook his head. "If you didn't set this up, I'd say someone's hacked you."

My ears stopped working when Cotten said, *the week your father passed.* What could this mean? My brain clicked through possibilities like I clicked through channels on a Saturday night.

A mistake. It had to be. Somehow in my distress after the funeral, maybe even before, I was ticking option buttons, typing in email addresses. Probably happened when I was informing people about his death. Probably. Yes, some poor associate of my dad has been getting copies of all my boring emails, and he's just too nice to say anything. I was sure that's all it was.

But what if it wasn't?

I mean, I didn't even know that I had a stalker until I hired Cotten. Who knows what might have happened if I hadn't gotten a solid buzz that night. What I wouldn't give for a buzz right now. But that wouldn't help anyone. The stalker, the murder, the car accident—oh, Edna! Inez's slashed tires. No, this wasn't some random accident. This was deliberate. I was in someone's crosshairs.

"What should I do?" I heard myself say. It took me another second to realize they had been talking to me while I was in la-la land, pondering my position.

"We're doing it right now," Cotten said. "Well, Cleeton is. He's digging to see if he can track down a location."

"An address?" I asked.

Cleeton cocked his head to one side. "Not necessarily a street address. Because it's a Steele Mail account, it won't get us that precise. It's not like on TV." He typed for a second more. "But I should be able to tell you a general vicinity."

Drawing a deep breath and releasing it, I rolled my shoulders forward and back. "Why does that make a difference?"

Cotten reached for my hand but stopped short. "It's a matter of jurisdiction. If it's a DFW location, and we can connect it to your stalking case, DuBois can use it to prove that this situation has been planned for a year."

"A year." I repeated his word because I had none of my own. "But really?" I asked, trying to make sense of his supposition. "Why would someone take the opportunity of my father's death to start after me?"

"Ms. Peters, do you need to sit down?" Cleeton asked, pointing to a chair against the wall behind me.

Cotten took my arm and moved me to the chair, but I

barely noticed. The words I'd just spoken—the opportunity of my father's death—rang in my ear like a bell. The last twelve months started stacking up in front of me.

"Daddy died." My voice was nothing more than a whisper. "And I've been muddling through a fog for the last ten and a half months. I could barely function as my own person, let alone be anything for anyone else." Where was Steve Havey when I needed him?

"Don't worry, Ronni." Cotten's voice was soft and low. "You aren't alone in this. You have friends. Let us help."

"When I hired you. That's when all of this happened. When it started."

A bruised look melted over his face. "You don't think I… Ronni, I would never do anything to hurt you."

"No. I know you wouldn't. But someone saw it. From the moment I emailed you the details of my schedule—remember when I hired you, and you asked for my routine? I emailed it to you. And to them. Whoever they are." The blood drained from my face, and a chill settled in my cheeks. "They know everything. Who my friends are. How the book was going. Who I'd hired. Everything."

"They saw you were regaining yourself." Cotten rubbed the back of my hand. "You'd spent months in mourning. You were going through the motions."

"And then I started taking charge of my life." I could see it all like a painting in front of my eyes. "But who's threatened by that?"

Cleeton turned in his chair to face us. "I, for one, find independent women quite appealing."

Cotten and I looked up, slightly startled at his statement.

He slumped his shoulders a fraction of an inch. "Also, I

have a location. The email address is definitely originating from the greater Dallas area."

"Are you okay?" Cotten squeezed my hand.

"Yeah."

He got up and walked back to Cleeton's desk. "Can we get anything more precise?"

"I can do a little more research and maybe find something to get us closer. The problem with these big mail providers is that they also give users an extra layer of anonymity. While that's great for some things, it makes tracking people much harder. And worse, most users choose a non-name. With this one, it's hard to say." Cleeton turned to face me again. "I don't suppose you know anyone named Victor?"

Thinking through all my friends and associates, I only drew a blank. "Nobody."

"Okay, give me an hour, and I'll see where I am at that point." Cleeton took a long sip from the water bottle at his elbow. "And I guess you'd like me to prevent all your emails from going to this address from here on out?"

"Yes, please," I said through a sigh of relief.

"No," Cotten said, shaking his head and turning back to me. "Keep it for now. We don't want Victor to know we're on to him."

I stood and walked back to Cotten's side. "Then we gotta get this guy quickly. The idea of someone reading all my emails is making me sick."

"I'll call you when I find something," Cleeton said as we walked back to the elevators.

"What else have you done since your father passed?" Cotten asked once we were again alone in our elevator car.

"Nothing," I answered. My mind was blank. "I get up, go

to work, grab something for dinner, and go home. On Satur-
days, I get groceries for the week. It's the routine I sent you."
I tried to think of anything else that might have sparked
someone's rage, but I was entirely dull. "I haven't even gone
to church since Daddy passed. I can't stand the thought of
him not being there. But honestly, the only person I can think
of that would be upset by that is your mother."

Cotten squeezed my hand. "Well, maybe I'll take you with
us once she's well."

"I think I'd like that very much."

We shuffled back to my office to work out a plan of action.
I sat at my desk, and Cotten relaxed into my Eames chair just
as Bev poked her head through my door.

"Hey, girl," she chirped with a broad smile on her glossy
red lips. "I just wanted to apologize for storming out of the
meeting this morning. I don't know what came over me. I
had brought up an idea at the last quarterly meeting, but then
I'd kind of forgotten about it, and then I was supposed to
have some big presentation or something. I don't know. I just
got nervous and embarrassed and flabbergasted." Her explanation rushed out like a train going off a bridge. "Maybe I
just had too much coffee, if that's a thing. But I'm sorry
anyway. It was your first time back this year, and I should
have been more supportive."

"I get it." I thought it was best to play along with whatever was happening, just in case she was the one trying to kill
me. As Cotten said, I didn't want her to know we were on to
her. If, in fact, we were.

She seemed to notice Cotten suddenly and turned to face
him. "Oh, Mr. Hammond, I didn't see you." She pulled her
shoulders and elbows in at her sides, squishing her bosom to

create a fuller cleavage—her MO whenever there was a man within ten feet of her. "I guess I should apologize to you, too."

"Not at all." He swiveled the chair to face my bookcase, away from us.

I stifled a laugh. "Did you need anything else, Bev? I have a few emails to send before I call it a day."

Bev walked back to my door and sighed. "I guess not. I'll see you tomorrow, then. I think I'll head home, too." She waved and hurried out toward her office.

As Cotten spun back to face me, I leaned forward in my chair and tried to push my bosom up with my arms. "How'd I do?"

"With what?"

"With the email thing. Did you notice how fast she left after I said that? She's probably going to check her email right now." I leaned back and let a contented grin settle on my lips. "Do you think she's Victor?"

Cotten chuckled. "I have no idea. Maybe she left in a hurry because you said you were leaving early, and she thought that was a good idea."

"Maybe." My mind filled with every worst-case scenario I could imagine. "But did you see the way she was looking at me?"

Cotten got to his feet and sauntered to the edge of my desk. "Did you see the way she was looking at *me*?"

I mustered my most sultry stare. "Was it kinda like this?"

He pulled me to my feet and took me into his arms. "Not quite, but close."

His breath puffed lightly on my lips before engulfing them.

And this was not a make-it-look-real-for-other-people kind of kiss. This was a for-real-feel-like-I'm-in-a-love-song kiss. And not even a cheesy top 40 love song, but an honest-to-goodness movie soundtrack love song.

I dropped back into my chair when he released me from his embrace. The leather felt cold on my hot skin. "I'll have to practice my looks, I guess."

"Nonsense." He waggled his finger at me. "I prefer yours to hers any day."

My phone rang, and I nearly slid out of my chair at the noise.

"Hello, this is Ronni Peters."

Inez's voice was breathy and low. "It's me. Inez. I think I found something. And it's bad."

CHAPTER 34
The Numbers

"CAN you meet us and show us your results in person?" My hand shook as hard as my voice as I spoke to Inez.

"Where?"

We'd already discussed not using names over the phone—to keep her cousin safe. But places? Probably ought to err on the safe side of that, too.

"Why don't we get together in the place where we met for the first time. The very first time. Do you remember?" I hoped she would pick up on my suggestion.

"In the back, where I helped you with your shoe?" Her voice strained.

"Yes. Is that doable?"

I could hear her smile over the phone. "We'll be there in half an hour."

"Perfect. See you soon." I hung up and turned to Cotten with a smug, self-satisfied expression. "Pretty smooth, right?"

He mirrored my expression. "Yep. Now we just have to

hope your nemesis didn't drop a tracker on you or Inez earlier."

Why did he have to say that? I raked my fingers through my hair, suddenly feeling as though I had a bug crawling over my scalp. If Inez hadn't been there, I might have asked Cotten for another pat-down.

As we drove to the bistro, all I could think about was someone sniggering evilly and watching a couple of blips on a black screen converging at the quaint little downtown eatery.

Cotten parked in the back, and we entered through the employees' access straight into the kitchen.

"You're not allowed back here," a man in a white chef's smock said.

"They're with me," Inez chirped, coming in immediately behind us, followed by another young man who I guessed was her cousin.

The cook winked at Inez. "Gimme a call later."

"Maybe tomorrow, Jay." Inez returned the wink and pointed us to the hall that led to the dining rooms. "Let's head to my office," she said. "Chuy, this is Ronni and Cotten. Y'all, this is Chuy. He's the genius."

When we got to the door marked *Ladies*, Cotten and Chuy exchanged a dubious look.

"We'll go in and check that the coast is clear." Inez propped open the door. "Anyone in here?"

No answer.

"It's good." She held the door, and I went inside. The men both stood in the hall.

"This isn't a big deal," Inez explained. "It's the middle of the afternoon. Nobody is eating right now.

And besides, ain't nobody gonna say boo to you anyway."

I laughed at Cotten. "Can you think of a more secure place to meet than a ladies' room?"

Chuy stepped inside cautiously, holding a laptop under his arm. Cotten followed. Inez reached under the counter, pulled out a *restroom closed for maintenance* sign, and hung it outside the door. "That should ease your mind." She gestured to the countertop, and Chuy plugged in the computer. "And I can guarantee you are not the first two men to be here. Not even the hundred and first."

"Okay, so what did you find?" I crossed my arms and forced myself to focus on the computer. The deep purple walls and crystal chandelier made sparkling reflections on the screen.

Inez regarded Chuy with a take-it-away gesture.

He cleared his throat. "I don't know what all Inez told you about my program, but basically, it takes all the information you feed it and puts it into a spreadsheet format, automatically categorizing the different elements. It's nice for book-keeping because you can create reports based on whatever you like. Account name, amount, transaction type—whatever. Most accounting software works the same way. But since mine was written initially for sports, it looks for repetitions. Seeks out commonalities that other programs don't." He typed into a dialog box and proceeded to open his program.

"And it found something in the Petra files?" I raised my brows as I leaned down to see.

Inez shook her head. "Actually, the Petra files are perfect. Not a decimal out of place." She leaned against the closest bathroom stall. "We got through those files in less than an hour."

Cotten crossed his arms, and his eyes narrowed to slits. "Then what did you find?"

My stomach sank when I saw the file name at the top of the page—Diane Pawley-Peters Memorial Women's Foundation. "Oh, no."

"Yes." Inez pointed to the columns on the page. "Everything looked fine here, too. I was just about ready to call it square when Chuy let out a yell. I thought my Tia Elena had won at Bingo again."

Chuy chuffed. "I couldn't help it. I got excited." He scrolled horizontally across the screen. "These are the grants awarded by the foundation for the last three and a half years."

"Three and a half years?" The words escaped my lips in a weak moan.

"At first, it was just one or two here and there. But this last year, more than half." Chuy stopped scrolling at a column that showed the same numbers all the way down the page. "This line here. It's the bank."

Cotten squinted and moved closer. "The bank?"

"What does that mean?" I wasn't too proud to ask. I was standing in the ladies' room with my accountant, a computer, and two men. I wasn't too proud for anything anymore.

"So when you first look over the records, you don't notice anything out of place. The grant recipients' names are all different, and the amounts they received, where they're from, what the money is for—it's all different. Until you get to the bank." Chuy pointed to the numbers again.

I leaned in. "But the bank names are all different. First

American Denver, Miami National." I didn't see what he was seeing.

"Not so fast," Chuy said. "These are all dummy names. Whoever inputted them mirrored a bank name from whatever city they had for the recipient. Here's the tell; they all have the same routing number."

I squinted and focused on the column filled with the repeating number. "Meaning the same bank?"

"Yes. The same bank."

"Could it be a coincidence or a mistake?" I straightened my back. "An input error?"

Chuy released a contented sigh and took a step back. "There's no way it's a coincidence. Every bank in the world has a different routing number. And no mistake, either. I looked it up. That routing number belongs to a bank in the Cayman Islands. That's as far as I can go with it. The accounts there are kept confidential. People use offshore accounts for pretty much one thing—hiding money."

"Someone's been stealing from the foundation," Cotten whispered.

The room started to spin. I'd been subconsciously holding my breath, and now I couldn't get enough oxygen into my lungs to make my brain function. I started sinking but caught myself by grabbing the cold marble vanity top.

"They aren't stealing from the foundation. They're stealing from all the women the foundation is trying to help." The boldness in my voice surprised me. "What kind of vile person would do that?"

"The same type of psychopath that stalks and murders people." Inez's tone and expression exuded disgust. "This should be more than enough for a warrant. All you need to do is tell the police who authorizes the grants."

My heart raced at the thought. "The process is a little involved. There's a committee that goes through the requests. I'm actually one of the members now—since Dad passed. But Greg Oberman, Bev Muncy, and George Lovett are, too. We review hundreds of requests and prioritize them based on need, urgency, and likely outcome. We approve the requests as far as the grant money goes." My heart lurched at the thought of how many people may have died because they didn't get the funds they needed for treatment. "By the time they get to us, though, they've been checked out to be sure they're legitimate. At least, that's what I was told. I don't know who vets them before we see the requests. There's probably a team on staff that does that."

"And who sends the checks?" Inez asked.

"There are no checks. We send all the grants by direct deposit. I get the final list of grants going out each quarter, and I sign off on it." My hand trembled as I raised it to my forehead. My fingers were like ice against my flushed face. "Then it goes back to the foundation office, and the money is transferred directly from our account to theirs. I suppose a staffer at the foundation takes care of that, too. I don't know, really." A question popped into my head. I didn't want to ask, but I had to. "How much money went into the offshore bank?"

Inez furrowed her brow. "From what we could find over the last four years' worth of records, just under seven million dollars."

"Oh, my—" But I couldn't finish because I threw up a little in my mouth. In just a few short years, someone had stolen seven million dollars, and nobody had noticed. Not even my father. My heart ached, wishing he was here. He would know what to do.

Another thought struck me. Did he find out? Is that what triggered his heart attack? Something like this would undoubtedly have killed him.

"This is unreal," Cotten said. "I ran the background checks on everybody hired at the foundation and Petra for the last nine years. I'll get everything I have to the police."

I patted his shoulder and hurried to the sink at the other end of the counter. I splashed cold water on my face, hoping to preempt full-fledged vomiting. "We need to take all of this to DuBois." I blotted my face with a paper towel.

Cotten agreed. "Yes. We should go now with this and bring the rest as soon as possible. The longer we take, the more danger we're all in."

CHAPTER 35
The Evidence

"AND YOU HAVE no idea who is doing this?" DuBois asked after seeing the evidence from Chuy and Inez.

"We were focused on the board members because I believed they were trying to squeeze me out." I gulped down a cup of cold water, desperate to stay calm. "If you make a Venn diagram—the kind with the circles that overlap—between the board members and the foundation committee members, that takes the ones in the middle down to three. Four, if you include me."

"So Oberman, Muncy, and Lovett?" Detective DuBois ticked off their names on his fingers. "They're in the overlap of your diagram?"

I swallowed hard. "They are, but it could also be a staffer at the foundation. I don't want to accuse anyone without knowing a little more. All three were good friends, hand-picked by my father. Greg Oberman has been with Petra for nearly twenty years."

Cotten shook his head. "I think you focus on the three. A staffer wouldn't have the motive to get her ousted from the board."

I glanced at Inez, who shot me a confident nod. I could do this. "Maybe look at the three, but also their staffers. There has to be someone doing the paperwork. These three don't type their own letters, lick their own stamps, or file their own documents. Why would they get their hands dirty with something like this?"

"You think they have a scapegoat in place?" DuBois angled his chin in my direction.

I drew a deep breath. "I'd expect so. And Cleeton, the IT guy for the executive floors, believes I was hacked. He said it'd probably take someone with admin rights. I think that was what he said. And he was in my accounts in a matter of seconds."

Chuy shrugged. "But a good hacker from outside might not take much longer than that. All they need is the right access." He twitched his lips from side to side when everyone shifted their attention to him. "That's what I've heard. From a guy I know."

Inez grinned. "The point is, everyone on Ronni's floor has access and admin rights. These three could be in and out of her office in seconds. She'd never know the difference. And they could have done the same with her father."

DuBois gestured to Chuy and Inez. "I'd like both of you to make statements, and with your consent, I'd like my forensic technology analyst to go through your program. You can give her a guided tour if you like." He turned and focused on Cotten and me. "Can you bring up your computers, too? The analyst could do some digging and help narrow our search."

"You don't have enough for a warrant with this?" Cotten asked.

"I think we do, but that will take some time to get a judge to sign off. Your computers could give us a head start, maybe a more specific target." DuBois gestured to me. "Plus, this kind of cooperation looks a little better in the grand scheme of things. If you're the one authorizing the grants, the real perpetrator might try to shift the blame to you. I can almost guarantee that's what their lawyer will do. But this takes that power away from them. At least minimizes it."

Imagining the scenario he suggested, I was more eager to help. "Should we bring in the foundation computers, too?"

"No." DuBois leaned his hefty body forward. "We'll let the officers get those. I don't want them to be compromised by a chain of custody problem. This kind of fraud may be a federal crime. I don't want to mess it up with something like that."

"But it's okay for us to bring in our own?" Cotten's expression turned skeptical. "I know how you don't like your cases getting fumbled."

"I think in this situation—her stalking case, which now includes attempted murder—the benefits will outweigh the downside. It falls under local jurisdiction." DuBois stared at Cotten. "If it later ties in with the other, and it probably will, a conviction at the local level will only boost the fed's case."

I looked around the room, thinking this little mishmash of people was the only team I could count on—the only people in the world on my side. No... Edna was, too. And probably April. I'd bet money on that. Everyone else fell under the shadow of suspicion.

My muscles ached. My mind hurtled from one crazy

thought to another. I'd return to my office, gather my stuff, and hand my computer over to the police. Once I did that, everything would change. Rumors would start. Accusations would fly. Former friends would look at each other with contempt. Daddy would have been heartbroken.

"How could I let this happen?" I muttered as Cotten and I drove back to the Petra building.

He huffed. "This isn't something you chose. You're the victim in all of this."

The stones in my gut weighed heavy. "Well, not anymore, I'm not. I have zero interest in being the damsel in distress from here on out."

As we drove past the bronze longhorn sculptures in Pioneer Plaza, I heard my dad's voice. *Time to take the bull by the horns, Ronni.*

We parked and took the executive elevator up. It was nearly 5:30 in the afternoon, and almost everyone had left for the day. Good. I was ready to be brave as long as it was just Cotten and me.

"The top three floors should be nearly empty by now. Most of the execs go home early after the board meetings." Cotten's voice reassured me. "Do you need any help dismantling your computer?"

"No, I can do it. Should I keep all the cords and cables together or leave them with the monitor?" I wasn't sure what DuBois would want.

"Leave the monitor cables and take everything else. Do you need a box for carrying it out?" Cotten asked.

"That would be great."

"I have a couple in the storage closet by my office. I'll bring one up."

We reached the twelfth floor, and he walked me to my office. The other offices were dark and closed up for the night. Only the automatic lights in the main halls and reception areas remained on.

"Looks like we're alone. Do you want me to stay with you?" He unlocked my office door and held it open for me.

"No. You go on after your computer and the boxes. I'll get mine ready, so we can get out of here as quickly as possible. Is there anything else we might need to take to DuBois?" I glanced around the room. Everything looked quiet. Everything was in its place.

Cotten glanced at my desk, and I could see that something had occurred to him by the change in his expression. "I think I figured out where your father's gun came from."

"What?" I asked. The idea of a gun swirling into this mess startled me.

His eyes looked wild. "The gun—your father's pistol that they found by Wexler's body—we couldn't figure out where it had come from because the security logs showed nobody accessing his collection or the gun safe at the Castle."

"Right."

"But it hadn't occurred to me until just now that your father sometimes carried. He had his permit. When he carried, he kept his pistol in his desk." Cotten patted my desktop. "He had a false bottom in his top drawer."

The implications of his statement hit me like a runaway train. "I had—" My breath gave out before I could finish. I inhaled to the full capacity of my lungs and held it for a few seconds. Releasing it through my lips sent a tingly rush to my toes. "I had no idea. But I suppose someone up here did."

He rapped a knuckle on my desktop. "You get whatever

you may need from up here. I think you should work from home for a little while—maybe even my mother's home. At least until DuBois gets this sorted out." He headed back to the door. "I'll go downstairs and get my computer and the boxes, then I'll meet you in your dad's office. I want to check it over one more time before we go."

"Good plan." I watched him start out into the hall and then hesitate. "What's wrong?"

He took two long strides back to me, folded me into his arms, and kissed me full on the mouth. I felt a shudder race from my lips to my toes.

I needed that.

He chuffed, making me wonder if I'd said that out loud. But before I could blush, he was out the door and headed to the elevator.

I slipped off my suit jacket, dropped into my desk chair, and grabbed the mouse, causing my monitor to flicker to life. My heart pounded as I closed programs, saved documents, and shut everything down. When the soft whirring went quiet, I slid from my chair to the floor and began pulling out the computer from the cubby on the left side of the desk. Carefully, I unplugged each cable from the power strip and wrapped it with the Velcro strap at the end. Twenty minutes later, I was done.

"What will I need to work from home?" I whispered to nobody. Nobody answered.

My laptop had access to all the documents on my cloud. My desk drawers held the most generic office supplies. The books on my shelves were mostly from my travels with Dad. The low credenza under my windows housed my little printer and a ream of extra paper, a box of ink cartridges, and other such supplies.

Like most of my stuff, I'd inherited it from Dad. I didn't need any of it to do my work.

My heart ached and pounded. Not just my heart but my head as well. I tugged at the lapel of my silk blouse to air out. I wasn't sure if the heat or my nerves caused me to sweat, but I needed hydration. I crossed the room to the small under-cabinet refrigerator below my bookshelves, eager for a water bottle. The fridge was empty.

I'd been planning to get rid of Dad's green bottles of sparkling water but had never gotten to it. I guess someone else figured I needed a little help. Probably Karen had done it for me. I wished she'd have left me just one bottle of plain water or a Coke or something. I needed an aspirin.

Flipping the bathroom light on, I searched the medicine cabinet for headache relief. I had two chalky pills in my mouth before I remembered that my glass was gone. I'd taken it home a week ago and forgotten to bring it back. The tap would have to do.

Bending down to the faucet, I filled my mouth with tepid water. I stood up quickly, rocking my head back to swallow before the bitter tablets dissolved on my tongue.

Thump.

I heard something but wasn't sure what it was. I spun around and poked my head out of the bathroom and into my office. "Cotten, is that you?"

No response.

Inching back into my office, I scanned for movement and listened for even the slightest sound. Nothing.

It was probably my imagination or, worse, it could be my brain rattling around in my skull after this week of trauma.

Just to be sure, I looked out my office door toward the elevators—still nothing.

Thump!

I spun around to see a bird crash into my window and sputter away. A gasp escaped my lips, and I slapped my hand over my mouth, trying to quell the scream that followed.

My nerves were shot, and I was beyond ready to leave. I picked up my phone to text Cotten to come and gather me. Before navigating to his name, my screen dimmed and flashed a low-battery warning. Of course.

Setting my phone on the charging pad, I turned my attention to the hall. Cotten should have been back by now. I peeked down the hall to my left and then to my right. No movement. I was about to park myself in my desk chair again when I heard a door slam on the opposite side of the twelfth floor.

I was not alone.

CHAPTER 36

The Truth

STANDING on the threshold between my private office and the hallway, I decided I needed to be braver than I felt. I stared to the left, toward the elevators. No movement. No sounds.

I turned to the right, toward my father's office. Still dark. Cotten hadn't come up yet, or if he had, he hadn't left any indication of his presence. I exhaled and enjoyed a quick rush of relief.

It was short-lived, though, as I heard a man's muffled voice from somewhere else on the floor. It wasn't Cotten, but I wasn't sure who it might be.

Easing my way into the hall, I listened more closely.

"Well, this—" followed by something I couldn't understand, "—time-table up. And puts us both at risk." The voice was deep and commanding, more like Oberman's than Lovett's. I crept around the corner at the elevator and saw light coming from under Greg's office door. That settled that question. Dang.

My heart ached. Greg had been one of Dad's closest friends.

It occurred to me that he was talking with someone else. Maybe his scapegoat. Maybe a partner. I edged closer, hoping to hear more.

"I'll have to move my London trip up a week. You'll need to stay here for a few days and ensure it's all right." He wasn't yelling, but his tone was clearly urgent.

"No! You can't leave me to clean up your mess." It was a woman's loud whisper. Definitely not Bev's bold, round voice. Probably a staffer at the Foundation.

I took another step and pressed my back into the doorway beside Oberman's office. The records room. It wasn't latched, and I felt the door push in behind me. I spun to catch the door before it hit the wall and alerted them to my eaves-dropping.

I stepped inside, leaving the light off and the door open just a few inches.

I stood silently in the dark room. It was a good place to hide if either one came out of the office. I focused on the conversation in the next office. "My mess?" Oberman said. I imagined him scowling, his fists on his hips. "No. This one's not mine."

"The whole rainy-day account idea was yours. You set it up!" Ooh, she was mad.

"And it was all going just fine until you got greedy. If you hadn't lost your patience—"

I heard him stomping.

"You know as well as I do that he suspected something. I

was trying to manage the situation." Her voice turned snippy, and I almost recognized it.

"By throwing yourself at him?"

Whoa! This was a full-on soap opera.

"It was better than hiring someone to kill him!" She was still keeping her voice to a hissy whisper. "I'm *glad* that idiot of yours was hit by a bus."

What? My heart pounded so loudly I almost couldn't hear. Did she say *hit by a bus*?

"Well, that bus cost me twenty-five grand for nothing, thank you very much." Greg's tone lowered, and I figured he was right up in the poor woman's face. "If I'd known you would kill him the next week, I'd have saved my money."

The sound of an open palm on a cheek indicated she'd had just about enough. I wished I was recording it all.

"I didn't intend to kill him. I only put the saline solution in his water to make him sick. I wanted him to reevaluate his life and change his will. I didn't know he'd drop dead of a heart attack right there in his office."

The words floated into my ears and began hammering at my brain. Heart attack? Here in the office? Seconds ticked by, and they were still yelling, but I couldn't hear anything more. All I could hear was the echo in my mind. *They killed my father.* Greg hired someone to kill him, and when that didn't work, the woman killed him.

"Oh, Daddy, you were murdered." That time it was my voice, and I had no idea how loudly I said it.

Apparently, it was loud enough. The argument in the next room came to a screeching halt.

"Shh!" The woman. "I heard something."

Panicked, I closed the closet door and locked it. Doing so

made a loud click and triple beep, which told them exactly where I was. I didn't care. At least they couldn't get in—unless they had the passcode—which, of course, they did.

As soon as I realized this, I moved to the back of the room and wedged myself into the narrow space between the last filing cabinet and the back wall. I'd only just squatted out of view when the light flicked on.

I squeezed my eyes shut and tried to hold my breath. Which most likely made more noise than if I'd done nothing.

"I don't see anyone." Greg's voice.

"Go ahead and lock the door." It was Karen's voice. Karen. Oh God, please, not Karen. "If anyone *is* in here, they won't be found in the ashes until morning."

"Time is short," Greg said, turning off the light and tapping the keypad in the hall. "We must check all the other offices before leaving."

"That settles it," Karen hissed again, "I'm going with you. I'm not staying here in Dallas to be burned at the stake. Not with two bodies left in the building."

They continued arguing but had moved away from the door until their exchanges became no more than a buzz here and there.

This was too much. I clutched my stomach, willing myself not to throw up. Their voices played over and over in my brain. I wanted to be wrong. Greg and Karen. Karen and Greg. Dad trusted them more than anyone else in the world, and they had murdered him. And now, if I understood correctly, they would murder Dad's company by torching the building.

She used the word 'ashes.' Maybe it was just a figure of speech, but it didn't sound like it. And she'd said two bodies left in the building. They meant Cotten and me. They were going to murder us, too.

I reached into my pocket for my phone. I had to call 9-1-1. Empty—I'd left my phone charging in my office. Wasn't there a landline in the room?

Feeling my way to the door in the dark, I found the light switch and turned it on. The phone was a clunky desktop model at least twenty years old. I picked up the receiver and listened. No tone. I pressed the big acrylic buttons at the bottom, but nothing happened. I checked that it was plugged into the wall, and it was. But there was no service to it.

How was I supposed to warn Cotten they knew he was in the building and would kill us both? Think, girl. But then I did think. They knew he was there, and they weren't any more worried about him than they were about me. I was locked in a room, and no longer a problem for them.

Tears flooded my cheeks. He wasn't a problem for them, either. What did that mean, though? Was he locked in a closet, too? No. He was the head of security. He had the codes for every door in the building. If he was conscious, he would be fighting them tooth and nail. He'd be rescuing me right now.

That left only one option. If I wanted to live, I'd have to save myself—and him.

CHAPTER 37
The Waiting

THE WEIGHT of the situation crushed down on my shoulders. Before I could even attempt to find Cotten, stop Greg and Karen from torching the Petra offices, and call DuBois, the fire department, or anyone else, I had to escape the electronically locked records room. I tried the latch, just to be sure, but it was locked from the outside, like any other storage closet.

Staring at the keypad on the wall next to the door latch, I tried to imagine what the code might be. Dad's code had been a master pass that got him into any room in the building. My code got me into the executive parking garage, elevator, and my private office. I could get into Dad's office now because I had inherited that code, too, but it wasn't the master passcode. Or was it?

I stared at the keypad through a squint, knowing that I would only have three tries before it would lock me out for fifteen minutes and set off an alarm at the security desk. I had to concentrate. The codes for these keypads were five digits plus the pound sign. If you made a mistake, you hit star-star-star before the pound and try again.

Holding my breath, I decided to try my code first. I was on the board, so I thought maybe it would work. I punched the buttons to spell out the name of my childhood pet cat. D-A-I-S-Y-#. The red light flashed, and the words INVALID CODE filled the small screen. One try down, two more to go.

Sweat broke on my forehead, but my fingers were chilled. I rubbed my hands together, trying to get a little circulation going.

Maybe Dad's office code would work. I punched in my name. R-O-N-N-I-#. Red lights. INVALID CODE.

Okay, I had one more chance. I had to make it count, but my mind blanked. Dad had always used my name for everything. Except for the safe at the Castle. For that, he used his birthday. And not the month-day-year set of numbers, either. That would be too easy to crack. No, he had to be different. But would he consider the Petra records room the same as his gun safe? I doubted it, but I couldn't think of anything else.

With my fingers crossed on my left hand, I entered the code with my right. M-A-Y-2-1-#.

For a split second, I thought it had worked. But then the screen flashed red. INVALID CODE flashed three times before the screen read LOCKED with a fifteen-minute timer that counted down.

Three strikes; I was out. My heart slammed against my ribs, and I could feel my whole body shaking. I was going to die in a fire. I dropped to the floor and stretched my legs out in front of me. My second-grade teacher, Mrs. Henderson, always said that if there was a fire, one should crawl as low as possible to keep below the smoke.

Now I had fifteen minutes to think up three more guesses. My birthday? No, he would leave that one for me. What other dates would be important to him? Maybe his anniversary? Or it might not be a date at all. It could be the name of his childhood dog. Buster or Bronco or something like that. Even if I could remember, those had too many digits.

This was getting me nowhere, and the timer was ticking. A thought struck like lightning. If Cotten was in his office, the lock-out alarm would be sounding, and he'd probably come up to investigate. I looked at the timer. Four minutes had already passed. That would be ample time for him to get to me.

Then I imagined him lying on the floor of his office, out cold. I wondered if the alarm might be loud enough and last long enough to rouse him. Would it sound for the whole fifteen minutes, or just beep a couple of times and then quit? That would probably be helpful information to know right now.

"What are they doing out there?" I whispered to myself. I was not eager to die, but I thought people would just start a fire and leave the building. Then I started thinking about all the forensic shows I'd watched over the years.

You can't just toss a match and leave. You have to make sure the fire will catch. And if there is anything you need from the place you intend to burn, you can't just take it—that's a sure sign of arson and points directly to the arsonist. So you must make copies of photos and files and leave the originals to the flames. Plus, you must ensure that whatever you use to accelerate the fire won't be an obvious accelerant.

Unless you intend to frame someone else for arson. Of course, anyone who's already tried to pin a murder on someone wouldn't think twice about framing that person for arson, too.

The timer showed seven minutes left. I had to come up with something. I could hear Greg and Karen shuffling around in his office and down the hall. Every once in a while, I heard one of them ask a question or gripe that they needed to hurry.

"Yeah, you wouldn't want your next murder to take all night," I called out. I doubted they could hear me; even if they could, I was sure they wouldn't blink at my sarcasm.

It would be easy for them. Torch the building, head out on a short trip to London, and wait to see what shakes out in the ashes.

Greg would be appropriately shocked and disappointed that Alexander Peters' own daughter was using the Foundation as her private piggy bank. Karen would probably weep real tears at the inquest, deposition, or whatever the police put together.

"It just can't be, Your Honor. She was such a lovely young woman," she'd say. "I'm sure that young man she'd been seeing talked her into everything. He'd always had his eye on her—and her money." Oh, Karen would bask in the limelight.

All I could think about was what would happen when it was all over. Greg and Karen would get away with it, and Cotten and I would be shamed and dead.

My heart ached. I had to figure out some way to reach Cotten. At this point, I was sure he was in trouble and needed me. I prayed that he was still alive.

I absolutely, positively had to escape this room, find him,

and get us out of the building. And somewhere along the way, call 9-1-1.

There were still two minutes left on the lock screen. I had to get the passcode correct this time. We couldn't afford another fifteen-minute lock-out.

My new mantra floated through my mind. "What would Edna do?" I didn't bother to whisper. "She'd use Cotten's name if only it would fit. I need something with only five letters."

C-O-T-T-E-N was what I had used for my new code at the Castle. He couldn't be dead. I needed him too much. I just couldn't imagine going on without him.

"Daddy, how did you go on without Mama?" I asked the ceiling. "You were always so strong. I guess you had to be." I dropped my head into my hands and sobbed. "That's what the Diane Pawley—" and the words stuck in my throat.

"Diane. D-I-A-N-E." My heart thumped so loudly it became an echo in the small room. I hopped to my feet and stared at the keypad, willing it to unlock.

Fourteen seconds.

"This is it. I know it. I'm getting out of this room."

Nine seconds.

"Only open the door a crack and make sure no one is waiting for you."

Five seconds.

"Just get back to your office and call DuBois first. Then you can look for Cotten."

The light changed from red to green and said ENTER PASSCODE.

I felt lightheaded. I whispered the letters as I punched in my mother's name. My eyes blurred for a second, and when they refocused, the screen flashed green three times, and the latch clicked open.

It took every ounce of control I had not to fling open the door and run down the hall to my office. Instead, I turned out the light in the records room and peeked carefully in either direction. Only the automatic hall lights were on. All was quiet on the twelfth floor.

I inched out enough to see if they were in Greg's office, but the lights were off in there, and not a sound could be heard but the hum of the air conditioning.

Tip-toeing toward my office, I whispered, "Please help me, Lord," over and over. The room was dim with the shade of the coming evening. I crept inside. Everything looked right, except my phone, which was crushed on the floor under my desk. I picked up the receiver on my desk phone, but there was no tone. No service. So much for Plan A.

CHAPTER 38

The Alarm

MY PHONE'S glass screen was shattered into a spider-webbed pattern, but I thought it might still power up. When I picked it up to see, the back separated into four or five different pieces, falling to the floor. Worthless.

I started to grab my computer and make a run for it, but I still didn't have a box for it and knew I'd probably end up scattering it all over the building. I also knew I only had a short time to get out before they started the fire. And I still had no idea where Cotten was.

Greg and Karen knew he was here. They had either run into him in his eleventh-floor office or on twelve, in Dad's office, or on the way to mine. It might be a long shot, but I had to check Dad's office before going downstairs.

I poked my head into the hall again and listened for even the slightest noise. Nothing. No change in the lighting or office doors, either. I had to risk it.

I pressed my lips into a tight, straight line and stepped out of my heels. I hurried down the hall, staying as close to the wall as possible while avoiding the art. At Dad's office door, I realized I'd left my key in my purse, so I had to use the keypad. I pressed my body around it as I punched in my name and pound sign, trying to muffle the beeping noise. I could smell the pungent odor of my stress sweat as the light flashed green and the latch clicked.

Too much noise.

I slipped into his private office and inhaled the still-lingering aroma of cherry cigars. It was as if he were still there. His black-out curtains were closed, but the automatic opener made a distinct buzz, so I opted to turn on his bathroom light instead.

The room was dim, but I saw nothing out of place. The desk was clear except for a phone, which was just as dead as all the others—I checked. It didn't appear that Cotten had made it back upstairs from his office.

My heart pounded hard, and my fingertips throbbed as I clutched at the back of Dad's desk chair to steady myself.

Something caught my eye in the corner of the room. There was a cardboard box on its side, leaning against the wall. On the floor beside it lay something reflective.

My mind raced a million miles an hour as I tried to figure out what it was. It could be a bomb. Maybe that's how they were going to start the fire. I froze in place, forcing my brain to work.

Do I try to figure out what it is, or just run as fast as possible?

The practical side told me to run, but curiosity convinced me to investigate. One of these days, that curious side would get me killed.

Creeping closer, I saw that the shiny thing was a phone. Thank the Lord, it was a phone!

I started to pick it up, then I realized it was smashed to smithereens, just like mine. The screen, the back, and the case were all in pieces. But the case looked familiar.

It was dark blue plastic, with a magnifying glass logo and the words Hammond, P.I. down one side. This was Cotten's phone. He'd been here when Greg and Karen found him.

I spun around to scan the room again. I heard my voice cry out before I could stop it. "Oh, Cotten, where are you?"

Thump!

I jumped a foot off the floor. The sound came from the window. Stupid birds. I couldn't take any more of this.

Thump-thump-thump!

Staring at the closed drapes, I shook my head. That was not birds.

I ran to my dad's desk and hit the button on the corner. The curtains parted with a buzz to reveal a mass of duct tape over a man's body. Cotten had been plastered up facing outward, twelve stories up. The tape at his head was loose, allowing him to move just enough to bang against the plate-glass window.

Coming around to face him, more or less, I saw Cotten's dark eyes, bruised and bloodshot. His mouth was taped shut. I grabbed a chair and climbed up to level with his face.

"Cotten, are you all right?"

I started to pull the adhesive from his cheeks. His eyes teared in pain as he rocked his head slightly. I stopped tugging at the tape.

He shook his head and tried to talk, but the gray tape made the words unintelligible.

"If I yank it off, it's going to hurt."

"Hrmmm-mmrr-rreerrrr!"

"Okay." I eased my fingertips under one end of the strip over his lips. "Three-two-one." And I pulled.

The tape peeled back with a terrible ripping sound, leaving Cotten's face scraped and bleeding. He gulped fresh air between exhausted gasps.

Trying not to pull out too much hair, I began on the adhesive over the rest of his head and neck. There were layers upon layers.

"I was afraid you wouldn't find me." His voice sounded parched and rough. "Thank you."

"I almost didn't." I cried as I pulled the strips back, an inch at a time. "They're going to set the building on fire."

"DuBois. Call DuBois," he choked.

"No phones working in the building, and they pulverized both of our cells." I climbed down to move the chair so I could start freeing his right hand.

"It's Oberman." Cotten coughed and swallowed a few times. "Cleeton called and told me he knew who hacked your email. Before he could tell me, Oberman knocked my phone to the floor and smashed me in the eye."

"It's okay. Save your voice. I know." The tape pulled out half the hair from the back of Cotten's hand. Moving up his arm would hurt even worse.

"We fought for a second. He slammed my head into the wall, I think." His words grew weaker as he spoke.

"Please shush," I said. "I already know. We have to get out of here soon."

As I worked on his wrist, the hallway lights dimmed, and an alarm sounded. "Smoke detected on the seventh floor.

Please evacuate the building," a calm, computer-generated voice said. "Do not use elevators for a fire evacuation. Use stairwell exits only." The automated message began again. "Smoke detected on the seventh floor...."

I grabbed handfuls of duct tape and pulled with all my might. But Greg or Karen, whoever had been in charge of the taping, had used such a disorganized method of overlapping tape it was impossible to remove a whole strip at a time. I peeled back half of one piece and then worked on another, leaving ends dangling, only to get stuck again.

"You go on and get DuBois," Cotten whispered.

"I'm not leaving you here to die." I pulled and peeled more aggressively, which only managed to get my fingers more entwined in the gluey side of the mess.

Cotten coughed again. "You have to go right now. I'm not going to die. The fire sprinklers will kick on in a few minutes. I'll be fine. But you have to go and get DuBois. He has to pick up Oberman before he gets out of Dallas."

"Shut up!" I tugged at the tape in a frantic, convulsive fit. "I'm not leaving you. Period." The sprinklers. They would come on soon. They should be on *now*. Had they been disabled, too?

"Ronni, listen to me." His voice became low and severe. "I think my ankle is broken. The elevators don't work, and you can't carry me down twelve flights of stairs."

"I can try."

"No." He stared at me. "You have to go. Right now." His eyes swelled almost shut. "You've got my right arm almost free. I'll work on the rest." He shifted his arm so that his hand reached the first ends of the tape that held his torso in place against the glass. "See? I'll be out of this in no time."

Leaning close to him, I cried and shook my head. "I can't. I can't go without you. I can't—" I choked back a throatful of tears and sniffed. "I can't live without you."

He thumped his forehead against the glass and almost smiled. "Yes, you can. But you won't have to. You're going to make it out of the building, and then you're going to call the police and the fire department and DuBois. You're going to save me, Ronni." Tears mixed with blood and smeared between his face and the window. "I need you to save me."

"I don't want to go." My heart pounded as though it would explode.

He gasped and coughed. "I know. But you have to. If you don't, neither of us will make it."

Daggers stabbed into my heart as I climbed down from the chair. "I love you," I said.

Cotten's hand patted the glass. "I know, Ronni. I love you, too. Now go."

The computer voice droned on. I raced barefoot down the hall to the stairwell. I was going to make it. I had to.

"Smoke detected on the seventh and eighth floors. Please evacuate the building." The message had changed. The fire had spread upward, and I was heading down.

CHAPTER 39

The Escape

I RAN AS FAST as I could in my bare feet and pencil skirt. I realized that I should have picked up my purse on the way out, but I was already between the eleventh and tenth floors and didn't have time to waste.

My brain wrestled with motives and methods as I ran. Why would Greg and Karen even consider any of this? Greg was second in command at Petra after Dad, and Karen never complained about anything. She got regular raises, bonuses, and vacation time. Why would they do any of this?

What had they said in their argument? Greg accused Karen of throwing herself at Dad. Had she been in love with him? No way to know, but I was sure Dad had not been in love with her.

After that, she'd said she only wanted to make him sick. Make him revise his will. The will that left everything to me. She apparently wanted more from Dad than a secretarial position. Had she even asked him for more?

And then when Dad passed, I inherited Karen... My stomach turned at the thought. "I inherited her?" I scolded myself out loud as I ran. "How many times have I said that phrase?" I didn't really mean it. She was a person, not a stapler or a car. Not a thing to be left from one person to another. Had Karen ever heard me say that aloud? Probably. I felt sick with regret.

She'd murdered my father, and I could only think about apologizing to her.

I knew I wasn't the reason she'd killed Dad. That had obviously been building for years. Something had happened that made her want to steal from him.

"Smoke detected on the seventh, eighth, and ninth floors. Please evacuate the building...."

I almost didn't hear it over all the thoughts whizzing through my brain. The fire was spreading. I looked up and saw the sign on the landing below me—the eighth floor. I was right in the middle of the blaze. I paused to peer through the narrow glass panel in the access door.

Smoke billowed everywhere, rosy with a pulsing orange glow. Why hadn't the sprinklers activated? I knew there was a slight delay to allow a false alarm to be shut down before extensive water damage occurred. But the water should be flowing by now.

I picked up my pace down to seven; my breath wheezed as I ran.

"What about Greg Oberman?" I asked, trying to distract myself from the voice warning me to get out. "Did he try to kill Daddy so he wouldn't get caught with the offshore accounts?"

My chest heaved as I struggled to run and breathe at the

same time. "Maybe he thought he would become the controlling shareholder. Maybe he thought Dad had left more to him."

"I guess killing him would be one way to find out what was in the will," I puffed as I flew by the door on six.

My hand slipped off the rail between six and five, and I stumbled on the next step, falling to my butt on the landing. I sat for a second and ran through a few breathing exercises.

"This is crazy," I wheezed. "I'll never make it. I should have stayed with Cotten. As it is, we're both going to die alone." I sobbed between gasps. "If I'd have stayed with him, at least we'd have had each other."

Every inch of my body ached, and gravity pinned me to the floor. From the landing, I looked at the door to the sixth floor and down at the one to five. The wire-embedded glass of the windows turned opaque with smoke. The automated voice warned that the fire was spreading both up and down. I was done.

The fire moved faster than me. My legs barely held me up, let alone outrun the smoke and flames. I couldn't save Cotten. I couldn't even save myself.

"Don't let your mind stop you." The words drifted into my brain and bounced around, echoing louder with each rebound. Steve Harvey's voice pounded his admonishment over and over, as he had on a recent episode. "Don't let your mind stop you. Get up. Don't give up. Keep going."

I stood up mechanically. Steve Harvey was right. My legs still worked. My body still worked, and until it didn't, I must keep moving. I didn't feel like going on, but exhaustion was no excuse. I wasn't sure I would make it, but doubt wasn't an excuse.

Daddy used to tell me even if my heart wasn't in it, I had to do what I had to do, and I had to keep doing it until I didn't have to do it anymore.

I couldn't imagine letting Daddy or Mr. Harvey down. I had to save Cotten.

Even as my knees burned, I plodded down the stairs. My body steeped in sweat, and I continued.

I was almost on the fourth floor when I remembered something. I was in the stairwell on the east side of the building, which was adjacent to the parking garage. I could access the garage and breathe fresh air when I reached the third floor. I'd be able to scream to anyone on the street for help. Only another twenty steps or so, and I'd be out of the building.

I could have escaped in his car if I'd brought Cotten's keys. But I didn't have them, and I was one hundred percent sure he didn't have a spare set hidden anywhere in the car—being the security-minded man he was.

I could see the waning daylight through the window of the door ahead. "Thank you, God!" I sprinted forward and pulled open the door to the garage.

Racing out into the almost-cool shade of the covered bays, I drew in a deep breath of automobile-infused air, but it was such a relief that I didn't mind.

Taking a moment to enjoy my escape, I turned a quick circle to appraise my surroundings. Cotten had taught me that.

His life depended on me right now.

Though I could hear sirens at street level, Cotten's car sat quiet in its space. Greg's pearl white car was only a few slots down from the black sedan. And at the other end of the executive spaces was a silver mini-van with a couple standing on the other side—Greg and Karen.

Panic shot through me like an electric current. I turned back to the stairwell door, doing everything in my power not to make a noise. I didn't want to go back into the building, but now it was my only option.

I held my breath, grasped the door handle, turned, and pulled. The door didn't budge. I pulled harder. Nothing.

I wrestled with it, jerking at the door until I strained my shoulder, frantic to get back inside.

Then my eyes caught sight of the warning posted below the stairwell sign. "Stairwell doors will lock in the event of a fire." I whispered the words to force my brain to understand them.

I was trapped out here with the two people trying to kill me. Maybe they hadn't seen me.

Turning slowly, I watched as Karen started her minivan and headed down the garage ramp. And then I saw Greg marching resolutely toward me.

CHAPTER 40

The Drop

MY THIN SILK blouse clung to my back, drenched with sweat. I pressed against the steel door to the stairwell and felt the heat of the building, compounding my exhaustion.

Greg Oberman stormed in my direction with a vicious expression. He'd obviously not expected me to escape the building and appeared determined to finish me off by whatever means necessary.

I strained to remember all the self-defense tips Cotten had taught me and scanned the parking garage for possible exits. If I ran to the right, I could overlook the street below, but the sounds of sirens and gathering crowds guaranteed that my screams would never carry. Not only that, but I'd be in the perfect place to be pitched over into a thirty-foot drop.

Going up wasn't an option, as the roof to the parking garage was filled with the deafening HVAC units for the whole office, and once there, I'd be in position for a forty-foot drop.

The only way down was to the left, taking the ramp bare-foot, running right past Oberman. He still marched toward me, merely a few yards away. Cotten's "last resort" technique popped into my brain. I prepared for launch.

I drew a deep breath and propelled myself forward, keeping Oberman in view. He looked genuinely surprised and even stopped in place. His arms stretched out when I made contact, but it didn't help him. I buried my left shoulder into his sternum and hammered my right fist into his groin.

As Cotten had instructed, I didn't wait to see his reaction. I raised my right knee for a second strike to his privates and then ran with all my might. I was sure he'd be out of commission for a little while, but I knew he might recover before I was out of the structure, and he had a car.

I charged ahead on pure adrenaline, barely feeling my aching feet on the rough concrete. It wasn't until I rounded the corner to the ramped area that I looked back to see Oberman on his hands and knees, vomiting.

Good. Serves you right for trying to kill me.

I ran until my lungs burned and my shins turned brittle. My knees and ankles throbbed. I thought I heard his car engine rev as I turned to the second-level ramp. Could I get down one more level before he caught up with me? I had to try.

I saw dozens of people below hurrying to see the spec-tacle of my father's legacy ablaze. More sirens blared from blocks away. I had to find someone to send help up to Cotten. I had to.

But as I reached the halfway point between the second

and first level of the garage, Oberman's car growled close behind me. I wasn't going to make it.

Running to the midpoint of the last ramp, I decided to chance a jump. I climbed up on the half wall, swung my bare legs over, and took another deep breath. Oberman's headlights glared as I inched off the ledge and let myself fall.

I landed on a flat-trimmed box hedge of holly, which hurt more than I expected. In movies, the hero just bounces off and keeps running. I, on the other hand, sank a good eighteen inches into the razor-edged leaves, and the stupid shrub held me fast as I struggled to extricate myself.

I considered lying still, hoping that Oberman might not find me, but it wasn't an option. All the pain I hadn't felt while I ran caught up to me as the sharp leaves and branches stabbed and slashed my body.

I pushed and pulled my way through the greenery and got free in time to see a fireman waving Oberman to park his car down the street away from the building. That was that, I supposed.

The sun dropped behind the buildings to the west, turning Petra into a surreal silhouette with smoke and flames breaking through. What should have been a beautiful twilight grew into a nightmarish setting.

I limped toward the fireman, but he directed me off before I reached him. I tried to explain that I had escaped the building and needed to speak to someone in charge. He couldn't understand my hysterics and waved me off again, saying I needed to get out of the way of official vehicles. I marched up into the park area to catch my breath.

From across the street in the park, I watched Oberman's

taillights glow red. I assumed he would just drive away, but he didn't. Instead, he parked his car and got out.

What a psychopath. He could have just driven away and taken his private jet to Mexico. But no, he had to come back for me.

I stood in front of the civic center, with doors facing the police memorial. If I made it inside, I could call DuBois on his cell. I shot a glance toward Oberman. He again made a beeline toward me. Okay, I'd just serve him a second helping.

But as I tightened my fist into a ball, I noticed his hand pushing something in his jacket pocket toward me.

A gun. Really? Right here in the middle of a crowd of a hundred people? He wouldn't dare.

But his face said he would dare. I saw the hate through the dusky, smoke-filled air. He'd shoot me dead and never blink. And right in front of that fireman.

I wasn't about to wait around for it. I ran. But before I reached the civic center, a man inside locked the glass entry doors and turned to walk away without seeing me. No go.

My only option now was the crowd. All that separated me from the mass of fire-oglers was the small memorial cemetery and the Pioneer Plaza sculptures. If I could maneuver through them, I'd find someone who would listen.

I held the home-field advantage in this park. I'd spent months of Sundays in this park, walking between headstones and monuments and naming the horses and longhorns in the bronze cattle drive. This was my playground.

I ran. Between the carved granite angels and crosses, I ran. Beneath low branches, past the engraved war memorial, and between the larger family plots, I ran.

I made the mistake of looking back just once. Greg

Oberman paced less than forty or fifty feet behind me. Panic took over, and I faltered—stopping myself only inches away from falling on the little wrought iron fence circling the grave of a fallen soldier.

Too close.

Scrambling back to my feet, I scanned the park for the fastest way back to the street.

"You can't outrun me," Oberman growled. "You're as dead as your father."

I wanted to yell back at him. I wanted to plead with him to stop. I wanted to bargain with him for my life. But I couldn't. Besides the fact that it would do no good—he was beyond reasoning—I had nothing left.

Clear of the headstones, I had only the short stretch of rocks and grass to cover. Then the terraced retaining walls beside the cattle drive. I could shimmy down the first one— only seven feet high or so—and then hide between my beloved sculptures until I reached the sidewalk where the crowd gathered. I was almost there.

I ran another fifty feet, hearing every curse and filthy name Oberman spewed at my back. I half-expected to be shot, but I supposed he decided to wait until the gun's report would be muffled by the din of the screeching onlookers.

The first retaining wall lay just ahead. I sprinted on and imagined myself sliding into home plate. I dropped to my belly as I reached the rocky lip of the terrace and grabbed the top row of stones as I slid. My legs fishtailed over the edge, and my toes touched the ground of the lower level just as my fingers let loose. I hadn't done this in years, but my muscle memory kicked in, and I squatted down in the shadow of the wall. I had to catch my breath.

"God, please help me," I whispered and gazed at the amber-pink sky. "Help Cotten, too. If I don't make it, I can't send help for him."

And then I saw it happen in slow motion.

Greg Oberman sailed over my head—I guessed he hadn't seen the edge of the terrace—and landed on the longhorn sculpture in front of me.

I couldn't move or even breathe. My brain barely registered what I saw. Oberman hung limp, six or seven feet away, impaled squarely through the chest on the bronze horn of the bull I called Quincy.

The pistol dropped from Oberman's lifeless hand, clattering on the rock below and startling me back to myself.

I needed to calmly get a fireman, police officer, paramedic, or someone to help. "Please help me!" I tried to call out. But nobody could hear me over the screaming.

Was it Oberman? Was he yelling? No, he was definitely dead. He had at least sixteen inches of bronze protruding through his back. I looked around for who else might have seen the spectacle. My throat began to hurt, and I suddenly realized it was me. I was the crazy woman screaming at the top of her lungs.

My screams turned into panting, and the panting turned to long, deep breaths. I was alive. I staggered toward the closest ambulance and called to an EMT. "I need help. There's a dead man. Over there."

I must have looked crazy—covered in dirt and cuts—because he ran to my side as soon as he saw me.

CHAPTER 41
The Rest

"DETECTIVE DUBOIS WILL BE HERE SOON." The young EMT dabbed an icy handful of gauze across the dozens of cuts and scrapes covering my body. As he finished each stinging section, he adjusted the blanket to cover my shredded blouse and skirt and to, in theory, keep me from going into shock. Too late.

Two other men loaded the body bag containing Oberman into the back of an official van, and I forced myself to swallow over and over to keep from throwing up.

"I need to know if they got my friend out of the building," I explained when I was finally able to talk again. "He was on the twelfth floor."

"I understand, but as I've said, I don't have that information, and I can't let you leave yet. I've requested DuBois twice. He knows you're here. He'll be here soon."

I dropped my gaze to my hands and watched my tears fall. I couldn't watch my dad's building collapse. The fire was under control—at least that's what the EMT could tell me so far—but it didn't look like they'd have it completely out for hours.

A hundred terrible thoughts careened in my mind. Would I be able to explain everything that happened this afternoon? Would anyone believe me? Cotten was DuBois' good friend. He'd be angry. At me? Probably. I sure was.

And Edna? Cotten died because of me. How could I ever face her again?

The rocks in the pit of my stomach grew heavier. I'd lost everything. The glowing smoke filled the air, mixing with the smell of burnt wood and charred stone. Dad's building, his business, everything he loved—everything I loved—was gone.

Everything.

"Ms. Peters." The EMT squatted down in front of me to make eye contact. "Ms. Peters, I just got word that DuBois is headed this way."

For one ridiculous, fleeting moment, my hand flew up automatically to straighten my matted hair. Why?

"Thank you." My voice creaked.

I stared up into the smoke-stained purple sky. Was I still the vain woman-child protected from the mad, evil world? After today I couldn't still be that, could I? There was no more protection for me. I had to toughen up. To learn how to live and how to love others. I wanted to be more like Edna. She never shied away from the truth. And maybe that's why everyone was scared of her. She wielded truth like a sword. But not to destroy—she slashed away at nonsense until all that was left was pure life. I wanted—I needed more of that.

"Ronni, thank God you're alive." DuBois rounded the

open ambulance door beside me. His huge profile blocked the view of the building, and I looked into his relieved face. He glanced over his shoulder and waved his hand before turning back to me. "It looks like the building is beyond salvaging; I'm sorry."

Tears coursed down my cheeks. The EMT handed me a tissue, and I mopped my face as DuBois continued. "As you know, Oberman is deceased."

My head bobbled.

"And thanks to a few of your best employees, we have Ms. Richter in custody. I think we'll have a full confession from her by the end of the day." DuBois forced a smile. "I know that's no consolation, but we're gonna take a win where we can get it." He started to turn away, but I reached for his hand.

"Wait." My chilled fingers clutched his warm hand. "There's more than you know. I heard Oberman and Karen fighting. I think they hired your CI guy—the one hit by the bus—to kill my dad. But your guy died first, and then Karen poisoned my dad. I'm not sure how exactly—she said something about saline. But she killed him. And tonight, they killed Cotten. He was on the window. Taped—duct-taped. They broke his ankle." I babbled, trying to make sense.

DuBois looked over his shoulder again. "You may have to give her a job. Or maybe I should. She's holding it together better than I expected." I didn't know who he spoke to.

"I taught her everything she knows about detective work." The voice was familiar.

My stomach tightened again as Cotten staggered from behind the ambulance door. "You're not dead!" I yelled.

DuBois laughed. "Yessir, Cot, that's A-1 detective work, there. Definitely your protégé."

Cotten grimaced. "I couldn't die. My mother wouldn't allow it, you know."

"That's true," DuBois said. "Lord, I sure wouldn't want to break that news to her. Might as well dig my own grave for that."

My mind finally caught up with the situation, and I grabbed Cotten's hand and pulled him to my side.

"Ow!" he whined. "Careful." He shot a look to DuBois. "Can I have a moment with her, please?"

DuBois gestured to the EMT, and they took a dozen steps away from us, still in view but out of earshot.

"I'm sorry for all that you've had to go through this week." Cotten sat beside me and wrapped his arm gently around my shoulders. "I can't say it's going to get easier anytime soon."

I leaned hard against him and held tight. After a few seconds, I could hear his heart thumping. Everything would be all right.

"How did you get out of the building?"

He raised his hand to point to the building catty-corner from the Petra offices. "Someone on the tenth floor of that office saw me hanging up there and called the police. Maybe even before you found me. You'd only been gone for a few minutes when I got pulled down. I told them to send someone for you, but the fire had already blocked that exit." He hugged me closer. "I've been out of my mind looking for you. They told me what you went through. What you saw. I'm just glad they didn't seriously hurt you."

"They tried. But I'm a lot stronger than I used to be." I

looked up into his beautiful, dark, brooding, glassy, blood-shot eyes. I knew I was emotional, but I was also in love.

"You are that."

Inhaling a shallow breath, I tucked my chin to suppress a cough. I noticed that we had matching bandages, *and* he had no wrapping on his foot or ankle. "Not broken?"

"What?"

"Your ankle. You thought it was broken. But it's not?"

His bruised face suddenly blushed. "I suppose I should confess. I knew it wasn't broken. I told you that so you would leave. I didn't think we'd both make it out. I wanted to give you a fighting chance."

I pulled away from him to glare. "So you lied to me? You think it's okay because you did it to save me? Listen, Mr. Hammond—"

"Mr. Hammond?" he interrupted.

"You know I am not okay with people lying to me."

"Would you have left me?" he asked.

"Certainly not."

"So I lied." He let his arm drop from my shoulders. "It's not as though you haven't lied to me."

"When have I ever lied to you?" I said without thinking. I pushed my bottom lip into a pout.

Cotten slipped his hand to the side of my cheek. "Hmm. How about when you called and hired me because you thought you had a stalker? You never actually believed anyone was following you. Not until I had proof."

Sucking my lip back in, I lowered my chin and my gaze. "How long have you known?"

He gently nudged my jaw up until we made eye contact again. "From that first call. Well, the next day, anyway. Once I knew you hadn't mistaken me for your lurker. I am a detective, you know."

"And you aren't angry with me?"

He shook his head. "You really did have a stalker. At first, I thought you had set me up. That maybe you had hired Wexler. When I realized you hadn't," he paused, "I was flattered. If I had realized before that you were interested, I would have called you up."

"You would have?" My heart pounded. After the day I'd been through, I wasn't sure I could handle any more excitement.

"Of course." He snugged me against his chest again. "Listen, Ronni. They'll have us go to the station and give our statements. And after that, I'll need to check in with my mother."

"Yes, you will."

"I know this won't be all settled for a long while. But I want you to know that I will be here for you as much as you want me to be. And you have an outstanding team of people on your side. Did DuBois tell you that Cleeton called him with Karen's name?"

"Remind me to give him a raise if I still have a company after this."

"Of course, you'll still have a company. Petra is more than a building; you know that. You've got a lot of work to do, but you're tough—like your dad. And I know he's proud of you."

I sat in the back of the ambulance in Cotten's arms, aching and tired, resting against his chest, and wished we were almost anywhere else. I ached with exhaustion and wanted nothing more than to be rid of all the charades and lies. We needed a clean start. My dad's voice crept into my thoughts.

No time like the present to take the bull by the horns and begin again.

I still had plenty of lust for Cotten, but if we were to have any chance at all, our relationship had to be based on trust and love. We needed to get to know each other. All the good and the bad. If I wanted a clean start with him, I needed to make it.

"My dad would want me to ask you something right now."

Cotten raised his brows, revealing more of the dark purple bruising radiating from the bridge of his nose. "I'll tell you anything."

I leaned forward, slipped my hands carefully on either side of his face, and whispered, "I know we've had a rough start, but would you please go out with me?"

I think he said yes, but I couldn't hear it over the kiss.

THE END

About the Author

Kim Black is an award winning author who enjoys mixing genres and blowing things up. She writes from her home in the Texas Panhandle where she lives with her husband and her pit-mix puppy, Bonnie.

Also by Kim Black

Little Black Dress, the LBD Project, Book 1

Red Heels, The LBD Project, Book 2

Bare Essentials, The LBD Project, Book 3

Shooting Stars Traveling Circus

CPSIA information can be obtained
at www.ICGtesting.com
Printed in the USA
BVHW042334140423
662364BV00012B/1043